ABOUT THE AUTHOR

Thomas Alexander is the author of over a dozen plays performed on four continents.

His first novel; A Scattering of Orphans was published by *Direct Light Publications* in 2015.

A second novel in the same series is due for publication in early 2017.

Also by the Author

PLAYS
Happiness
Murder Me Gently
The Family
Begat
The Crossroads Country
Great
The Visitor
When Dusk Brings Glory
The Recruitment Officer
Writer's Block
The Last Christmas
Writing William
The Big Match

ONE ACT PLAYS
Four Widows and A Funeral
For Arts Sake
The TV
Life TM
The Dance
The Pink Cow

ADAPTATIONS
William Shakespeare's R3
Othello

NOVELS
A Scattering Of Orphans

No one asks after dead children. That's the long and short of it. No one asks how they're doing at university or whether they've got that job they were going for. No one asks after their partners, or their spouses. No one asks about their children. No one wonders if they call.

Baroness Armstrong, a retired High Court judge and member of the House of Lords, is asked by the Home Secretary to interview a young woman who has just returned from Iraq with a view to using her as a poster child for a proposed bill limiting the return of jihadists who have joined the conflict in the Middle East.

In an unmarked bunker on the edge of Heathrow the Baroness meets with the woman who is anything but unsympathetic. Bright and articulate, it is the Baroness who finds herself having to having to defend the position of the state, and her role in it, while trying to extract the young woman's story and burying the memory of her son, killed in Afghanistan many years before.

As the night draws on, the Baroness finds herself coerced into becoming a tool for unnamed security forces, eager for information they can use against outside forces.

An immediate and timely novel, Thomas Alexander's The Door That Closes Open draws from the lives of two women, both of whom want to change the world, and looks at the conflict between the Establishment and Islamic Extremists, the world order they are trying to protect, and their reasons for doing so.

Children of the Jihad by Thomas Alexander

Bear Books Publishing
45 Dudley Court, Endell Street, London, WC2H 9RF

Permissions may be sought directly from:
Publishing Rights Department, 45 Dudley Court, Endell Street, London, WC2H 9RF
Email: info@bearbookspublishing.com
Library of Congress Cataloguing in Publication Data
Application submitted.
British Library Cataloguing in Publication Data
Application submitted.
04 05 06 07 08 09 10 9 8 7 6 5 4 3 2
uuid:6452fce2-cd8b-440b-8205-8a7a1a32ea04
ISBN: 978-0-9956680-0-3

—

Edited by Sean Davids for Bear Books Publications.

Available in Epub and Soft Cover from Bear Books

Cover design by SimplyA
© 2014 simplya

For Foad & Mina

Thomas Alexander

BOOK ONE
THE BARONESS

Thomas Alexander

No one asks after dead children. That's the long and short of it. No one ask how they're doing at university or whether they got that job they were going for. No one asks after their partners or spouses. No one asks about the children they never had. No one wonders if they call.

You can see it on their faces when they meet you. So conspicuous in their absence, these questions. It's the second thing you ask after, isn't it? How are you? How's the family?

Mustn't ask her, child is dead.

You can see the thought cross their minds. You can see the absence of it as they stumble over the greeting process, looking for some form of sub-question that won't reveal they've just remembered that your only child is no longer with us.

Absences. When your child is dead you become an expert on absences. Christmas is a time when not to buy presents. Birthdays are a time when no one orders cake. Conversations are awkward and filled without words.

Else Peterson. Dame. Socialite. Her mother is dead, but you don't see me not asking after that, do you? It's not the same with parents I suppose. My own parents have, of course, passed on as well, but that's not what passes through their faces every time they meet you.

Else Peterson. Dame. And like so many of these people nowadays she runs something. Online. Sub-Huffington. I know everyone; they think. Why not tell everyone everything I know about them? In-crowds for in-crowds. Concentric circles you hope you're in the middle of.

All it takes to be a socialite these days is an internet connection and a lack of forethought.

I tell her; I write for The Independent. It's a matter of titles, isn't it? Times, no, never the Guardian. Independent has a ring to it. Telegraph at a push.

Come on, Rachel, she says to me. You're not a judge now. Independence isn't all it's cracked up to be.

But in all honesty, I simply don't want to write for her blasted thing. I do accept dinner however. No real harm in that. I wouldn't normally but black-days are black-days, and it's not good for me to be alone when I'm thinking about Richard.

On these days I want nothing more than to be angry. Richard. Lucas. I simply find it easier and when it comes to anger, Else Peterson, Dame, is as good a switch as any.

I shouldn't be horrible.

She's been a good friend.

I find these days that there is so much one has to do and so short a time in which one has to do it, that I simply can't stand people who are trying to fill their lives and the lives of others with clutter to keep out the noise. I can't stand the boarded-up windows of lives where the only thing that looks outward is whatever they were just told by the media.

Still. I welcome the distraction.

She insists on the Groucho, I settle for the Hospital Club. More actor types. Less people who know who I am. She's not happy with it, but intrigued nonetheless. She's never been there and winds up disappointed. A desperate lack of famous faces, as she puts it. People who want to be someone but can't afford the dues.

It is raining when we enter and raining when we leave. I haven't seen the sky in days, and I miss it.

After dinner I stand there, waiting for the car, watching the rain. A doorman in a suit is uncomfortable next to me, standing with one hand on the door with his eyes averted. He wants to talk to the pretty blonde behind the desk. I suppose I can't blame him.

There are two types of beauty when you get to my age. The aesthetic and the young. Why would you want to wait with an old woman for a car that never comes when its antithesis is mere feet away, waiting to be charmed.

From behind her desk the young woman places a handset back in its cradle and speaks in vowels that have undergone professional smoothing.

Your driver says he's on his way now, Baroness, she tells me and I nod. And wait. And while I wait I think of Else Peterson and how simple it must be to get through life without ever having to engage in it.

It comes shortly after the entrée. The anger.

Do you hear from Rutherford, she asks me, by which of course she means Lucas. And I tell her naturally, all the time, which is what one does when one hasn't heard from an estranged spouse in over six months, and then only by email.

Hong Kong keeping him busy?

I tell her that Hong Kong is keeping all of us busy, but I have no idea what I mean by that, and dare her straight in the eye to challenge me on it further. But she does tell me one thing, Else Peterson. She tells me about a girl in North Korea. In London now, of course. Her publication has just done a piece on her. She tells me about her miraculous escape from such a terrible place. How big of an ordeal it was. How difficult it must have been. Her own little cause célèbre.

She believes it. Or used to anyway, and I'm not quite listening so I have to ask what it was she believed in.

Their leader. Whatever his name is. A god, she tells me. That's what the girl used to think of him. That's what she used to believe he was. Funny little man. A god! Can you believe it?!

Don't we all though, she tells me. Believe in someone. Not all of us, naturally, but the wasted, white and unwashed.

She looks around the room, waiting for the great waiter uprising that would never have happened at the Groucho.

A god! All of them. And when they can't find it in their leaders they find it in the mirror!

That's not what flips the switch, however. Not what raises the dragon. That comes after.

She drones on for a bit, waffling, and I think about what she's said. The mirror bit if nothing else. Perhaps we are all gods, looking into the mirror, despairing of our own creation.

Frankenstein, I tell her, is one hell of a book, but she's not following and tells me a story about someone in the movies who I have never heard of, and how she is currently reinventing herself in the West End - as if such a thing were possible.

Gods.

Then, and I've no idea of how we get there because I was only half listening and mostly avoiding eye contact from Waverly Grant, the American, who has been looking at me as though he knows me from somewhere. I've no idea how we get there, but now we're talking about Madeline. Her youngest. And I don't mind listening to peoples' stories of their own children. I'm not that old of a humbug. But I'm listening to her foetid life as a member of some New York elite, something overlooking the park and, my God, Rachel! The money! It's simply obscene! And then out of the blue she says it. Just, up and asks. As if that's the way it should be.

And Richard?

I look at her.

Do you think of him?

What kind of a question is that? And so I ask her. What kind of a question is that?!

And she tells me that, well, it's… She'd heard it somewhere, of course, but it's his birthday and the situation… My darling, she says to me. My darling, it's just a wonder why we ever went there in the first place!

The doorman is still waiting and there's still no car. Only rain pulls up outside the window, so he makes his apologies and goes for an umbrella. It's still light outside, but it's London finger-light now. Stretching between buildings. Big blocks of shadows abounding. The best part – and with it, the worst part – of the day behind me.

The reason she has left me, Else Peterson, waiting for a car that is presumably not coming is not because of my temper. A bore, yes, with horrid, horrid children, but a Lady nonetheless. No, she's left me because she has a meeting with New York that she has to get back to, or take from the car, I'm not listening when she tells me. Something lawyerly anyway, which she's sure I will understand, otherwise she'd offer me a lift, which she doesn't. And I tell her not to worry, that Jan will be along momentarily, but now, standing here, watching the light catch the rain, I'm wondering whether I should just head back up to the bar while they call me a cab.

The pretty blonde with a taste for musclemen in ties asks me if I would like a seat, please, Baroness, but I dismiss her with a curt no-thank-you and remain standing. The suit returns with the umbrella and waggles one eyebrow at her as if I can't see. She smiles and ducks her face behind the screen on her desk.

What a strange thing to say.

Dame Peterson hides her mouth behind her napkin but her eyes are eager, seeking pain.

I would just imagine it's hard, Rachel. On Rutherford, as well. It being in the news so much.

Will we ever get tired of the misery of others?

You will write it though? You're such an important voice. To the right people. It would mean so much for so many, many people. To hear your story.

But if I've survived thirty years on the bench then the bullying of flattery certainly isn't going to work on me now, and I start thinking about a piece to spite her. In The Economist, maybe. Or The Atlantic.

When the car finally does pull up, the rain is so strong that the doorman has to angle the umbrella against the drive of the fall as he leads me the five feet from the foyer to the car. Completely unprotected, I watch as raindrops slick off his bald head and fail to soak into his polyester suit as he passes the baton to Jan, who stands with his languid frame and grey spectacles under an altogether too peach umbrella.

Jan addresses me as he holds the door open: Baroness. But I ignore him and climb in, my face catching raindrops in the three to five inches of uncovered pavement between the umbrella and the car.

He closes the door behind me and I run my hands through my hair while I wait for him to store the umbrella in the boot and return to the driver's seat.

He gets in but doesn't start the car. He simply waits, sitting, looking at me in the rear-view mirror for the question he knows is coming. I can hear the rain beating off the aluminium, like an old church roof. Echoed to cacophony.

We called for you fifteen minutes ago.

I'm sorry Baroness. He has dark eyes, Jan. Darker than his hair and I've always thought that's the reason he keeps them framed behind glasses rather than adjust to contact lenses. Quite frightening. Despite his build.

I'm sorry Baroness. There're road-works at Holborn.

So I cast my glance away. Permission to start the car and go home. I stare out of the window while he presses the ignition button and listen to the indicators tut over the sight of a young couple caught in the rain, running towards a rose strewn bar promising sanctuary down the street.

Else Peterson. She had quite a thing for Lucas back in the day and is no doubt entirely pleased about our living arrangements; though it is a sign of the hour that I care about such things at all.

The young couple are soaked and I envy them a little. Romance is wasted on the over-sixties. I've always thought it is a fool who commits to such personal endeavours when there are far more important things to do with the few moments left.

Still, I envy them. The rain. The laughter of it. They duck under the thick flowerpots that adorn the lintels of the bar and kiss, cleanly, my view of them transformed by the thousand contorted raindrops that stain the tinted windows of the car.

Perhaps I was never quite so young. Certainly I was never quite so so pretty.

So lost am I in this that I barely notice when we begin to pull out, and am only aware when we come to an abrupt and jolting stop some eight feet away in the middle of the street.

I shift uncomfortably in the seat. A hand out to restrain my movement. A flash of a car accident decades ago suddenly clear in my mind. A surprised sound passing my lips. In stubborn opposition to the law, I rarely, if ever, buckle up.

I peer around and see a man. He stands dead centre in front of us in the middle of the street. His hands splayed out across the bonnet of the car, leaning in.

His face holds the surprise of one who thinks himself lucky for something as ordinary as breath, and I watch as it quickly turns to anger.

I didn't see him in the rain.

Jan's hands are locked on the steering wheel, ten and two, and I ask him if he's all right.

The man has started yelling now. Understandable obscenities. He is dressed in a worn hoodie and t-shirt. I can't make him out from the waist down but I'd posit jeans, and perhaps shoes that are a touch too shiny for their own good. That or sports shoes. He is thirty, black hair, slicked by rain and I watch him between the wipers as he slams his palms down firmly on the bonnet once more, anger and fear apparent on his face.

Richard.

Jan has lowered his window an inch, and I am splashed by both the rain and obscenities as they drift in together through the window.

Jan leans out through the window. Raising his voice.

I didn't see you in the rain!

But the man slams his hands down for a third time, fists punishing the bonnet for his near miss.

Jan opens his door. There's a thing with drivers. Whether or not they are new to the job, it's their car. It doesn't belong to them in the true sense, and one doesn't care as much about a work computer as one does one's own but when it comes to cars… They don't like damage to it, they don't like someone putting hands on it and by now the man is doing both.

Jan no doubt intends to get out and try to soften the situation a little bit, but just as he opens the door the man starts moving around to the passenger side of the car where I am. His hands never leave the wet metal of the car, feeling his way like a blind man or, more accurately, a man who fears the commitment of his legs beneath him. The windows are tinted enough, and if one is that close all that can be seen is one's reflection, but the windscreen less so and I suppose he saw where I was in the car from his starting position.

The man works his way around the car, his hands guided by the bonnet. Slapping and banging in short bursts so as not to allow us to drive off, even though Jan is halfway out of the car already.

The obscenities have stopped and he is just shouting one word, again and again.

Hey! Hey!

His eyes firmly on me.

Behind us a car blares its horn.

Jan, it seems, is at a loss. He can't really start chasing the approaching man, nor can he scoot across to the passenger seat and intercept him. I hear him mutter something in Czech and then he's out, into the storm, standing at the side of the car and leaning across the roof, trying to intercept him with apologies and a firm voice.

I can only see Jan from the midriff down now, his voice muffled. It doesn't matter though because the man is ignoring him, heading around and towards me as fast as his shaky legs and enraged hands will take him.

I watch him as he moves around the blind spot of the wing mirror, arching his body so that he remains pressed as close against the side as possible, the better not to let it move, I suppose. The better to prevent his legs from giving way.

We have all been there. One second, one step, one turn away from sure death, and one day we will all be on the other side of it, I know. A breath too late. A step too short. A turn too far.

What are we angry about, do you suppose? Are we angry at ourselves? The world?

It's almost as if one is angry to find oneself still in this land of the living.

Jan is standing opposite now, yelling determinedly, but the man never looks at him. He just keeps hammering at the car, shouting monosyllabic tomes until he is almost level with my window, and it's then that he really comes back to life.

I see you! I see you!

I hit a button and let the window sink into the body of the door. As it slides down he places a hand into the gap, using all his weight to push down, no doubt expecting it to stop or rise again.

I lean forward from my position in the centre of the back seat and he stops, hands on the window, thick hair slick against his scalp, deer-eyes angry and black. His hoodie slipped to one side, his hands still shaking from the adrenaline.

Richard.

And for a heartbeat I feel the panicked joy of hope.

No one asks after dead children.

I see you!

Yes, I'm sorry about that! So sorry. My driver didn't see you.

And I can sense Jan back in the car, door still open, no doubt thinking of the master controls on the front armrest.

Are you all right?

You people are all the same!

And he doesn't have Richard's voice. And he has a cadence that Richard never had, but the rest of his face…

I'm terribly sorry. It's the rain. Are you all right? You're getting soaked!

I know who you are!

But it's a class comment, not a personal one, so I ignore it. Best Judge's voice forward.

As long as you're not hurt! Are you hurt?

You people. You think you're all the same!

Jan is leaning over from his seat. One foot still outside the car door. Baroness!

You seem to have had quite a shock, I say to the man, reaching into my pocket for my card case.

Richard is fading. I don't think this is my dead son. I don't think that I've just nearly killed him. He's becoming his own man and I want him to go before hurt fills the vacuum of the experience.

You can call the police, if you like. If you'd like us to. We were completely in the wrong. Here's my card.

I hold it out for him and the deer-eyes look at it as if I've just passed him a hand grenade.

I really am terribly sorry about the whole thing.

There is beer on his breath and Richard doesn't drink.

I gesture with the proffered card insistently, and he takes it, holding it gently between his forefinger and thumb as though it were unclean in some way before looking at it. Then in one angry motion he throws it back in my face, hitting me flat-sided on the check, causing me to pull back.

From the front seat a cry and I feel Jan reaching past me, aiming for the man's hand which is still stretched in through the window, but the man pulls back and when I look, hand to cheek, he is leaning forward once more, his face a tower of rage.

I have, during my time at the Bar, been victim of many a foul-mouthed rant. I have heard death threats from the dock that are both believable and sustained. I have had suffered slurs and cusses that are both accurate and wholly against character. I have wept, I don't mind telling you. On the Bench. Silently. Wordlessly. Wept at some of the judgements that I have had to pass down, that the law has prescribed. But I have never had to endure a tirade from someone who looks like a dead son before.

You are all the same, he tells me. One rule for you, one rule for the rest of us. I was, in order; a stuck-up bitch, a fucking cow, and a dried up old cunt. Yes, cunt. That came out three times and once he'd got there I suppose there was nowhere else to go, so he simply stuck with it.

He is screaming into the car and I just sit, staring. Jan has gotten out and is shouting, making his way towards the man, trying to scare him off, I suppose, to avoid a physical confrontation, but I can't hear him over the roar of the man. I can't even hear the rain.

I can feel his venom catching my arm. And for a man who I suppose is not actually that much of a talker, he gets a lot out before Jan gets to him.

Even then he doesn't want to stop. Jan gets an arm under his shoulder and pulls him back, away from the car, but he hangs on for a good few moments, spitting words at me, his fingers gripping the window like icicles, rain sluicing off them and splashing onto the backseat upholstery.

I watch.

Thinner. Bearded. Older. But Richard to me once more. Standing there. Something in the eyes. The anger. Breath and voice have nothing to do with it. What else is one to do but sit there when a dead son comes back from the grave in order to call his mother a cunt?

Jan drags him back. There's a chip shop just up the road, tourist type, and people are staring now. Listening to the tirade from the doorway, from the window. I tell Jan to leave him alone, which he doesn't, of course. He pushes him back into the street, and the man stumbles and falls backwards into some rubbish bags. Jan, pointing a warning finger, tells him not to get up.

I press a button and the window re-emerges.

The fall silences him, or maybe it's the people watching. And he sits there. Waist deep in trash. Jan keeps his finger marked on him and makes his way back around to the driver's seat.

The man tries to rise but the bags are slippery and he can't get traction, so he has to make do with calling Jan a cocksucker instead.

A few of the staff are in front of the chip shop. They have umbrellas, nice ones, out on the street for people to sit under so they just stand there, shielded from the rain, watching. Jan's door is open and through it I can see one of them, his phone out, filming, hoping something worse will happen. But the man just sits there, silent and miserable, while Jan gets back in the car, the rain seal-slicking his suit and hair.

He starts the car and apologises, checking I'm unhurt.

We start moving, faster than we should, and I press the button to lower the window once more so I can see him, this other-Richard. I watch him struggle to find his footing in the wet bags as the window falls, letter-boxing him in dark lines until we pass.

It takes all I have not to turn around and watch him through the rear windscreen.

Jan is talking but I'm not listening. Richard, years younger, screaming at me in the midst of all those hormones, hoarse, asking, pleading, calling me a bitch, though I can't for the sake of me remember why.

Baroness?

I look up and he asks me if everything is all right. If I need to go to hospital. But I tell him no, I'm fine. That it's nothing.

And it is nothing, nothing I haven't seen before, on the street. In the eyes of strangers.

The blood is calming now, and I can see it for what it is. A man, small and frightened, screaming at the world for the injustices of his life while I see the injustices of mine in the world around me.

Home, I tell Jan and he nods, agreeing, watching traffic, watching me in the rear-view mirror, pensive all the while.

If only he hadn't been late.

And London is London. The people. The rain. I watch it all pass me as we move through the mess of a wet Wednesday. I watch the people and the umbrellas and the movement and try to keep Richard from my mind with something this other-Richard has said.

What about the rest of us? You own the cars, you own the houses. Where do we live? Where do we walk?! What do we control?! What do we get out of it, you fucking bitch!? What do we get once you've decided every fucking thing we're supposed to do! We have to live here too, you cunt!

I keep rooms at Temple. I shouldn't, I know. It has long ceased to be convenient for me, but Surrey is too far and I don't see the need for Westminster. It's too quiet in the evenings and too impossible in the mornings, but I stay here nonetheless. I tell myself it's to remind me of justice, but I just can't bear to be back in the big house.

The usual array of successful lawyers and broken barristers fill the bar at the end of the road, but it's a thin crowd and I watch them in reflection as Jan swings the car into the underground parking.

We pull into the allocated lot and Jan moves out of gear, and then we sit there, thinking, the pair of us. Engine running. Like a suicide pact without the motivation to set up the hose.

Are you all right, Baroness, he asks me and I tell him, yes. Flat. You? But he knows better than to answer that.

I'd feel better if we called the police.

Do I doubt that? Probably. It's not me that pushed someone into the rubbish after all and there was the filming. Still. Not a crime. All in all.

Why were you late, Jan?

I can make out the Czech in him when he tells me about the road-works in Holborn that we both know didn't affect him and I wonder whether it comes out more when he's lying, but I don't know him well enough to pass judgement.

I think, Baroness, after tonight, I should resign. You could have been badly hurt.

You'll do nothing of the sort I tell him, but he's insistent.

And, perhaps, I'm too indignant. Too strident when I tell him that it's beyond imaginable. It's out of the question. I stare at him firmly in the rear-view mirror and tell him that we'll hear no more of it.

He nods. Sullen. Spoiling for a fight.

Are you planning on going out later, Baroness, he asks and I tell him no, he's free for the night.

I'll keep my phone on me, he tells me, which is standard procedure and I nod. It is rare that the House calls a session this late at night. We are not, after all, the Commons, but it is not unheard of and it is one of the duties of my driver to be on-call late into the evening, just in case.

He looks at me again through those fashionable grey glasses, this time turning around to do so, twisting in the seat so that he can give me his full attention.

I know a lot of good drivers, Baroness. They would be happy to take care of you.

Perhaps it's the tiredness. Perhaps it's the emotion of the day, but I don't reply as I move out of the car into the dark of the garage and walk across the white-yellow-white lines that are almost always carless towards the elevator and home.

Behind me the alarm beeps, which means Jan has alighted, and I wait for the doors to close on the renewed hum of his own car starting, but I never look back.

I do not keep exceptionally busy rooms at Temple. Some personal items. My photographs, of course, but predominantly the things that I am surrounded by are law books. There are, of course, a few on the constitution too, including a particularly fine copy of the American Declaration of Independence which now hangs on my wall but was originally sent to the Court of St. James in 1823.

Of the five rooms, three are used. When I took my seat in the Lords I had to return my chambers, and the majority of space is taken up with the trappings and furnishings that used to make up my offices there. Old presents remind me of past successes, though which is for what I would be hard-pressed to tell you.

The hall therefore is lined, in no particular order, with bound copies of judgements and court documents. On the right are copies of

Blackstones, Judicial Reviews, and more editions of The Law of Refuge Status than I care to count, while on the left are thinner, more personal forms of many of the exact same copies. I pass by the IPLA 1996 Review, as well as the Asylum and Immigrations Act itself that I myself had a large hand in writing, lying as it does on some poems from Joyce that are signed by a playwright who shadowed me in the eighties.

There are lines of thin green-bound books with strange denotations, like UKSC 30, [2011] 1 AC 338, WLR (D) 226, and other grander titles; RT (Zimbabwe) and Others (Respondents) v Secretary of State for the Home Department (Appellant), Civil Partnership Act; Asylum and Immigration Tribunal (Procedure) Rules 2005, Nationality, Immigration and Asylum Act 2002; British Overseas Territories Act 2002; ZN (Afghanistan) (FC) and Others (Appellants) v Entry Clearance Officer (Karachi) (Respondent) and one other action.

I pause at the last one and pull it down. I know why I do it. The cover is more worn than all the others put together, including the Joyce.

I take it into the kitchen and set it down on the counter while I pull a chilled glass from the fridge and pour. The Hospital Club served us martinis with dinner and while I have no wish to approach inebriation, there is still adrenaline in me from the incident.

This appeal raises a short question on the true construction of the Immigration Rules, House of Commons Paper 395 (HC 395). The question is, what rules apply to family members seeking entry to the United Kingdom, where the sponsor has been granted asylum and has subsequently obtained British citizenship.

Ah, Richard. Why did you ever have to go to Afghanistan?

I drink, knowing I will not find Richard in all the angry people who dominate the streets, nor in the family of a former Mujahid who may now travel at leisure back to the place where my son held his last breath.

UKSC 21 was my final judgement on the Bench.

The telephone rings. The house phone, not my mobile. I can hear it in the other room, singing out from its stand next to the bookshelf. But almost as soon as it does my mobile rings as well, and out of instinct I pick that up first.

Baroness Armstrong? And I do not know the voice.

The phone, the house phone is still ringing and I make my way towards it, pinning the mobile to my ear with my shoulder, the glass in my hand.

My name is Travers, Baroness. I have a Black Pouch for you, Baroness.

And what can one possibly say?

I see.

Only the doorman has gone and the courier doesn't seem to be able to find a bell. So I tell him there is a letter box at the front he can use instead.

It's a Black Pouch, Baroness. He'll need you to scan for it, I'm afraid.

I see. Would you tell him I'll be right down? And then I add quickly, if you could be so good as to ask him to come around to the garage. It's underground. Thank you.

I have reached the bookshelf and allow the mobile to drop into my free hand, turning it off without waiting for a reply, simultaneously putting the glass down on the shelf before picking up the house phone.

Yes?

Rachel?

They are the damnedest things, long-distance phone calls. There is, no matter how good the connection, that very particular satellite delay that makes each party believe it's their turn to speak.

Rachel?

I'm here, Lucas. Is everything all right?

I have a picture of him, Lucas. It sits on a table by the elevator door and I look at him now, his voice on the other side of the world. A picture of Richard lies at the other end by the kitchen; one for coming in, one for going out. My son's face beneath a light switch and above a rather fine copy of The English Reports of 1852.

He is younger in the photograph, Lucas, by twenty years at least, and it's only by calculation I can tell you that it was taken just before Richard passed. The thick blonde hair greying at the temples in the photograph is pure white now, giving his already statesmanlike eyes a reverence the image doesn't show.

I thought I'd call.

It's good of you. Which I genuinely believe it is.

I'm afraid I can't talk this minute, Lucas. There's someone waiting for me.

A pause, and then we both start speaking. There is never a good way to do these things, even for someone like Lucas who no doubt does it for a living.

I just wanted to check you were all right. Given the day.

That's very sweet, thank you. Perhaps I can call you back?

I'm just heading into a meeting.

Of course.

I just wanted to check you were all right. I'll call properly on the weekend.

I nod, though he can't see it.

It's good of you Lucas, I say, because there really isn't anything else one can. I've already pushed the button for the elevator above his head and don't expect a response when I ask him if he's well.

I've got to get into this meeting.

We'll talk on the weekend. And then, because it's needed;

It really was good of you to call.

And there's a pause while my words traverse the globe before he tells me I'm to take care of myself again. And a click that tells me that Hong Kong is no longer in the room.

Car parks have never bothered me. I was, of course, on the Bench long enough to understand how dangerous they can be. Though it wasn't an area of expertise for me, the Criminal Bench, one cannot get to the High Court without doing one's time and I know all too well the horrors that are perpetrated on women within the four dark walls of a car-park. On a scale of one to ten, unlocking your car door is on a par with letting a strange man buy you cocktails at a nightclub when it comes to sexual assault.

Nevertheless, I've always found them something of a comfort. There is something personal about cars left abandoned by their owners. Personal belongings left neatly in clearly defined boxes, ever-changing yet always the same. Hallmarks of their owners. Standards for the modern world.

Judges are, I suppose, nothing if not nosey.

When the elevator door to the car-park opens however, the sight of a helmeted motorcyclist standing dead centre under a single light, with no bike in sight, is enough to give pause. I stay where I am, not moving, and stare at him expectantly. He – presumably because he doesn't know who I am – does likewise.

The door begins to close, so I stick out a finger and hit a button, arresting its movement, mindful, perhaps that the button to close it is just one to the right.

Baroness Armstrong?

The voice is muffled by the helmet and I don't move.

I'm going to have to ask you to take the helmet off, I'm afraid.

Though I don't know why I say it. As if rapists and murderers are afraid to show their faces.

He switches, body language understanding, and slips his helmet off through a muffled apology.

Sorry, madam. I've got a package for you.

I step forward into the dark, the light behind me, away from the safety of the doors. He reaches behind him into a hitherto unnoticed satchel and produces a package.

I hear the slide of the elevator door as it closes behind me.

Where's your motorbike? And he nods back to the ramp, indicating the street.

It's a bit late for you to be doing this sort of thing, isn't it?

He smiles. Older than I think. Ex-military all over him.

I'm just the messenger, madam.

The package is in a faux-leather pouch with one of those plastic governmental seals on it that are impossible to duplicate. It's about the size of a shoebox but half the depth. A photo frame perhaps and is lighter than it looks.

I take it from him and he produces a tablet from his pocket, about the size of a mobile but much thicker.

Please put your finger here, madam, he says, holding it out to me

I comply and it blinks at us, informing us when it has finished. I tell him that I've never done this in a garage at nine o'clock at night and he nods, as if for him it's a daily occurrence.

Biometrics are the new signatures, though just as easily forged if you ask me. Time, patience, and a laptop. That's all, I'm reliably told, is needed to get past them. It's a fad, like electronic badges, and exists far more for the persecution of the person being scanned should something be lost, than the security of whatever is being transferred.

He nods, thanks me, and turns to go, leather and zippers pinging and rubbing with every step.

I turn, push a button; but the elevator has moved on without me and I'm forced to wait, the sacred black pouch clutched to my stomach, wishing I had brought the wine.

Black Pouches are for national defence. Black Boxes are their far more famous counterpart, but boxes are conspicuous and only used by Ministers directly. Black Pouches, with the tightened security that couples them, are their lesser cousins, sent by the great and mighty to those in outer circles, usually for advice or counselling. It is not uncommon for a member of the Lords to be a recipient of such tributes. Constitutional advice is what we are there for, after all, but nonetheless only one person ever asks my opinion on such matters, so I lay the mobile next to the pouch in expectation of the call and set the thin tablet that the pouch contains along side it. The wine has, unpleasingly, now reached room temperature.

I stand there, sipping, looking at the technology on the table. I have, of course, tried turning it on, but the tablet is password protected so I simply sit there, waiting for the call, patient with my wine.

Rachel.

Helen, because I can remember her being sick in my toilet at Kings, and once one can do that, Home Secretary sounds too formal.

She apologises for calling so late and I tell her I got the Black Pouch.

There's some form of password. On the tablet. I thought these things were all biometric these days?

That. No, the damn things keep freezing on us. We've had to go old school, I'm afraid. Just pop your security number in and it should open.

How can I help, Helen? And I only ask because I sense we are coming to that awkward third question and it's Helen, and being Helen she's bound to know what day it is, even if she wasn't at the funeral.

Well, we're going ahead with the legislation, it seems.

Through the House?

Not yet decided, I'm afraid, but the PM is very eager to put a human face on it.

I've picked up the tablet again, the ten digit keyboard shining up at me, asking me to trace the numbers I know by heart: along with my phone number and the passcode to the elevator.

I think we've talked about the dangers of that.

And I hear the click of her jaw when she replies.

We have – we have – but you know how he is.

Which, of course, I don't.

The home screen of the tablet is naked apart from a few icons and I click them randomly, opening a cascade of documents and images. A video starts up, but I can't see through all the windows which one it is, so I simply turn the tablet in my hand and place it face down onto the kitchen counter before stepping out into the hallway and closing the door behind me.

You think you have someone?

At Heathrow. Can you go there?

I pause. I'm not sure what I'd be looking for.

That's just the thing, isn't it? The problem with any new legislation. No one is.

I take it he's just flown back into the country? But she cuts me off.

Sorry for the expediency but the PM thinks if we get our ducks in a row now, we can push it through before the summer break. That sort of thing.

There's a pause, and then she adds.

Which the PM is very interested in.

Which reminds me we're old friends. Which reminds me we were at University together, even if she was a good few years behind me. Which reminds me it was her who put me up for the peerage in the first place.

We'll send a car.

No, I tell her. My driver will take me, I say. And I ask her once more where it is.

Heathrow, she answers. One of those god-awful bunkers they've got out there, I should think. It's all on the tablet. Oh, by the way, she adds, and for a moment I think she is going to talk about Richard. It's a she, she says. The subject. Though I can't see why that should make a hoot of a difference.

I hang up. The music from the kitchen has stopped, which means that either the video has ended or everyone in it has gone quiet.

I glance instead at the picture of Richard, pull up the number for Jan under recent contacts and dial.

BOOK TWO
THE CONVERSATION

Thomas Alexander

Airports are like two worlds crammed into one. Like a city built on a river, the city is not there for the river. The city is built for itself. Water comes and water goes, airplanes land and airplanes leave, and while the river is the reason it survives, the city keeps itself as far from the banks as it possibly can.

Nobody goes to an airport to see the aeroplanes.

Baroness Armstrong watches as a distant plane falls to the runway. The thick, high fence slices the plane in two before it bounces neatly to the tarmac, gravitized once more and heading away to the lights of the main buildings beyond. The tinted window and the rain obscure it from the Baroness' view and she watches the little flashing red lights that denote its shape until another comes to take its place. The car has stopped while Jan takes instructions on his mobile phone. It sits on the grassy verge, its own warning lights ticking in annoyance while the Baroness reads from the tablet in front of her.

Twenty-three. Youngest of five, apart from a brother. And there are notes there, telling her that this fits the profile. Fits the pattern of this kind of thing. Younger children rebel. But, she notes, thinking of Richard, first children are more fundamental. So there's that.

There's a photo. Passport. A note tells her that it's five years old. Taken before a family trip to Algeria. A cousin there. Forty-three. Doctor. Dated a girl in university who died in a street bomb in Yemen ten years after they separated, but there's nothing strange about that.

She looks at the thick brown eyes of the photo, but no one seems real in a passport. Everyone looks as if they are auditioning for the role of a James Bond villain, that's why the press always use them.

The leather of the back seat is warm and comfortable. The heat from the air conditioner fogs the windows.

Sleep, the Baroness thinks, but switches off the florescence of the tablet instead.

Jan is looking at her in the rear-view, the phone switched off. She meets his gaze, blinking him permission.

They're coming to get us, he tells her and she nods.

How far away are those lights, she wonders? One? Two miles? Heathrow is a city.

She breathes out, adding yet another layer of tint to the window.

Are you the oldest, she asks Jan. There are vague memories of talk of siblings so she doesn't ask if he has any brothers or sisters, and he tells her that he is. A younger sister living in Prague.

Why do they put these things so far away from everything? But they both know it's rhetorical so Jan turns his hand back, the tick-tick of his wedding ring keeping time on the wheel with the beat of the hazards.

Another plane comes in to land.

Is this where they're looking at the new runway? You'd think MI6 would have something to say about that.

The blink of the tablet waves at her, denoting something, but she doesn't know what, so the Baroness lays it face first on the seat beside her.

She can hear it now, the rain. Heavier even than the planes falling beside her.

There is a rap at the front passenger side window, startling Jan. He pushes a button and it drops an inch, letting impatient raindrops fall onto the passenger seat. Keen eyes peer in under wet hair.

Baroness Armstrong?

And it's Jan who answers on protocol.

Follow me please.

His voice is high. Reedy and eager all at the same time. She can feel a smile behind it. Even senses the permanence of it, sight unseen.

She hadn't noticed a car, and she cranes between the headrests in the direction of the departing man, his footsteps firm on the wet road as Jan closes the window behind him. Then the lights come on and Jan slips the clutch, arrests the hazards, and pulls the tires off the slick verge.

The Baroness sits back again. Missing the rhythm of Jan's ring on the steering wheel. As they pull into formation between the car ahead of them and the lights that creep in from behind, she taps the tablet instead and listens for the sound of aeroplanes.

She remembers a sensation from her childhood. Buckingham skies were full of the drone of aircraft overhead and on bright summer days she used to like to look up, watching for the white lines that told you where they'd been before they got here. Except they were never where the noise told you they would be. She'd heed the hum, look in the direction it was coming from, and then have to scour the sky to find out where they were.

The car ahead is driving slowly, trying not to lose them, and she can tell from Jan's shoulders that it annoys him. Ex-military pride, she supposes, and taps the tablet once again.

They turn off about a mile down the road and slow at checkpoint gates that open suddenly but they do not stop.

The car ahead of them is speeding now and Jan's shoulders drop as he switches up a gear. The Baroness looks out of the window. For a moment she thinks they are on some sort of highway until she sees that in reality they are on a runway, water sluicing up against the side of the car, the purr of an engine set free, the rain marking the window in sideways streaks.

She thinks about asking Jan to slow but doesn't. It would wound his pride and besides, there may be planes to outrun.

They drop gears, decelerating quickly, following the car lights ahead of them, and slip off the runway onto a side road that runs around a manmade hill. To her left she can see an aircraft hanging feet above the tarmac, quite far away but god, they're big! And then it's lost behind the hill and for the briefest of moments Baroness Armstrong is caught by the sadness of never seeing the moment the aeroplane connects with the earth.

They turn again, still moving fast, and pull up alongside a bunker. One storey, windowless except for a porch-like office stretching out from the front. One way in. One way out. Functional. Impenetrable.

Jan pulls the car up next to a small portico at the front and the Baroness looks at her watch. A little after eleven. They made good time, all told. She waits while Jan gets out and even through the rain she can hear him talking with the man from the car in front of them.

She looks at her door, registering the way the rain falls differently around the oils left behind from the finger grip of the man outside the Hospital Club and waits.

Her door opens and a man ducks his head in. Wet hair and dark eyes above a practised smile.

Baroness Armstrong?

But this is a perfunctory question, a British question, and not one in need of an answer.

Do you have an umbrella?

The man shakes his head and before he can answer the Baroness steps out of the car, accepting his proffered hand while shielding her head with the other. Neither stop moving and the hand is cold.

Ian St Thomas.

He releases her hand and pulls back his hair.

You have her here?

Again, British. Rhetorical. But you cannot have silence and be British at the same time.

They stop at the porch, just before the doors, and St Thomas shakes the rain from his coat theatrically.

We were hoping to move her, frankly, but we were asked to wait until you had a chance to speak with her.

She can look at him here, under cover of the porch and lit by the yellow of the room lights in front of them. Slight. Fortyish, but looking late-twenties in that tie. Thin man. Close shave. Pale. A thinker, not a soldier. A dentist rather than a spy.

Where did she come from?

Russia, Baroness Armstrong. Moscow. Aeroflot of all things. But Turkey before that. Batman. In the east.

We know that?

He shrugs, a thin shouldered affair that's not far off a shudder.

It's in her passport. She wasn't trying to hide it.

The Baroness motions to the door ahead of them which remains closed. Jan is standing at the edge of the porch. Close enough to hear, not close enough to intrude. A damp wind pulls at her hair and the Baroness has to put a hand up to stop it whipping into her eyes.

Of course. St Thomas opens the door and motions for her to enter. Glad to be out of the cold and wet, she opens the inner doors herself.

Jan, she notes, does not follow.

The office inside is simple and efficient. A counter to the left channels visitors to a further set of doors, hiding the office on the other side. A desk, a chair, a laptop, and three armed men, one with his hand on a release button, are all that the room contains.

Military.

Which is odd. None of them wear uniforms. All three men are dressed in sturdy black and grey fatigues covered in pockets that rightfully beg for insignia. Still, she knows military when she sees it.

All three stand to attention and watch her with trained caution. She offers them a tight smile, which they ignore while St Thomas shakes his coat and shapes his thinning hair.

Military but no insignia or rank. And the Baroness wonders if the people they bring in here notice that.

We'll need you to sign in, the man with the finger on the door button informs her in a steel voice, but St Thomas waves him away with a hand.

No need for that. The Baroness is here… under capacity. We will need your phone though, I'm afraid, Baroness. And any other electronic devices.

Eton? Perhaps. Cambridge, definitely.

He takes the tablet from her hands. Is this the tablet we sent you? And turns it on.

Keys too, please, ma'am.

He is large, the Button Man. Accent with a hint of Brummie, but that was a long way back. He has a chip on his round shoulders that the Baroness can spot instantly from a hundred meetings across the dock with the accused, and a thousand more meetings with members of the Commons. He glares at the Baroness with all the jawline strength of a class warrior passed over for promotion in favour of better bred stock, and extends a hand in waiting.

She slips off her coat and puts it on the counter instead.

Why don't you just take this?

Is this the tablet we sent you?

Button Man takes the coat and the Baroness feels the cold of the grey interior more acutely, wishing she had worn something warmer than a blouse and trouser suit.

It is.

St Thomas is rifling through the screens, flicking this way and that.

Have you added anything to it, Baroness? And it's as cold as the room when she tells him she hasn't.

He hands it back to her.

You can keep this, Baroness. Thank you. Do you have anything else in your pockets?

But she has had enough of this.

Do you plan to search me?

No. With that smile.

Then let us assume I do not.

Which seems to please him no end. His hair is falling down over his face again and he pushes it up, pinning it with a finger until it heels.

A couple of ground rules, Baroness. Before we go in there. Ms....

He pronounces it like this, though they both know she is married. Ms. With a Z.

Ms. Guelmoussi is, technically, not on British soil…

That may fly with Whitehall…

The Baroness is cold. Tetchy. She should be at home. Warm, and in bed. The last of the alcohol has long since left her system.

That may fly with the people in Whitehall but it will not fly with me, Mr. St Thomas. British law extends into British airspace. The myth of airports is like the myth of fingerprints.

That… is true. Yes. However, Heathrow is, technically… He is choosing his words carefully. Unsure of his footing. Heathrow is, technically, international waters, so to speak. Or at least, so my betters have led me to believe, which, I suppose, is one and the same thing.

May I see her now?

St Thomas weighs this for a moment. Looking, perhaps, to see if he can survive a refusal. But he can't and he knows it, no matter what branch he works for, and so he nods to Button Man who once again exerts his button finger, allowing a third pair of glass doors to open up ahead of them.

They step through.

Quick set of rules, Baroness. The room is monitored in a number of ways…

The Baroness thinks about what he means by this, but remains silent.

…so your safety is assured. Should, however, you feel in any way uncomfortable, Baroness… If you should feel endangered, perhaps… A simple word, perhaps the ubiquitous; 'guard', will alert us to that and we will come in.

A safe word, she questions.

Well, he smiles. I think we'd both be uncomfortable by that. No. No, banana. No, geranium. Not for us I think. 'Guard' will suffice entirely.

They have turned down a narrow hall. Uniform grey doors dot right and left. There are no names, no demarcations. Each door as the last, a single black card reader on each left jamb. They turn right again, into another corridor. No different.

And maybe it's a change in his gait, or maybe it's just coincidence, but she stops him there, in front of the door they are about to enter and looks at his lank hair, his thin tie, his caffeine buzz, before saying:

Mr. St Thomas, you seem to be under the assumption that this is my first time in such a place. Or perhaps that I am some kind of lawyer, here to see a client? I take it you know my background, so let me ask you: how many asylum cases do you think I heard during my time on the bench? Hmm? And let me tell you – she continues before he can answer – that is exactly how I am viewing this. As an asylum case. Nothing more, nothing less. This young woman. She has broken no British laws. Am I right?

He smiles. Does he ever stop smiling?

Not that I'm aware of, no.

And awareness is everything in law, Mr. St Thomas. Everything! She has broken no British laws or you and I would not be standing here today.

Neither has any country asked for her extradition. This is not a rendition. This is not an interrogation. This is an extraordinary hearing to assess a legal case, and make an appraisal of it to the Home Secretary! Am I making myself clear?

St Thomas smiles his thin smile, and the Baroness has to fight the urge to wipe it.

No touching, Baroness, he adds. The final rule. And with that he presses an unseen card from his left hand against the pad and the door buzzes open.

The Baroness looks at him a moment longer, asserting her peerage, and then enters the room.

It is twenty years earlier and the Baroness finds herself again at Heathrow under unusual circumstances.

She is waiting, like all people at airports, for the world to conform to her travel plans, but unlike her usual transits, she finds herself in a small suite while a woman in her twenties checks through her itinerary, the Baroness' passport open in her hand, rapidly writing a succession of details on a clipboard.

Smiling, the woman hands it back and offers her a seat but not her condolences, so clearly there is nothing on the clipboard about Richard's death.

Baroness-to-be. High-Court-Judge-to-be. Rachel Armstrong, still just a Judge, is travelling to Kabul.

The room is cold. Chilled for men in suits weary of the summer heat. Rachel turns as a door opens, but it is just someone checking on the woman with the clipboard. He raises an eyebrow at her, and she shakes her head. The man, in his late thirties, heavy set and suit-neat, tilts his arm to indicate a watch he is not wearing and ducks back out, leaving the two of them alone in the VIP lounge together.

Rachel has never travelled by private jet. She is, of course, accustomed to the large open spaces inherent in the first-class lounge but this is another level of extravagance altogether. This is Lucas' world

– perhaps it was even Richard's – but it certainly isn't hers. The room is thick with leather. The woman, if asked, will bring her whatever food or drink Rachel might want, as long as the cooking time corresponds with the departure time of the aircraft. There are three televisions in the room, oversized wide and undersized thin, though clearly the room is meant for no more than a dozen people at a time.

There is coffee brewing in the corner.

The young woman steps across to a wall phone and taps in a number. She waits, instinctively turning her back on Rachel just as the call is received.

From where she is sitting, uncomfortable on the sofa, a purse at her side and an empty space where her bag – whisked through without her upon arrival – would usually be, Rachel cannot make out what is said but it is clear from the woman's body language that it is not good news. Finished, the woman waits, pausing for a long beat after replacing the receiver, before turning to the Judge and asking if, perhaps, she would like to call her husband.

Rachel stands on a white balcony overlooking buses that shuttle passengers from the terminal to their planes like cows to an abattoir, a phone pressed to one ear.

This is the smoking area, a grand view over the planes coming in and out, and is not intended for phone calls that can easily get lost amidst the roar of incoming and outgoing aircrafts less than a hundred metres away.

She barely hears Lucas pick up, and doesn't register until he starts his apologies.

Surely there must be, she thinks, a protocol to conversations between parents of the same dead child? Some formality that might allow each one to communicate. Her father would know. Lucas does not.

He speaks in monosyllables. The negotiations are at a standstill. He has spoken to Richard's people in Kabul. There is nothing they can do. There is no possibility of being able to get away.

Let them handle it, Rachel, he tells her. They know what they're doing. The country is a mess.

He's even spoken with Bethany.

Rachel had no idea that Richard was in Kabul when the call came. Bethany did, of course, though the judge in her rather doubts the other woman knows where it is.

They had received the news at three in morning. All bad things arrive at three o'clock in the morning and there is not a parent alive, the Judge will later bemoan on numerous occasions, who does not fear the call that comes during those deep, black hours before dawn. But in truth it never occurred to her to think of Richard.

Her first thought had been for her parents. Lord Osborne had retired the summer before, surrendering his place in the Lords with a signature that abruptly cut the ties that had let him switch from one House to the other for nearly sixty years. He was on his fifth heart attack and no one, outside of the man himself, believed he would be immortal enough to see the summer out.

And then her thoughts had jumped to her docket. The barristers before her. Her work with the United Nations. The young woman who had broken down in the box the day before while giving testimony over the men who had raped both her and her fourteen-year-old daughter before they managed to flee the Congo.

Everyone except Richard.

Bethany had been crying but she knew it was her. The moment she heard her the Judge knew it was Richard and knew what it meant but kept quiet, waiting for the other woman to gain control of herself. She placed a weighted hand on Lucas' arm, stirring him without trying to alarm.

Their son was dead.

Two years of marriage was too short a time, the Judge thought, to be engaged in such histrionics.

The news passed on, the Judge returned the phone to its cradle and informed Lucas. She had, in her time on the bench, told many people a great deal of bad news, but never a husband, never a father to her child, and the Judge in her watched carefully for the signs so apparent in the courtroom that an outburst was about to ensue. There were none.

What on earth was he doing in Kabul?

They talked for a little while. They accepted the shock for what it was and accepted their roles within it. Then, assessing time zones, Lucas had taken over the phone and had a board member from Richard's company on the line from America within fifteen minutes.

There was a voice to Lucas when he talked business. A tone that was used, no matter what the situation, when he spoke with other people in finance or in business, whatever the circumstances. And it had been there then, in their apartment, while the Judge sat in bed, waiting to hear if the body of their only child would be flown home for a funeral. It was a tone that lacked warmth but invited conspiracy. A tone that was inclusionary, while at the same time remaining wholly devoid of emotion. Her own voice, as a judge, was more manipulative. She was a ringmaster, moving people through a carefully orchestrated set of dance moves they had no prior knowledge of, and that demanded a greater deal of gravity than the calculations she could hear as Lucas spoke to someone from the oil company, half a world away. Legal proceedings demanded a lack of emotion, but never the lack of passion the business world seemed to grasp with both hands.

She made tea while she waited. Thinking about little things. The funeral: at home she thought, in Surrey. The church where they were married. They lived and worked in the capital now but who was buried in London? You were buried at home, though no doubt Lucas would be upset that Surrey was where she still called home. Might he fight for Cheltenham instead? She doubted it. She would have to call the priest.

And then there was her docket. Full, as always. Break just over. Christmas a way away. She would have to take time. For the funeral at least, and they would probably insist on a few more days. Stephenson was the obvious choice. He wouldn't like it but he'd understand. Still, he would have to be handled carefully. The Judge did not want Finch getting her hand in.

It was an hour before Lucas returned, and the tea was cold.

They're going to call back, he told her, pouring his down the sink and switching the kettle on. For the arrangements. But he'll be back by tomorrow.

Did they tell you what happened?

They did, and he related it to her, hand steady on the teapot, eyes balanced on the sugar.

We don't have an embassy in Kabul. Haven't since eighty-one.

Lucas nodded. He'll be back by tomorrow. They're sorting things out.

But he wasn't.

Phone calls dragged into days and now Rachel was on the phone with her husband, listening to him tell her that he couldn't come with her to collect the body of their son because he simply couldn't get away.

What about Bethany?

He asks her this as if she is looking for comradery for the flight, so she ignores him.

Someone needs to do something.

Leave it to the company. The place is a mess.

I'm sorry, Mrs. Armstrong, the young woman tells her once she returns to the VIP suite, but the pilot says that it's time to go.

I am addressed as 'Your Honour', Rachel replies, and I am ready to leave.

Bethany did not want to see the Judge and neither did the Judge want to see her. Perhaps it was mother-in-law de rigueur or perhaps it was because the woman was quite clearly incapable of ever surmounting anything that even remotely approached a career, but the Judge held no place for her daughter-in-law in her heart. Still, she had to go round.

What was he doing in Kabul?

His job. He was always doing his job.

How long had he been there?

Just since the start of the week.

I thought he was in Bahrain?

He was. He said they use it as a base.

They?

The company. Apparently it's rich for oil. Or a pipeline. Or something. Afghanistan. And now they've killed him for it.

Not them, the Judge said, rising at the sight of fresh tears welling up in the girl. The Soviets, apparently. Ten years ago. When they planted that bomb on the side of the road.

The young woman looked up at her, cheeks glistening wet. How much beauty had she lost in those two years? When that was all you had to give to the world, wouldn't you think you'd work a little harder at keeping it? Or at least, work a little harder at covering up its lack?

The Judge could never understand people who simply didn't try.

What am I going to do now?

Do you need me to lend you a black dress, the Judge asked, not altogether unkindly. One perhaps with a lower hem?

These rooms are always the same. There are no one-way viewing mirrors as you used to see in the movies where people stand behind while you try to catch their eye, but apart from that nothing much has changed in the past century.

Uncomfortable chairs. Grey table. No sharp objects.

The woman at the table is young. Too young. Younger even than her five-year-old passport photo. Bathed in fluorescents the purity of her skin is obvious and few lines cross it, despite the hours of discomfort. She is small behind the desk. Good posture. Strong eyes that would no doubt have carried charge even if she were wearing some kind of veil, which she is not.

The Baroness crosses the room and sits quietly, placing the tablet carefully on the table as she does so, and looks across at the young woman in front of her.

Behind her the door clicks shut. The Baroness hadn't waited for St Thomas to follow her and the lack of footsteps promise privacy with her charge, at least in the physical sense of the word.

Thin, but not skinny. Attractive, but not pretty. The woman in front of her – twenty-three, the fourth of five – dressed in jeans and a sweater, long sleeved, Moscow ready.

She has long hair, uncovered. An oddity, perhaps. Perhaps alluding to subterfuge?

My name is Baroness Armstrong.

But she is silent. Eyes cast away on purpose. Tired and angry. The girl's arms are crossed, breaking the line of the sweater.

First things first then.

She stands, goes to the door, and waits there, her back to the girl, not knocking.

The room is monitored in a number of ways.

She glances back and smiles. The young woman looks at her, and then looks away again.

There is a buzz and the door opens. A uniformed man – not Button Man, younger, less confident – stands there, allowing her to exit.

The Baroness looks at him.

We need food, she says. Pizza, I think. Chicken. Pieces of some sort. And hot tea.

The man looks at her.

Now. Her best Baroness voice.

We don't have food on site, he says, confused.

Young man, we are in the middle of an airport! She is speaking louder than she needs to, not talking to the man at all. Young man, we are in the middle of an airport! If memory serves, one that has a plethora of possible choices. We'll take pizza. Large. Chicken of some variety, and a lot of hot tea. Understand?

And because it pleases her, the Baroness reaches out and pulls the door shut herself. There are no handles on the inside but she puts in enough momentum to click it shut - enjoying the look on the man's face as she does so - then returns to the table.

There, that should do it. Start us off on the right foot.

The young woman looks at her. Exceptional skin. Tea coloured. No doubt from the sun. Ah, how youth is wasted on the young!

I'm not hungry.

The Baroness picks up the tablet and makes a show of turning it on.

Of course you are. Aeroflot? And before that, what was it? Something Turkish? Let's not pretend with one another. You are too famished and I am too tired.

Now, she says, the younger woman watching her every move. Now, my name is Baroness Armstrong, but you may call me Rachel, if you like. I am a member of the House of Lords. Do you know what that is?

I know what that is.

And her voice is beautiful. Lyrical. No trace of an accent, British or otherwise.

Good. It is a bitch of thing to explain when one does not.

Are you my lawyer?

No. Before I took my seat I was a High Court Judge. Which means that I dealt with a lot of asylum cases such as yours.

I am not seeking asylum.

I'm afraid it's a bit more complicated than that.

I live here.

That is what I am here to determine.

This is my country.

There is silence while the two women look at each other, broken by the younger.

Are you saying it's not?

The Baroness sits back, reading the file on the tablet. Looking for something.

You are not wearing a niqab.

No.

Do you usually wear one?

Silence.

Hijab of some sort? Chador? Burqa?

No.

Did they take it?

The young woman looks at her. How many hours has she been in this room? How long since her plane landed? How many questions ago? She has long since discarded the need to answer everything.

What did you same your name was?

You may call me Rachel.

Rachel. You want to know about my headscarf?

It seems strange, that's all. If you are who they claim you are. To not be wearing one. I was just wondering if they removed it.

They didn't remove it.

And the Baroness looks at her over the rim of her glasses, over the rim of the tablet.

I see.

You think I'm not who I say I am?

But the Baroness has played this game more times than her, in Court as well as in the Lords.

Who do you say you are?

What it says on my passport?

The Baroness smiles at that and reads.

Zahra Guelmoussi. Twenty-three. Newport, Gwent. Undergraduate, Cardiff. Masters, Birmingham: Political Science. Single…

No.

And the Baroness smiles. The young woman's hands tremble slightly. They have moved to the table, her body reclining in the seat, more relaxed, tired. She has fine nails. Very fine nails for someone who has purportedly been in a terrorist camp for the past two years, and the Baroness is acutely aware that her own are in dire need of care, steady though they may be.

The shaking could be attributed to low blood sugar, it could be as simple as fear. Who knows what time zone the woman's body thinks it should be in. Certainly later than now.

Not single?

No.

No marriage certificate. No record of an application.

I did not get married here.

There is an old trick to getting someone to talk that has served the Baroness well over the years. Everyone has something they will fight over. A weak point they will defend. Age usually works. Tell someone they are older than they are and they will fight you on it, insisting you get it right, or at least deduct the added years. But the subject isn't important. Everyone has something to defend. That's what matters. That is all it takes to open the floodgates. Once a person has started defending something, it becomes second nature. The trick is to start the process, then lead on to more important things.

Video.

But the Baroness hasn't understood and the girl has to repeat it.

On the internet.

The Baroness picks up the tablet again and taps an icon. A window opens.

You mean this?

The room is filled with the sound of rushing air and voices, and the Baroness wishes for a moment she knew how to mute it, but lets it play, placing the tablet flat on the table and spinning it so that it faces the young woman.

The video has been downloaded and was obviously filmed with a phone. The sound bounces and crackles, loud in the soundproofed room. It shows a young man, bearded, desert robes. He looks bright and happy and young. A voice from behind the phone is saying something, but it is muffled by bass. The young man in the video is speaking Arabic, laughing at the man behind the camera as he pans to the floor and back up again, ostensibly checking to see if the phone is recording.

When it comes back up a young woman is in the frame, also laughing behind her Saudi-styled niqab. The young man places an arm around her, and the Baroness doesn't have to speak Arabic to understand that this is a wedding party and that Zahra is the bride.

The young woman is transfixed by the images. She wants to reach out and touch them, but doesn't. She keeps her perfect nails pressed lightly to the austerity of the table. The Baroness drops her voice when she asks if she is the woman in the video.

Yes.

Your marriage?

And the young woman pauses before answering in the affirmative.

Where was it taken?

It doesn't matter.

If we know where it is, we might be able to find records…

The background of the video shows a typical backyard of a typical Middle Eastern house. White walls. Chapped paint. Old doors, indistinguishable from a million other houses. Could be part of a compound. Could be a house in the centre of the city. Only the light tells you that it was recorded nearer the equator.

Is that why people get married? Records?

It can be, yes. There are benefits to being married…

It is not of the state.

The state! The Baroness locks that away for later, interested. The video has ended. The screen faded to black. She can tell from the young woman's posture that she wants to touch it, to make the images reappear, but controls herself so the Baroness moves the tablet back to her side of the table.

Actually, it is. Marriage. It is a legal distinction, not a personal one.

The young woman finds this appropriately repulsive and tells the Baroness so. She pities her, she says. If that is all marriage is to her.

Perhaps, says the Baroness. But in matters of immigration it is the law that dictates the status of the individual, not romance.

Zahra leans forward, and this is the first time she has looked the Baroness in the eye. Such deep browns. Such utter conviction.

I am not an immigrant!

The Baroness nods. Pleased. No, she tells her, but your husband would be.

The plane is larger than it looks from the outside. The leather of the VIP lounge has seeped into swivelling armchairs that rotate to fit into mahogany tables, watched over by the now somewhat ubiquitous flat screen televisions. Two sofas sit centre, easily able to welcome up to eight people, and it is only the discrete appearance of seatbelts and the curved roof that differentiate the space from a luxury hotel.

By the end of the second day after that 3am phone call, two things had become clear. Firstly, if they wanted to get the body of their son transported out of Afghanistan, then someone with authority would have to sign for it. And secondly, it was the Judge who was going to have to sit by the phone, waiting for information, not her husband.

The first call relating to work came at the end of the second day. Lucas took it in his office, but the Judge knew the shape of it and what it meant. The second came in the early hours of the third day and was shortly followed by a driver knocking on the door. with Lucas saying that he would only be a few hours. There were just certain things that couldn't keep.

Like the body of our son, the Judge thought but didn't say, simply closing the door and plugging her phone in to recharge once more.

She was on her own. In life, if not on the plane.

At the far end of the jet a man in short sleeves and cheap shoes taps angrily at a weighty laptop. He doesn't look up as the cabin attendant ushers the Judge to her seat, nor does he look up as she tells him they are ready for take-off.

The woman, older and wiser than her counterpart in the VIP lounge, knows how to address Rachel.

We're so sorry for your loss, Your Honour, she says, before telling her to call if there is anything she needs.

She watches as the other woman makes her way through the cabin and hears the man ask her for a bottle of bourbon in a thick Texan drawl before the woman tells him for a second time to secure his seatbelt for take-off.

We're taking off?

In just one minute, sir.

About fucking time!

How weak men are, the Judge lets herself think. She watches with anger as the ground falls beneath her, the roar of the jets stinging the cabin and reverberating the table.

Had she always wanted a girl?

The funeral has been set for Friday. Four days. Enough time surely to secure a return. The Judge hadn't known any funeral homes but her mother, always well-versed in social necessities, had obliged with the arrangements. All they said they needed was the time and location of the jet carrying the coffin and they would take care of the rest.

Would you care to choose a casket?

But the Judge hadn't and Lucas wasn't around to object, so she'd told them to choose something appropriate and left it at that.

How can anyone feel loss at a bereavement?

Death was loss, but only the beginning of it. Loss didn't start at the moment life was over. It grew and grew, like the heartbreak of a lover who can never recover what once was.

Perhaps, with a child – a small child – or even a spouse, the inability to reach out to them at any given moment was tangible, raw, even directly after they departed, but she hadn't expected to see Richard this side of Christmas so there was, so far, nothing to lose. Bethany even, for all that a wife might feel, had on her own admission not expected to see Richard again for days to come. Perhaps even weeks.

The Judge had seen loss on thousands of faces over the years. The loss of a child who could not be returned. The loss of a parent whose face disappeared too soon. The loss of a lifestyle that could no longer be returned to.

Loss was compounding. It grew over time. Any tears shed at the moment news was received were shock at best, at worst self-aggrandizement.

Perhaps she had wanted a girl. Richard had always been Lucas' even from an early age, and despite her husbands steady climb up the corporate ladder of industry he had been a good father, taking pride in his son's achievements and nurturing Richard's interest in following in his footsteps.

And yet here she was. Alone. Heading towards a war zone to claim the body of a son she had never truly felt was hers.

The weakness of men.

You mind if I sit?

The Judge hadn't seen the man approach. The window had taken up her view ever since take-off, England slipping by beneath them, the sunlit waters that separated them from the rest of the world falling far below.

Politeness or genetics, the Judge nods assent.

Robert Darlington, he says, extending a hand.

The Judge shakes but doesn't reciprocate the introduction.

The man seems surprised that she's heading to Kabul but doesn't question the reason, though whether this is because he knows better than to ask or he simply doesn't care isn't clear.

And what are you heading there for, Mr. Darlington?

The man shrugs. Thick shoulders over a heavy chest. Layers of fat over youth beneath a cheap shirt that doesn't look like it should afford to travel in such luxury.

I'm just getting my things and getting the hell out! You step out of a country for five minutes these days and there's nothing left to come back to. I've got a picture of my kid. In the hotel. Only one I've got of him. That age, anyway. Usually carry it with me. They pulled me back State-Side at the last minute to attend some symposium and I left the goddamned thing on the dresser table.

Has she brought a photograph? She didn't think to. Not a recent one anyway. She carries one in her wallet; Richard reaching up towards the camera, no more than a toddler, sun hitting off his left eye. She'd carried one of him on his wedding day for a little while, carefully folded, but she went back to the original. That she has. But what use is an image of a child when one is trying to prove identification of a grown-up?

I'm surprised they fly you via jet just for that!

The man smiles. It's a good smile. Face wide. Eyes pulled into it, whether intended or not.

They're still hoping I can get a sign-off from both sides. Not that that's possible. The whole place is about to go to hell in a hand-basket.

You have a good grasp of the situation on the ground?

That smile again.

Well, I ain't been shot yet!

The stewardess brings ice and shoots the Judge a sideways glance, offering assistance should she want to return to solitude, but the Judge ignores her and accepts the drink when it's poured, noting the date of the bottle, the expense of the liquor, and the contrast with the man in front of her.

It's the usual damn thing. Outside interests blowing it all up.

How so, asks the Judge, choosing to ignore the irony of an American and a Brit discussing the downfall of another country in a private jet.

Flight time is nine hours, the stewardess informs them, and withdraws.

First thing you've got to understand about people is; no matter what creed or religion they follow, no matter how enlightened they are, they're out for themselves. Self-interest is the one thing you can rely on. That, and habit. Harder to break a habit than a vow any old day of the week.

The Judge tells Robert Darlington about a case she once worked on, careful in the telling to remove herself from the equation, allowing him to believe that it might be something she read about in the newspaper or heard about at a dinner party.

There was a man, she tells her travelling companion, who every day of his life had come home from work to find himself greeted by the same dinner on the very same day. Mondays were left-overs, Tuesdays; corned beef. Wednesdays were always chicken chasseur, Thursdays a pie, Fridays fish, battered. Saturdays a stew, and Sundays the roast leaving the leftovers for Monday.

I believe, she confides in him, that the contents of the pie on Thursday differed week to week but that was the extent of the variation.

And it drove a wedge between them. Man and wife. This was, on the whole, a very loving and natural couple but why always the same food? Week in, week out. Always the same. He'd come home, day after day, year after year, thinking that this time it would be different, only to be greeted with the same thing, the same vegetables – I believe you'd call them 'sides' – the same portions, cooked the same way. The husband; he loved his wife. But why this! They would argue, over and over. 'Cook me something else!' But there it would be, on his plate, every night, same meal as the week before.

Then one day. After eleven years of this, he comes home on a Tuesday and smells steak.

What was Tuesdays?

Corned beef.

Not such a great departure.

Maybe not. But it drove him insane! Why the change? Had she come into some money? No. Had there been a sale on at the butchers? No. Had she suddenly had a change of heart? What about, she asked him, but he couldn't say.

The next day, things were back to normal. Same dish, same day. And it broke him. Why steak? Why now, after eleven years? And she couldn't answer him. So he began to think there must be more to it. An affair? Or money she was hiding from him? Some change of fortune. A mysterious guest?

He started spying on her. Going through her mail. Contacted old friends of hers. Quizzed her.

Months went by and still the same old routines. Monday, Tuesday… Nothing.

And he began to think he imagined it. Not the problems. The change! Maybe there had been no steak. Maybe it had been corned beef all along! He questioned her, but she didn't seem to find it strange. And so things went back to normal. It was an aberration. A false memory. Every day the same thing.

Then a few months later the menu changed once again and he beat her to death with a chair. In their kitchen. The neighbours heard the screaming and had to drag him off, but she was already dead.

The man tilts his head, thinking.

What did she serve him?

It was Wednesday. She served him chicken chasseur.

I don't get it.

She'd added an onion. She never added onion to chicken chasseur.

The man laughs and wipes bourbon from his nose before speaking.

Afghanistan is not that fucked up.. The Russians… This was the war of a generation and they simply can't get over it. Who screwed who out of which land? Whose grandfather didn't come to the aid of the other's. You've got an entire generation that knows nothing more than sitting on hillsides and taking pot shots at people they hate with guns we supply them with, so that's what they do now. Only this time there are no Soviets. The Prime Minister takes shots at the President's men. The President's men, they take shots at the Prime Minister's. Doesn't matter that they're both in the same government. The whole thing gets a lot worse once you get outside the capital. All they can think to do is to shoot each other out of habit!

The Judge sips and watches him. A strange man. Incongruous to both his surroundings and body at the same time. Intelligent and charming, but willing to dress as if he believed he was neither.

I thought you said it was outside influences?

The man finishes his drink and swills the ice cubes around the glass before pouring himself another.

Oh, it is! Iran, they got their hooks in real early. With us, by the sounds of it. They were funding arms to about half the warlords during the time of the Soviets. Which was fine by us! Why not? Together with Pakistan they had the most to lose. So… fund away!

Problem is, Saudi Arabia hates Iran. More than even the Jews they hate Iran. Okay, maybe not more than…

The Judge cuts him off.

So they are funding..?

Well. Dostrum. To the north. That's virtually a state of its own right now. But it's the Taliban that they're getting the most out of, funnelling the most to. See, they're anti-Iran. Anti-Pakistan too when it comes to it, but the Jihad you know...

And what do the Taliban want?

The man pours himself a generous third, and sits back.

Peace, mainly. But peace on their terms. Which doesn't include money. At least, not from the likes of us people anyway.

The Judge puts her drink down on the table and watches her companion.

What is it you do, Mr. Darlington, if I'm not being indelicate?

Me, he answers, as if the question couldn't be further from anyone's mind. I'm just there to make sure they all just try to get along. And maybe get a pipeline or two built in the process.

There is, historically, as the American tells the Judge, only one reason to be in Afghanistan.

For hundreds of years the country has bridged the biggest, most powerful nations in the world. To the west, you have the Persians. Huge empire on its last legs that still has a ton of oil and, more importantly to almost everyone else right now, a warm water port that's a gateway to the Middle East. To the North, the former Soviet blocks. Again oil-rich, and significantly a strategic nexus between Russia to the north and China to the east. In the middle of all that sits this tough little mountain country that's the modern day equivalent to goddamned Sparta! They won't fall. They won't crumble, and they resist just about everyone who sneaks their forces across their border.

Next hundred years is going to be about oil. We all know that. And this little hillside shanty town is sitting at the crossroads of three of the biggest suppliers – and demanders – of that liquid gold the world has ever seen.

So, yes. They're fractious, they're stubborn, and more than a little backwards if it's just between you and me, but the company that controls the rights to the pipeline that will inevitably cross their borders, is going to be the company that controls the twenty-first century.

I've got, in this plane, ten thousand soccer balls. Why? They love them! Adults, kids… They love them. So I go in there, with my trinkets and my promises, and I get them to sign over deals for nothing more than exclusivity when and if they ever get their shit together and start making things work.

The Judge smiles. Which you don't think is ever going to happen?

Robert Darlington throws his chubby arms out into the air, catching the tip of a finger on the cabin wall as he does so.

Hey, I go where they tell me! I get them in a room, I back a truck full of money up to it, and I tell them that it's better to play nice with each other than not at all. Who knows! Guns ain't worked, politics does jack shit, maybe self-interest can win the day!

And is that what my son was doing? In Afghanistan? Backing, as you say, a truck up in hope of getting everyone to "play nice"?

The American picks up his glass again, his thick Texas drawl pronounced when he tells her that he should have guessed who she was.

The Honourable Judge Armstrong. Yes? Richard Armstrong's mother.

He raises his eyebrows and swallows deeply.

Nice title!

Were you with him? But it's a stupid question and she knows it.

Hell, no! I was in the States. Look… He picks up the bottle and for a moment the Judge thinks he's going to pour himself another but he just holds it, hanging in the air, a Foucault's pendulum, swinging in an unsteady arc.

Look… It's just one of those things. They give us the top security firms. The top. I've been down that road…

Which road?

They didn't tell you? He was driving between the airport and the

UN compound. No idea why.

You know it?

We've driven down it a hundred times.

There were two men with him…

The bottle reaches an apex and he tucks it under his arm, rising as he does so.

Good men. Security detail. Listen… It's a tragedy. I've been down that road a hundred times myself. Landmine's probably been driven over a thousand times in the past week alone. Why'd it go off now? Nobody knows! It's a tragedy.

Robert Darlington moves his bulky frame out of the thick leather seat and shuffles his way to the aisle, the bottle of overtly expensive bourbon tucked under one arm, a heavy crystal glass in his hand.

I'm sorry for your loss, he tells her. And I'm sorry for shooting my mouth off as well. I just didn't know who you were.

Why does it matter who I am, the Judge retorts, but the American has already turned and is heading back up the cabin to his seat when he mutters;

Probably should have guessed from the black.

And then never utters a word again until they land in Kabul.

The Baroness watches Zahra eat in silence. She has had dogs at the big house for as long as she can remember and is familiar with the look, the expectation, the belief that no matter what you are to them, you will take the food away so she waits for the first slice to become the second before asking;

Where is your husband now?

But she neither expects nor receives an answer. Instead, the Baroness allows a finger to pull at a piece of cheese on one of the slices. It stretches and breaks and picking it up with her forefinger and thumb, the Baroness puts it in her mouth.

It tastes like nothing. It feels like rubber.

This must be strange for you.

The Baroness allows puzzlement to cross her features and the woman repeats between chews.

This must be strange for you. Pizza. I can't imagine a Baroness eats a lot of pizza.

The woman's voice is calmer now. Deeper. Mastication breaking the words into bite-sized chunks.

They forgot the tea. And the Baroness' voice is loud, accusatory: For the number of ways in which the room is monitored.

I can't imagine you eat a lot of pizza?

The Baroness thinks about this before agreeing.

It does seem to be something that's not popular in the Lords, that's true.

Zahra discards the crust and opens the box of chicken.

I missed British food, she tells her, taking a thigh. That seems strange, doesn't it? British food? All this is American. But I did. The bad stuff. The stuff I would never have eaten while I lived here.

The Baroness touches the side of the tablet, careful not to wake it from its slumber. The fried chicken smells cloying and sickly, irritating her.

This was taken two years ago.

Yes.

A month after you left Britain.

Another nod.

Is that why you left in the first place?

Zahra sits back in the seat. Sated a little she licks the oil from her fingers.

I have answered all this.

Not to me.

And you are?

I thought I'd explained.

You're not my lawyer.

No.

And you're not part of… She waves a hand around the room, flinging grease into the air. You are not part of… this.

I am. Absolutely. I am.

You said; asylum.

Nod.

From what? My passport is British. This is my home. I've committed no crime. I have broken no laws. And yet, here I sit. Banned from entering my country. Ready to be sent to some secret base somewhere where they can torture…

The Baroness raises a hand. Years of work on the bench have instilled her with a keen body language for discipline. A hand, palm front, eyes down to the left, tilted head. A micro-movement in the palm towards the person. A micro-tightening around the eyes. This will still speech in almost anyone.

Let me be completely clear, Zahra. I may call you that, yes? Zahra? Good.

Always use the name. Always gain control. So many puppies growing up.

Let me be completely clear, Zahra.

She looks the young woman in the eye.

I am not your lawyer. I am not interesting in any laws you may, or may not, have broken. I am concerned with your religion, but only insofar as it pertains to your predicament. I am not concerned with your life. I am not concerned with you, on the smaller scale of it, at all! I am here as an advisor, to the government, regarding your legal status within the country. Nothing more, nothing less.

I have a British passport.

But she does not say that she is British, and the Baroness takes careful note.

A passport, like a marriage… These are legal terms. They are papers, given to you by the government of the country. They are not absolutes, you understand? They are at the discretion of the government.

The young woman tells the Baroness that she was born here, and the Baroness nods.

Which is why I am here and not, perhaps, someone from immigration.

So, says Zahra, and she impresses the Baroness with her grasp of the problem in front of her.

So, if I do something that the government doesn't like they can revoke my passport? Prevent me from returning to the country. To my country. To my home. Even if I was born here?

Is this your home?

But the young woman is a quick learner.

I would have thought that was a legal distinction.

The Baroness nods. Asked and avoided.

The government who I vote for, voted for! And am part of a democratic process…

But it is just that, the Baroness interrupts her, a process. Just that. Officially we are all subjects of the Crown. We are not a republic.

The young woman sits back and think about this.

Birmingham, says the Baroness. Masters in political science. Unfinished, I might add, but I did read one of your essays in the car, coming over, and it showed… intellect.

If education was a standard of passport ownership… But the Baroness cuts her off.

One year at Birmingham should be more than enough to understand the process, don't you think? I would expect, at least, that you'd understand the country you come from! The constitution of the United Kingdom is written by people like me, in places like this, to reflect the society we live in. It is an ever-shifting, breathing thing.

Like a guard dog, making sure people like me don't get in.

Eighteen months ago you left the country to join what this government deems a terrorist organisation. An organisation that has killed a number of British citizens. That is directly linked with acts of terror affecting citizens of this country. That has claimed responsibility for acts of terror throughout the world. You joined them freely. Committed funds to them. Spoke for them. Acted for them. Ostensibly you married a member of their ranks. Surely you can understand the British government being reticent about allowing you to return on a whim? You can understand that there might be distrust!

The young woman looks at her. Straight in the eye. If this was intended to shock, it has done nothing of the sort.

And this is yours, is it? To decide? This country? Communist.

Libertarian. Christian. Suffragette. You get to decide which parts are us, and which aren't?

The door buzzes again and the young soldier enters, tray in his hands. Paper cups. Green tea from the smell of it, though why is beyond the Baroness. Silently he relocates the cups from the tray to the table, the fragrance blanketing the chicken.

Neither woman looks at him.

He tucks the tray under his arm and moves back to the door, rapping it twice with the side of his fist. It opens and he exits. The two women look at one another. Waiting for the closing click before speaking.

The tea is steaming. Paper cups, but steaming tea. What kind of fools are they?

The Baroness picks hers up and sips, disgusted but thirsty, holding it lightly between her forefinger and thumb in an attempt not to get burnt, feeling the give of the paper as the liquid rocks over the pressure point where her fingers meet the cup. What was this obsession with green tea these days?

Do you believe that?

The young woman scrambles forward again, picking at a piece of pizza, tearing it from the body, but this time she doesn't eat, she just sets it to one side, a thin slice of precooked meat hanging off the edge, crumbs from the crust covering the table in front of her.

Look at Palestine. That's democracy! You gave them democracy and they voted for Hamas. What is so great about democracy? And Communism?! What was so bad about Communism that we had to spend fifty years killing each other rather than letting the people decide whether they wanted it or not? I voted for this government. Don't I get a say in how it works?

I'm sure it must be lovely, being a Baroness. But – she's counting now, tapping off fingers with the pad of her index – but Afghanistan, Vietnam, Cuba, Czechoslovakia? Were they worth it to keep communism from destroying the ruling class? Was that the price we had to pay for your peerage?

The establishment has always found a way to use people to protect itself, hasn't it? Class war, fascism; it's one and the same thing. Nothing has changed since the First World War except for the weapons. The Establishment gets the rest of the country to fight on it's behalf. You get the rest of the country to fight to protect you!

The banks. Islam. Communism. Anything that threatens to destroy you, you tear down or prop up using your kind of people to do it. What are you? Five percent of the population? The moneyed and the powerful? Five percent? And yet we'll do anything to make sure you stay that way! Go broke so you can prop up a bank? No problem! Die, so that the world stays the way you want it? Pass me the suicide vest! Kill millions of people who we never had an interest in, who will never be of threat to us, who live so far away that the only thing they will know of us is the whistle of the bomb as it drops on their children – and for what? To stop them living their lives the way they want, just in case it encourages the people who work for you to do the same!?

The Baroness shifts, looking to rise.

Well, if that's your take on this.

And for the first time the young woman seems shocked.

The woman can't go!

I'm sorry, Baroness. That was rude of me. I know how this works. Please!

She watches the Baroness readjust. Maybe not leaving just yet. Maybe thinking over whether or not she's worth it.

At Kabul airport there are no security checks. The jet taxis to an abrupt halt outside a hut and the aeroplane door opens allowing the heat in, before the two sole passengers are ushered off. The tarmac, thick with the sound of the jets engines as they ping and cool, is warm under their feet.

No one asks to see passports. There are guards, armed with imposing machine-guns, but they are preoccupied, deep in a conversation, and don't give more than a passing glance to the two passengers as they move along the tarmac towards the exit.

Robert Darlington strides ahead. The Judge watches as the salesman takes the ground at a brisk pace, nothing but a lumpy laptop bag at his side. She follows him as he enters what passes for a building but is nothing more than two porta-cabins pushed together. The Judge has brought a wheeled cabin bag with her, and it bumbles over the pot holes that grow more numerous as the building approaches. She berates herself for forgetting her sunglasses, and squints into the late afternoon sun instead.

Had she expected someone to meet her?

There had been a flurry of phone conversations over the last day in London, each more strident than the last. Lucas had, on the second day, had a less-than-productive conversation with a civil servant he knew at the Home Office. There was no consulate in Afghanistan, and indeed no presence at all it seemed. Lucas had questioned this, pointing at British interests which included, after all, the body of his son, but was told curtly that Richard was with an American company and as such they would have to deal with them.

Could the Home Office help in any way?

They wished they could and wrung their hands woefully until Lucas hung up and rang the American Embassy instead.

No one wanted them to travel to Kabul. The American government were insistent about having issued a no-travel directive for the entire country, and had themselves withdrawn all but the most essential of staff. And anyway, neither Lucas nor Rachel were American citizens, nor was – so sorry – their son, and as such there was nothing they could actually do for them.

The company was equally unforthcoming.

Yes, they had people on the ground. No, they didn't have an office. Their people were operating out of a hotel.

Richard's body was being stored at the United Nations compound just outside the city. As such they had to go through the proper procedures with the Afghan government, which was too busy shooting at each other to get around to sending over the correct paperwork to fill out.

The Judge had reached out to her contacts in the UN, but they had been just as unhelpful as both she and Lucas expected them to be.

It was news to them that one of America's largest oil companies was using their runway at the airport. It was news to them that they had two

British citizens and an Italian, all deceased, in their compound waiting for removal and repatriation, and once it wasn't news to them they weren't entirely sure how they could help.

The Judge had worked with the UN on a peace treaty between Chad and Libya over the Aouzou Strip a couple of years before, and had been able to get someone senior enough on the phone to help put pressure on the company.

Five hours before the Judge learned that her husband was too busy to fly to Afghanistan to retrieve their dead child, Christian Lambert, a senior French diplomat tied to the UN had woken her from a dream in which Richard was small and worried about tooth decay.

I've spoken to someone in the Hekmatyar government, and, in lieu of the proper paperwork, they are happy to sign the body over to the next of kin. The company is pulling out. They've got a turnaround jet flying in to get their people before the end of the week and it'll be refuelling at Heathrow in about four hours. The problem; I can't promise the Hekmatyer government is going to last, so my advice to you is to have a ceremony at home and visit the grave later. But if you or Lucas…

Just before the door Robert Darlington stops and waits. Outside, through stained glass panels the Judge can see three men, all in fatigues, all well-armed, and all alert in a way that shouts military, waiting by a black sedan.

The American stands there, patient for her to catch up.

Mr. Darlington.

Shouldn't have been so rude. It's just… They were good men. All of them, he says, fingering his own pair of sunglasses as he pulls them out of his shirt pocket, revealing a thick brown stain that tells her that the freshness of the shirt is older than trip.

Some of the warlords, they don't like Americans. But they don't mind the Brits so… Your son? He was helping us with that. Seems they got over the whole Great Game problem, so we put a British face to it, alright? My idea. My call. Anyway. He was just doing his job. Nothing more. Wrong place at the wrong time, that's all it ever was. He seemed like a good kid.

The Judge looks out of the door at the car and the road beyond it.

You're going to have to give me a lift I'm afraid, Mr. Darlington. It seems your company forgot to send me a car, as well as the body of son.

The American looks at her, sizing up the possibility of refusal.

You got a scarf, he asks her. You better put it on.

Was it a car like this that Richard died in? Black, heavy, German.

Two men in the front. They weren't expecting two passengers, so one of the security guards has to remain at the airport. He grumbles something unintelligible and American and goes back inside the porta-sheds.

The armrest is hot against her arm. Was the car armour-plated? You would have thought so.

My son was Vice President of Finance, she says, matter-of-factly.

Robert Darlington looks at the Judge over the rim of his shades and nods.

They're all V.P.'s. That's the point of it. I've forgotten what the fuck title they've given me this week, he tells her. Some bullshit that'll impress the locals.

Oh, Richard. What were you doing in a place like this?!

Who wants to take a meeting with a junior financier who has been out of college for three years? Anyway... He trails off. I'm sure he was good at his job.

You requested him.

It's a question, but not one the American looks inclined to answer until she repeats it once more.

Didn't you?

I requested a Brit. Someone good at sales. Someone with the right amount of class. It's all sales at the end of the day. Sales is where the money comes from so, V.P. in Bahrain, used to sucking up to the locals? Great, put him on a plane over.

He looks out the window, remembering.

Outside is a surprisingly large and uninhabited road. Houses and shops dot each side. Low rises, single storey, small windows. Dirty white for the summer heat. All closed.

What time is it? The Judge had adjusted her watch on the flight over, but never quite trusts her calculations. Shouldn't this be rush hour?

We'll drop you off at the hotel, but I've got business to attend to in the city.

He looks at her.

Did they give you a room?

But the Judge doesn't answer.

Take me to the UN compound, she tells him.

We ain't going to the UN Compound.

The Judge nods.

Still. I'd be extremely obliged if you could take me there, nonetheless.

In the front seat the driver looks into the rear-view with amused eyes, waiting for a directive.

Robert Darlington shrugs and the car swings left, cutting off the road into a smaller turn. The man in the passenger seat adjusts his weapon and stares more carefully out of the window.

They are going to the UN compound.

Once a colony, always a colony. That's what everyone in the car understands from that little conversation.

The UN compound in Kabul sits just beyond Udheiyl, twenty minutes outside the city, in a conclave of buildings that are best accessed from the Nangarhar highway in the south.

The car approaches from the west.

During her time in Chad the Judge had grown used to the heat. She had grown used to the windowless houses that let out the air and kept the interiors cool. She had grown used to the poverty. People went about their daily lives in the midst of heartbreak and the threat of death. A market that survived a bombing or an incursion would be open for business mere hours after the event. In Chad people often forwent Western-style windows to keep the heat out, preferring shutters if they could afford them and open holes if they could not, here in Kabul, window frames are evident but bullet holes and mortar damage speak to a lack of glass that has more to do with safety than economics.

The suburbs of Kabul are a ghost-town. Few cars are parked on the street, and those that they encounter seem to be heading out of the city, loaded with as many worldly goods as they can carry.

The Baroness watches as the houses slip by one after another. Small houses pushed together. Large houses with high walls, only visible due to the extensive damage evidently from mortar attacks or tank fire.

Kabul is a war-zone. It is Paris after the liberation. It is Spain during Franco. It is Baghdad, live on CNN.

Robert Darlington sees her looking and motions out past the window.

All during the Soviets this place was as quiet as the grave. No one dared do anything here. Even coming in, they didn't really put up a fight. You'd seen this place ten years ago, he tells her. It was as like a shining jewel. The countryside was for shit, but this place… Now, the countryside is pretty much at peace and this place can't stop shooting each other.

He looks at the Judge, watching her assess the situation.

People hold grudges I guess, he adds, and goes back to looking out the window.

A family is walking down the street ahead of them, the father pulling a cart laden with belongings. The road has taken some shelling and the men in the family are trying to navigate the potholes at the side of the road while the women, head-scarfed and skin-covered, try to steady the consequences and prevent their belongings from tumbling off the lopsided cart.

The driver brakes and hammers at the horn. A child, no taller than the wheel of the cart, turns and looks at them but everyone else keeps on with the task ahead, so the driver hits the horn once more.

Go around or go back, his compatriot tells him. The driver swears under his breath and slams the car into reverse, twisting around the headrest to better see what he is doing.

Robert Darlington ducks down to give him an unobstructed view and the Judge peers over his other shoulder, out into the eyes of the boy as he grows smaller and smaller the faster they pull away. His family are concerned with saving what they can. Only their son stands witness to the black Mercedes reversing away from them.

The driver leans on the wheel and the reversing car shoots through a small intersection, then swings a hard right, causing the Judge to steady herself by holding onto the handle above the window, barely preventing herself from falling into the lap of the American.

Oh, Richard. What on earth were you doing in a place like this!?

The familiar blue hats of the UN soldiers bob about in the sunlight.

The car must have plates because it barely slows as it approaches the armed officers and they barely hesitate before moving to remove the crash barriers that line the road, designed to corral approaching vehicles into a manageable line of fire.

The drivers wave as they pull up to a dense metal barrier and righteous footsteps approach.

Robert Darlington presses a button to lower the window and offers a hearty bonjour.

Monsieur Darlington. We were not expecting anyone from you today, I'm afraid.

The American waves a thumb at the Judge.

I've got a someone's mother in the backseat boys, he starts, but the Judge isn't about to allow flagrant informality to get the best of the situation.

Please inform Mr. Laurent Viviani that the Honourable Judge Armstrong is here to retrieve the body of her son, if you would be so kind, she says. Then repeats it in French, just to irk the American.

Laurent Viviani is the diametric opposite of Robert Darlington. Overly thin and overly careful, neat with an office that borders on austerity.

The American has not come into the compound. No sooner had the Judge got out of the Mercedes than the driver hit reverse once more and they disappeared from view.

A soldier in a blue regulation hat denoting the international organisation took the Judge into a room at the side of the building and checked her passport, then handed her over to a young wordless woman who led her through the maze of the compound, out of one building and into another, before knocking on a door and leaving her to wait.

We were told you would not be coming.

Laurent Viviani's accent is Belgian. He wears a neat grey suit that belies a wiry frame and stays standing when the Judge refuses a chair.

My husband, I'm afraid. Everything was very rushed, as you can imagine.

I see.

The Judge looks at him, waiting for him to speak and when he doesn't, continues. A wave of tiredness comes over her. Anger sustained her for most of the flight. Anger at Lucas, anger at the company Richard had worked for, anger at the American, anger at her daughter-in-law, even anger at her own child. But now the energy is leaving her, and she fears that once it does the impetus might not return.

Mr. Viviani, you will have to excuse me. I understand that you have a proper way of doing things, as do I, but if it's all right with you, I'd like to see my son now.

Laurent Viviani's nail scratches the wood of the desk below his hand, revealing the thoughts that have not for one single moment crossed his face.

Of course, he replies eventually. I'll have someone take you down.

He picks up the telephone and speaks in German, asking whoever is on the other end of the line to come in. Then he waits. His finger nail tapping on the edge of the desk, thoughtfully.

I wish I had better news for you, Mrs. Armstrong. I wish I could say that you may simply take the body and go home. We would all wish it so, but my hands are tied.

They look remarkably free to me, Mr. Viviani.

A smile at that. Coy, like a cat.

They are bound by the law, Your Honour. Surely, you of all people understand that.

But the Judge isn't about to let him off that easily.

I was told if there were a next of kin…

The thin man nods. Of course, of course. But, as you can see, it is the end of the working day and no office is open until tomorrow, and even then…

He lets it hang. Like a promise.

The problem, you see Mrs. Armstrong is that the United Nations is not a country. We are not a sovereignty. We are not subject to the benifits of, say, an embassy or consulate. Had your country maintained its roots here… But no, we must abide by the law of the land. As must you. As must we all. Paperwork is the language of government, no matter what the situation, do you not agree?

A door behind her opens and Laurent Viviani looks about to usher her from the room, but tiredness or no tiredness, the Judge does not want to let the man off without a response.

Mr. Viviani. I am not here as a judge. I am not here as an employee of the state, any state, nor in my role as a legal counsellor with the United Nations. I am here as a mother – a grieving mother – who has lost her son. Please do not confuse me with someone who will ever understand or care about anything other than burying my child.

Laurent Viviani's fingernail forgoes the tap and nestles itself in the palm of his other hand.

As you wish, Mrs. Armstrong. Mariela will show you where he is being held. I hope you understand that we have made all possible provisions in the interim. My condolences again, he adds, though he had never offered them in the first place.

Richard rests in a black body bag on the floor of the basement of the central building of the compound.

There are three mounds of black. Each identical.

How does one know if she is looking at the right one?

The assistant who brought the Judge down here is a bescarfed woman in neat attire, close to her own age. She stands modestly towards the back of the room as the Judge looks down at the formless bags at her feet.

She finds a tremor in her voice as she speaks.

The other two were British?

Madame?

The other two? His… Security detail? They were British?

She repeats herself in French but is pleased when her companion addresses her in English.

No. One was. He was a soldier. Ex-soldier. The other one was Indian.

This surprises the Judge.

I thought he was Italian, she asks, but the woman seems insistent.

There are a lot of Indians in the security details. They pass more easily for locals.

But are not Muslim, questions the Judge and the woman nods her assent.

The Judge gestures down near her feet.

Which one is..?

The woman motions to the furthest from the Judge, but she is not sure the woman has understood the question, so she rephrases, indicating with a casual hand.

My son?

Yes, madam.

And for the briefest of moments the Judge can remember the weight of him in her arms. Twenty-eight years ago. Fresh and wet and soft and…

You speak French?

The woman shifts her weight, unsure of her footing.

I am French, madam. My father was born here. Just a few hundred feet from this building. But I was born in Marseilles.

The Judge nods. The moment has passed.

I'm sorry. I've forgotten your name?

Mariela, madam.

The Judge repeats it, enjoying the feel.

What will happen to the other two?

Mariela shrugs. She has been on the phone all day and still doesn't have any answers she thinks the other woman will like.

It's UN policy to bury all unclaimed remains on site after five days.

But there's no accounting for time zones.

And this is?

Day four.

The Judge nods, looking down once more at the bag containing the remnants of her child. She shifts her footing so she is standing closer to him than the others, but does not feel comfortable abandoning any of them.

Tomorrow it is, then.

I wonder, Mariela, if you could get me the details of the family of the other British man. From the security detail. I would very much like to try to see if I can help them get their son back again.

Mariela knows the answer to this but sure, why not. Let her think what she will. What harm can it do?

I'll see what I can do.

We should all rest in our beds at home in the end. Don't you agree?

Ask me anything you want.

The Baroness' fingers tap gently on the metal of the table. The ring on her wedding finger catches on every third beat, sending out a ringing noise.

If I can be honest with you, Ms. Guelmoussi. Zahra. It's not actually about questions at all. You see. There is a bill, proposed by the Lords…

Because no M.P. could do it and be re-elected.

The Baroness smiles;

You're not wrong. It would be political suicide for most Members of Parliament to introduce such a bill, which is one of the reasons that the House exists in the first place. I'm glad to see the years of education didn't go to complete waste.

But she regrets that. The barb. And adjusts her tone to convey it.

The bill, at its essence, would allow a revoking of citizenship on anyone who leaves the country to partake in acts of terrorism.

Which I haven't.

Or join a terrorist group, which you have. And that's what I'm here for. Not to question. Not to question! But to assess.

Me.

In essence. To see if this is such a case, were the law passed, that would fit the bill.

The young women is silent. The pizza is still beneath her fingers. The tea, warm in her hand.

It's not exactly against expectancies, the Baroness continues when the silence gets too long. We already prevent people from travelling overseas to such places. Under the law. Had we known about you, for example…

And that's what you're here for. To assess me. As a poster child.

Yes.

And you answer to – whom? The Prime Minister?

Ostensibly, the cabinet. The Home Office. The Lords. It's a grey area.

To what end?

The Baroness seems taken aback by this. She's staying now, is firm in her seat when she answers.

The law. Naturally.

The government wants to ban people it doesn't like from being citizens.

That is the thinking.

I was travelling from Russia…

Your passport was flagged, I'm afraid. The moment you boarded the plane to London. They knew you were coming. Such is the nature of information these days.

The young woman leans forward.

I'm going to be tortured, Baroness. I'm going to be locked away in some cell in Albania or Iceland. That's my legal status and we both know it.

The Baroness looks at her and then, for nothing more than equal parts effect and an attempt to remove the smell of green tea from her nostrils, she picks up one of the serviettes and uses it to pull open one of the grease-thick cardboard boxes that house the remaining chicken pieces. Adjusting the serviette so that her fingers don't touch it, she pulls out a wing and holds it, mid-air, halfway between the two of them. A bartering line that one of them must cross.

There was a girl. Her voice is measured now. Calming, authoritarian. There was a girl; not much younger than you, perhaps. This was a number of years ago. And she came to my court. Immigration, asylum. She had fled a country, I won't tell you which one, but she had fled that country and found herself on our shores. No passport. No means. And she was… of a religion. Of a religion in a region that we knew was suffering persecution. Blatantly. But she was on our shores. And so, it fell to me. It fell to me to talk to this girl. To make a judgement. Should that young woman, who had been raped, who had been beaten, whose sister had been killed! This is what she told us. Should that woman be granted asylum? I remember she was a small woman. Very frail, physically. There had been a boat from Holland, I believe. A small woman, but great power behind the eyes. A lot like I see in you. Strength. And I believed her. I believed everything that she said had happened to her. Every horrible event. All of it. You see, the law talks about objective facts. If you watch the TV shows that's what the law talks about. Facts that back up the case. Only, we rarely have facts. Well, perhaps in a criminal trial. Perhaps even in corporate law more so, but eighty percent of all law is made on judgements. It's why they call us judges. Eighty percent is us, listening to someone, talking to someone, and trying to discern the facts. Within the law, it's true. We could not, you understand, give a judgement that, for example, rendered this young woman's rapists dead, or the killers of her sister brought to trial in our country for crimes in their own. But, within the law, it is for us to judge. Good or bad. Laws are prescribable. One Judge will give this sentence and another, another. It is our job to interpret the law. As it stands. And occasionally, like today, it is our job to advise on its creation. To help guide it so that one Judge cannot give life for one thing while another gives freedom for exactly the same offence! The law is a living, organic thing. It is in the writing. It is in the judgement. And today, it is here in this room, if you let me listen to your story.

The young woman is quiet. Her little fingers, those perfect nails, toy unconsciously with the piece of precooked meat hanging from the edge of the slice in front of her.

What happened to her? The girl?

I believed her and I shouldn't have.

Zahra asks the Baroness if the girl had lied.

Lied? I don't know. I doubt it. But I was alerted to her. In another case. This was years later. You see, the woman... We shouldn't call her a girl. Not really. I had granted her asylum. Her life was clearly in danger. But what had she used that life for? This was maybe five, maybe six years later. The young woman. Ilsa was her name. Ilsa was convicted of killing three women. All in their seventies. You see, what she did was, she would live with these women, terrorise them, find an older woman looking for a lodger and then terrorise them. Brutalise them. For years, some of them. She would strip them of all their savings. All their benefits. Physical and mental torture. You see, she didn't want the women going out. Didn't want the women talking to anyone. She needed to make sure they were bed-bound, and bound to her. And she lived that way until they died. Or until they were of no use to her, whichever came first. You see asylum, protection; this is a Good Samaritan act. It is the act of one person, or, in this case, one country, saying: we will help you, we will protect you! But there is a de facto responsibility on the person being protected to act in a manner befitting of that kindness.

Zahra doesn't want the slice. She toys with it once more and then puts it back in the box, recovering the ring of oil soaked cardboard it belonged to.

Pulling her sleeve down over her hand she wipes the table.

You don't believe in immigration.

The Baroness smiles. On the contrary. I am one of the most vocal supporters in the House on the issue. What I did, I did within the law. I did what I could do. But I regret it, you understand? I don't doubt what she told me. I don't doubt what happened to her was real. But I shouldn't have granted her asylum. Rights – the rights of a citizen within a country – they are dependent on the behaviour of that person within that society. They must be! I saved Ilsa. Perhaps her life. The law did that. But that same decision also took the lives and the years of a number of other women. Do you see the dichotomy? Law must always be tempered with judgement. Otherwise…

She lets it hang there. A thought in the air. The wing has served its purpose and is carefully returned; the serviette rolled and placed neatly on her left-hand side.

A nation is only as strong as the people within it.

Zahra is looking at her over the rim of the cup. Obviously she likes green tea and the Baroness wonders if this factored into their choice. Perhaps she had asked for it before. Perhaps it was one of the measurements they were taking. A barometric enjoyment of beverages.

It's such an antiquated notion though, isn't it?

You don't believe in nations?

74

I believe in the corporate identity of them. I believe that they are making sure that there is trade. The creation of wealth.

Isn't that what you were doing? Forming your own.

Really?

She is leaning forward now. The pizza box is in her way and it gets pushed to one side a little aggressively, so the Baroness sits back in her chair.

The room is monitored in a number of ways.

I read your essay. Your proposal. For your Masters. Your thesis, I suppose, had you finished. On nationalism. You don't believe in it.

The young woman looks at her. Folds her arms across her chest.

It's an outdated concept.

And yet there you were, in Iraq. Fighting for one.

We don't live in one place anymore. Not one place. We live here, the young woman tells her, tapping her head. Or here, tapping the tablet in front of her. Kick racism out! Am I right? That's the hallmark of today. You can't hate someone for the colour of their skin. You can't hate them for their religion or where they come from. But you can tax them! You can make them pay. For the ability to live in one place over another. To enjoy their share of the spoils, no matter how long they've been there. You can say, no room at the inn. You can make them fill out forms and carry cards and restrict their movements and monitor them and – you know what – kick them out if they don't meet your standards! You can do all that! And why? Because they're not born in the same country as you? How arbitrary is that! As if the land is somehow important? We are not farmers. We don't need land! A flat. A small garden. Things that already exist. That's what people need. People don't live on land anymore. They don't buy from land. They live in their heads, in the gardens they create and the worlds that are sold to them. These people can live here, these people can't. These people can have running water, but these people need to die of dysentery now. How is that any better than judging someone based on the colour of their skin? On their beliefs?

Nations work on fear, Baroness Armstrong. Nations work on fear! The haves and the have-nots. If you treat land as if it's a person. If you give it an identity. If you give it a name, then it becomes distinct from everyone else and fears that one day, they will rise up and want what you have.

Your story? I despise that girl. Preying on the weak? Using them for her own gain? Keeping them alive so that they can feed her, clothe her, and then discarding them when they have no further use. And I despise you too, Baroness. You are her, in that story. Britain's laws? Choosing who lives and who dies? A country? A nation? I honestly can't tell the difference between the two of you.

Fear and discrimination are natural by-products of nation states. The only reason we keep them is so that we can trade currency.

They will need a car to get the Judge to the hotel.

Mariela tells the Judge this and disappears, leaving her standing enveloped in the sunlight streaming into a high walled garden.

It is hot, but not August hot, and the sun has a cleansing quality. The Judge just closes her eyes and feels it scour at her skin.

I have not seen you before.

The Judge opens her eyes and looks around, but being blinded by the light it takes her a moment to make out the shadow in the corner of the courtyard.

A large man sits behind a thin wooden table, positioned to allow him the best view of the garden. He is tall and dark, blending deeply into the shadows, resplendent with a thick moustache and a regal bearing.

I didn't mean to disturb.

A jug of water and a glass pin a stack of papers to the table and they bristle softly in the breeze.

The Judge raises a hand and covers her eyes to see him better.

You are not disturbing in the slightest.

The man rises, tall and formal.

There are so few interesting new faces that yours could never disturb, he adds, closing a book in front of him as he does so.

What are you writing?

The man looks at the cover.

I am translating, he says simply. Peter Hopkirk. I gather from your accent that you are British?

I am.

The man smiles, driving the thick moustache up and out like a raven preparing for flight.

Splendid!

The Judge can see him better now. He is older than he first appeared. The greying around his temples has been attended to, but he is probably the same age as Lucas. Perhaps a little older. He has a thick, square jaw that speaks of fatness as a youth, but his thick-set his body is strong and trim.

I have been having trouble with a passage…

He leans down and opens the book again at a notated page before stabbing at the offending section with his finger.

And what can one do when in such a situation but to acquiesce?

With an eye to the door Mariela left through, the Judge makes her way over to the shade and the table, pulling her reading glasses out of her pocket as she does so.

His hands layered with hair.

Which passage?

He stabs at it again. Thick fingers. Not unblemished, but controlled and exact.

It was at this moment that Wellington's government fell, taking Ellenborough with it, and the Whigs came to power…

The text is old and worn, but the Judge recognises it instantly.

I see.

Perhaps you can help?

The Whigs? Well, yes. I suppose I can.

I have asked a great many people, but I do not think that this is the same as the American party, and the library…

The Judge removes her glasses once more and looks up at the man. His well-made shirt, his even tie, the gold watch on his left wrist. A jacket, hung on a beanpole behind him.

Not quite the same, no, the Judge tells him. Same time, different country, I suppose you'd say. Think liberalism. Monarchy without the expense of the people. You can have a supreme ruler, but he must not be above the people. Liberals, I suppose would be a definition as good as any when it comes to translation.

The moustache spreads itself once more.

There! See! You British are the answer to everything!

The Judge looks down at the papers, flapping in the wind.

You are translating The Great Game?

And the great man nods.

Afghanistan, he tells her. We are destined to repeat the same mistakes again and again.

Behind her the Judge hears a door open and Mariela calls out to her from inside the building.

Mrs. Armstrong?

The Judge smiles, offering a hand.

It was a pleasure to meet you, Mr…

And he takes it, engulfing it within the palm of his own.

Doctor, he tells her. Doctor Mohammed Najibullah. Or Mister President, should you have a desire to follow formalities.

Forget pride. Forget stupidity. Think about Solh.

You told me a story, Zahra says to the Baroness. The young woman leans forward and starts piling pizza back into the box. Let me tell you one. About nations. About belonging. But she doesn't wait for an answer, just goes on, talking and packing, putting the food down on the floor once it's boxed, wiping the table free of oil with of the edge her sleeve.

The woman cannot leave.

People come from everywhere. Where I was. In the camps. People come from everywhere. Every corner of the earth represented. You should see them. The… joy.

She is cleaning, wiping, no eye contact. She takes the last of the serviettes and rubs the table, remembering.

When I was a small girl. Six… Eight… No more. There weren't many of us. A very small community. Tight-knit. My father… My father is an engineer. Bridges. For the government. And… There was no mosque. Not then. Not really. Prayers were in a room above a fish and chip shop. So in the summer it was good for the family to go… somewhere else. To one of the cities. Birmingham. We have family there, and we would stay. Sometimes three weeks at a time. Sometimes with my father, sometimes without. I still remember, as a little girl, spaghetti junction. As exciting as anything I had seen. We would have those little packets of cereal. We didn't have cereal at home, but there we would have those little boxes of cereal. Selections, I think they were called. And it was never enough. In the boxes. You would pour them into your bowl and there was never enough. But the choice! The excitement of being there, of being amongst our own people. Of not standing out. Of fellowship. It was exactly like the camps. And I loved it. I really did. For the first years. And… it was a huge community, Birmingham. Lots of family. People coming from all over. All places. Exotic, and yet familiar. People talking about seas I had never seen. London. And there was this boy. Ahmad. When you are a girl there are always boys like Ahmad. And I suppose, thinking back, he must have liked me. In some way. I must have… reminded him of something. So he would hit me. He would… pull my hair. Squeeze me until I couldn't breathe. One summer, he found tickling. He would sit on me, holding me down until I could't move, and then tickle me until I… until I wet myself. And… I began to dread it. Going there. It would be, maybe twice a year. Maybe two years this went on. And I would dread it. I would scream at my mother: I don't want to go! I don't want to go! And she would pack me in the car, and we'd go. And I would pray. Everyday. I would pray for Ahmad not to be there. Just not this year. Not this year. Don't be there. Not this time. I couldn't have been there more than five, six times at the most, but for me, even now, it feels like… a lifetime.

The children. We were always so well behaved. Not like the other children. Not wild like the Western kids. But we would play together in the playing fields behind the mosque. With the trees. Our parents would talk and we would play. Small, small children. And Ahmad. He was… I don't know if he was big or I was small. But we'd play hide and seek, or tag, or whatever. Only, one time I was 'it'. I had to close my eyes. And he… Ahmad… he came up behind me and my eyes were closed and he pulled…

And I stood there. Naked. From the waist. And they were laughing. And I tried to pull my skirt up but he had grabbed me from behind. Pinning my arms. Lifting me off the floor. And I could feel him behind me. And laughing. Everyone laughing. I can still feel the heat of him behind me. His breath on my ear. I couldn't have been more than eight or nine.

Ahmad never came again. I was crying so hard my mother had to ask the other children and someone… I don't know who. He never came again. His parents neither.

And it is strange to hear the sudden Welsh in her voice. Strange to hear the vowels elongated. The negatives at play.

So, anyway…

And her voice is back to its crisp delivery, lacking a lilt.

So, anyway. I never really thought of him again. Ahmad. Until I got to the camps. His parents had moved back to Syria where they came from, though I doubt that was in relation to… Anyway, I went to the camps and there he was. Working there. And I could recognise him, you know? I could tell just by looking at him. Who he was. Still there. He wasn't big anymore, or I'd grown, but it was still there, in his face, I knew it the moment I saw him, recognised him. And… all those feelings, those… humiliations. And I nearly left. Right there. I couldn't stand it, you know?

His parents had been killed. I don't think he recognised me. I mean, why would he? I was just this little girl he used to terrorise, right? And the niqab… The purpose of a niqab is to prevent sin, to protect, and… His parents. His sister… She was much older than me. His sister, all of them, they were killed. In Damascus. No one tells you. No one tells you what's happening! They were in a car. All three of them. I don't know where Ahmad was. They were in a car and they were shot. Still in the car. I saw pictures. Just a family, out for a drive. Dead. And no one explains it.

I told my husband about him. I had to. I couldn't stay. It wasn't him. Ahmad. It wasn't… He wasn't that boy anymore, but for me… I told him – my husband – and he talked to him. To Ahmad. They had this long conversation.

She leaves it in the air. Words unspoken. The table clean.

Everyone there is a warrior. It's why they are there. In the camps. Everyone is a fighter. Answering the call.

That was the longest night of my life. The shame, you know? Sitting there, waiting for my husband to come back. And, they are together, when they come back. And Ahmad he has…

She gestures with her fingers.

He has tears in his eyes. And he kneels before me. I am… He kneels before me and he has tears in his eyes. This man. This holy warrior, he has tears in his eyes, and he begs, he begs, right there on the floor, he begs for my forgiveness. He asks God to forgive him. Right there. Right in front of me. And my husband, he's looking at me. And Ahmad – this holy man – asks me, he asks me; how do I make this right? How do I receive God's justice? With tears in his eyes. And I tell him that the sin, the sin was on a child and it can only be taken away by a child. It can only be forgiven by a child. And I know that I am right on this. I know that this is good. This man. This holy man of peace…

She sits back, the memory finished. And whether it's the exhaustion or whether it's the rhetoric of the answer, she finds a little catch in her voice, an uncharacteristic catch in her voice when she tells the Baroness about the schools in the camp. About the madrasas where they teach the Quran. Where they teach math and science and religion and languages. Where children play and sing and dance and grow in safety. Far from the eyes of man. Safe from the drones. And she tells the Baroness about the man who has committed himself to this. About Ahmad. The warrior whose parents were killed in an assassination. Who has waged Jihad in line with the Sunnah. Who now taught children how to read and write and play and sing and grow in the words of God.

You talk to me about justice. About the law having a human face. About the application of law? This is law! This is justice! There are no borders when it comes to justice. No difference between this country and that country. The sin committed by a man stays with him throughout the world. This is why nations are destined to fail! This is why they cannot be allowed to continue. We are one people. One. Not a thousand. The sin you commit there is still a sin whichever border you cross. And justice always has a human face. No matter what laws you tie yourself up in.

The Hotel Intercontinental Kabul is a monolithic beast, rising up from the surrounding hillside like a reminder of days gone by.

It was built by a British company some ten years before the Soviet arrival as part of the Intercontinental Hotel Group but it stands, battered and broken, a memorial to the departed Soviets and no one here remembers the British involvement in it's creation.

Of its some two hundred rooms almost three-quarters are now missing a floor or a ceiling or a wall of some kind. What the Soviets didn't plunder, the fighting Mujahedeen destroyed with mortar as regime after triumphant regime took up residence in its halls following their return from the mountains.

Like all great institutions however, it perseveres. The front door is unusable, as is the grand foyer, and guests must enter through the back, past a system of security guards and police checks that far outweigh those done at the United Nations.

It is, after all, now home to the Western media.

Those displaced by the end of the war in Iraq have bunkered down to report here. War always continues somewhere in the world, and this the West believes may well be its next stop.

The BBC occupies many of the last rooms left standing on the fifth floor, with CNN using their satellite link like a salivating puppy next to a sated dog. The rest are largely print journalists, a few American thrill seekers and heads of business. The last remnants of the great capitalist machine, still hoping to secure deals in a country that has grown tired of waiting for the markets to save them.

They do not seem to have a room for the Judge, but they allow her to call Richard's company from the phone at the front desk in order to get permission to use theirs.

She calls Lucas first, but there's no answer. Not at home and not on his mobile, and the Judge does not have the fortitude to be put on hold by one of his numerous assistants.

The desk has the number of the Bahrain office though, so she calls there instead, listening as a loop of transfers and hold music inch her towards someone who can secure her a spot to rest her head.

We thought you would have been able to make arrangements immediately, Mrs. Armstrong.

The Judge does not know the man she is speaking to, but it is clearly someone Lucas has been in contact with over the past few days.

The Judge explains about the problem of time zones and the man apologises before asking to be put on the phone with the concierge.

She hands the phone to the boy behind the desk and turns away. There is a weariness in her now. Dusk has crept in, both in the world around her and her soul.

They could hear the sound of shelling as Mariela drove her from the compound. It was, at first, distant, like thunder, and then came the answering response. Loud, and close by. The Judge craned her head out of the car window to see where it was coming from, but the highway was empty and calm.

Most people left days ago, Mariela told her. A lot of people, including those in the army, believe that the Taliban are going to be a positive change for Afghanistan. No more infighting, no more shells. Still, they're not stupid enough to think that either Hekmatyer or Rabbani are going to run away without a fight so they have taken to the hills to wait and see. Even in August the city is never as quiet as this!

And you?

Mariela checked the rear-view mirror and shrugged.

I am here on a UN passport and I'll be going back to France as soon as I can, she told the Judge and pulled them off the highway, headed for the hotel.

The boy behind the desk finds her a room and someone carries her bag up for her. Mariela has gone. She is meeting some friends, though where that might be possible the Judge doesn't know.

The boy takes pride in the room as he shows her around and the Judge regrets that she didn't exchange any money to give him. She pulls out her wallet but all she has are pounds, so she passes him a fifty instead.

At least, she thinks, I had the sense to go to the bank before the car arrived for the airport!

The boy bows with almost comic intensity and the Judge has to push him out of the room, mostly to stop him from offering her a plethora of delights, many of which are thankfully illegal back home in England. But as soon as he is gone, she regrets it.

The room is vast and sad. Curtains hide a window half made up of boards haphazardly nailed together, and later, when she finally lies down on the bed, the Judge will notice three neat bullet holes strafed across the lily white ceiling.

And the panorama from the windows still afforded glass? There lies Kabul. Dust and spit. A city broken by every hand that ever held it.

She pulls the curtains together and exits the room. Weariness is not a companion she has any desire to meet. At least, not alone.

The bar at the Intercontinental Hotel Kabul is in the basement, and like all good wartime bars it contains the last vestiges of alcohol found within the city. The closer the frontline creeps, the harder the guests drink.

The Judge orders a scotch and asks for the bottle. She rarely drinks, and even then no more than one or two, but she has been to bars like these before and knows that the fastest cure for loneliness is to have a bottle ready to be poured.

The bar is half full and she can see Mariela speaking earnestly in the corner, but not wanting to intrude she stays at the counter instead.

A few seats down from her two Germans are talking about the heroin farms in the north. One man is telling the other about a tour he had of the opium productions there. Vast fields of poppies, staining the sky as far as the eye can see. He tells a story of the men and women of the region, each gainfully employed – able to feel safe within their land – working to produce vast quantities of the drug. He tells of the factories that are being set up to maximise production.

Seriously, the one asks the other. Isn't this the perfect example of capitalism in action? Egalitarian ownership of land funnelled through a central pipeline, answerable only to profit and production?

The one tells the other about a man he has seen who had stolen from the region - or perhaps just disagreed with the product. He was hung up in the town square, his fingers flayed from their bones before being shot and left for the crows to peck at their leisure.

Perhaps he was from one of the other provinces, his friend offers.

The Baroness sips her drink and thinks about Richard. She is trying to remember the sound of his voice, but can't hear him. When did they talk last? Three weeks before? No, it was before the summer break. May, at the earliest. He had come back from Bahrain for something and wanted to borrow a car.

He was only allowed back in the UK for up to ninety days a year, he told her then, or his income would become taxable, so he wanted to get in and get out before the days started to add up.

She had asked about Bethany but there was nothing to report. There was never anything to report. Her life moved forward through a social string of hair appointments and pleasantries.

Has she ever considered a career, Lucas had asked him once while the Judge was within earshot.

And do what, her son had replied. Preside over other people's problems?

And then she can hear it, the laugh, and through it his voice. She can hear him telling her that Christmas might be a problem because they were looking at flying to New York for some shopping. And now here's her own voice, telling him that Bethany can go shopping the other three hundred and sixty-odd days of the year, but Christmas is in Surrey.

Lord Osbourne would not be long for this world, she had told him, which was ironic now she came to think about it.

She had called her parents the night of the phone-call. That's what they were calling it: The night of the phone-call. Her mother had cried. And even Lord Osbourne had a catch in his voice before she hung up.

Grandparents, she knew, were so much more enamoured with their children's children than they ever were with their own. Life is strident when you are young. It is full of important choices and realisations, and simply staying ahead of the game takes precedence over loving a child completely. You fall into your mistakes with your own children, and then you make up for it when they have children of their own.

I will never get to make it up to him.

These are the moments that hit you. The drink in her hand. The thought in her head. The rising fear in her chest.

I will never have grandchildren of my own.

Mrs. Armstrong?

Mariela is standing next to her, fear in her face, fleeting because she knows the Judge had seen it and so, gracefully, conceals.

Are you alright?

The Judge looks down at her drink and, uncharacteristically, finishes it in one.

Under the circumstances, yes.

You are drinking alone?

The headscarf has gone now and her face, though weathered, is not without beauty. The Judge chides herself for thinking the woman Muslim and tells her so.

No, not Muslim. Though I don't really tell anyone that. My father was Bahá'í but I don't know what I am now. Won't you join us?

The invitation is met with sudden thunder. Glasses shake and the bar grows quiet. A few people stand, gathering the cameras and equipment lying around the room.

Another follows. Softer this time, and the bar lets out a raucous cheer in celebration and relief.

That's just outside the city, one of the Germans tells the other and his friend agrees.

Think we'll hold out longer than the weekend, he questions, hopeful.

The Judge follows Mariela back to her booth, bottle in hand. The pair are joined by a few others and they struggle to find chairs for them all.

So what brings you to Afghanistan, asks a young Canadian with unnaturally bright eyes and a failing beard.

She's advising at the UN, Mariela interjects before the Judge can answer.

I'm a Judge. Immigration mostly, so I advise the UN on a number of issues.

Do they listen?

This from a small American woman who sits at the back. Small, hard, and a little younger than the Judge, though not by much, she is dressed in a t-shirt and jeans and has producer written all over her.

Not so much, the Judge tells her. No.

Her reporter, obvious from his middle-American, good-for-all-time-zones consonants as much as from his fine head of hair, interjects with a toast.

To War, he says. May it live long and prosper!

But no one appears eager in their appreciation of the joke.

I think it's easy to forget, starts the Judge and regrets it immediately, that 'war' is a legal definition.

Is that important?

But the Judge has already resigned herself to her glass and issues a 'probably not' while gazing back in the direction of the bar.

We'll never be involved in a war again. Not like you mean.

The small producer is looking at her. Clear eyes that belie the bottle of whisky half empty in front of her.

I don't think we're ever going to call it a war.

Isn't that problematic, asks Mariela.

Not for us!

But no one is listening to the reporter.

It's about people now, not countries, says the small producer, her eyes never leaving the Judge. What we want, where we want it... Every state that is comfortable acting outside the law when it comes to a foreign power will eventually be comfortable acting outside the law with its own people. That's what it's like. In South America. In Africa. Iran. Asia. The police come to the door one night and take you in, for questioning you understand, and you're never heard from again. No warrant. No record. Just another body in a half covered ditch that nobody even looks for. That's what we'll come to.

Hell, interjects another, we won't even knock on the door. We won't declare war on you, we'll just take you off your front porch!

But the reporter is tired of this.

Did I tell you, he announces to the corner, I'm writing a play!

The small producer rises at this and heads to the bar.

Fuck, she says as she exits, pushing past the Judge to do so. Not this again.

Or maybe it's a TV play, I haven't decided yet.

The corner booth collectively peer into their drinks, praying for mortar fire to save them from being subjected to a plot they have heard a hundred times over, but the Judge hasn't heard it and listens intrigued.

It's called "Which? War", he says. With a question mark at the end of the which. Like the magazine.

It's British, isn't it, says the Judge. The citizen advice bureau?

But the reporter doesn't know. He just likes the sound of it and tells them so.

Anyway, so we open on a hotel room. Reporter and producer checking in. Looks like Vietnam. The guy at the door gets tipped, they check out the room, talk about work. Maybe even fuck around a little.

His gaze drifts up to the bar and his producer.

Anyway. They call for room service and up comes this guy, only it's not Vietnam anymore. Now it's Angola or Mogadishu or some shit. And they're a bit confused by this. This isn't Vietnam? Shit. We better get our shit together. What the fuck do we know about… wherever it is?!

He takes a swing of his drink while another man makes his excuses and heads to the toilet.

So, they've got an interview coming up. Big one. Got to know everything there is to know. So they set up the camera and go over some questions but when the guy comes in, it's not…

Wherever it was, interject someone ironically, his accent revealing him to be Dutch.

Right. This time it's Iraq. They're in Iraq! So all the questions are wrong. All the stuff is disjointed, you see? One continuous war.

What happens in the end, asks a man in a military uniform that the Judge can't place.

But the American is bored with his own story.

Oh, they get kidnapped, by the next guy who walks in. Probably Afghan. Anyway, see. I think this is how the American public thinks about war overseas. It's just too much learning. You just get your head around one place and the next one kicks off and you got to learn about that instead. To them it's all just one big battle. Over there. In places they never wanted to visit in the first place. Never learnt about in school.

He thinks for a moment.

At least the Soviets used to invade places they'd actually heard of. Well, some of them, he adds, and heads to the bar himself, slipping an arm around his small producer in a manner that displeases her.

Everyone is a little on edge, Mariela tells the Judge. The Taliban are religious, but there has been talk, in some of the provinces, about the level of control, not to mention how much money they have behind them, so people are leaving. Even the UN is bringing in planes on standby in case there needs to be an evacuation.

I thought I might find you here.

The Judge turns to find Robert Darlington standing behind her, a large orange football tucked under one arm.

I brought you this, he says, handing it over to her. As a keepsake.

The Judge takes it from him, noting the bright blue 76 in the centre.

It's what we brought in on the plane. The soccer balls. For the kids, he adds, seemingly disappointed at the possibility that she might have forgotten.

The Judge looks at the ball, remembering Richard one summer back in Surrey on the lawn, kicking downhill and running up.

Why is it orange, the Judge asks, taking the proffered ball and turning it in her hands.

Robert Darlington looks at her, his ever-present sunglasses now pinned to the top of his head like raised eyebrows, expressing shock at the question.

It's our logo, he says, incredulity slipping out with every syllable. Unocal? The company your son's been working for these past five years?

The Baroness sits back in her chair. A memory of celluloid under her fingers flashes through her, though she can't bear to remember the picture it contains. Just the feel of it, cold, slick, almost wet to the touch.

The young woman in front of her has finished her story.

What you are talking about is justice, the Baroness tells her. What I am talking about is law.

Zahra asks her why they are not one and the same.

What of the people who choose to live alone? Choose not to congregate. Isolate themselves. Don't those people have the right to be left to their own devices? To form their own society? Hasn't, after all, that been the cry of all religious minorities at one time or another? The story you told? It's a pretty story. A man who is moved by his past crimes.

By his religion!

Alright, by his beliefs. Moved to help children after bullying them as a child. But what did you call him? A warrior? A soldier? Someone who kills people. A killer affected to atonement for a sin, but not that sin! How many had this man killed? Does he atone for them too?

Doesn't everyone deserve a second chance?

The Baroness leans back and looks at the woman, with her fine nails, her perfect skin. Her clear eyes. Her youth.

Indeed.

We have democracies. Here in Britain, we are a democracy. We're told this. That means we are responsible. For our government. The tyrant? The man who subdues the people, the people have no say over him. Over what he does, what he is like. They have no say and no blame. No blood on their hands for the countless children their leader has killed. Not the everyday man, at least. Not the man in the street. But in a democracy we are responsible, directly responsible for the acts of our government! We are responsible when they strip a country of its wealth. We are responsible when they set up a dictator who slaughters his people because it will further their interests. We are responsible when drones fly over cities and prey on children playing in the street. When soldiers shoot innocents while defiling their beliefs. We are responsible for all of this. We are a democracy and we cannot wipe the blood off our hands.

I was born in the green fields and the coal quarries. This is my country just as much as it is yours, but I would say that we have about as much in common as either one of us does to... an Eskimo. An Inuit. I grew up on a street made·up solely of white working-class Christian drinkers. Grandsons of coal miners and dock workers who now sweat for Sony or Tesco. How much do you think I have in common with them? How much do they have in common with you? Do you have the same values? The same insights? The same politics? Do we want the same thing for our country? I have more in common with a woman in the Philippines than I do with the people on my street. More in common with people from Botswana, Pakistan. These are my constituents! These are the people I want representing me! And where do you live, Baroness Armstrong? Don't say London because I've been to London. I've been to Catford. I've been to Tottenham, and I didn't see you there!

I don't pretend to understand your world, Baroness. But I'm sure it isn't EastEnders and rugby down the pub on weekends. I'm sure it isn't fish and chips. The Sun. The club on Friday. That's where I come from. That's my home! And it isn't me, either.

I'm sorry, Baroness Armstrong, but you seem to want it both ways. Either this is my country and you have no right to hold me here, or it's not. You want to say that I acted against my country? Against the people in my country? Then go ahead. But you better arrest the girl who grows up on American TV. That boy who plays on the internet all night with his friends from China. The old man who hates darkies. Because this is not their country either. You may want to define this country as 'like you' or 'like them'. But either this is my country and you have no right to say where I can go in it, or this is yours and I'm just another visitor.

The Judge leans back.

Are you finished? But apparently she's not.

Are you my better? Do you tell me who I am and where I can go? I don't know, maybe you have the legal right to. But then; they were right. The children on my street. In my school. This is a white man's country and you are kidding yourself if you think you are any better off than me! The people? They are not you either and one day – one day – they are going to notice that and come for you in much the same way as you are coming for me right now! I am your foreigner. And if that's true then all I have done is fight for my people, which, frankly, is none of your business.

Why not make a new state? A real state. Where all men are truly equal! Not under the laws of man, which only go to serve himself. But under the laws of God, where no man can ever adjust the law to suit himself, as you are doing now!

The Baroness leans forward. There is nothing to gain here outside of empty rhetoric.

You believe in your religion.

Yes.

You believe that governments are set against you. Your religion.

I believe that people are not defined by a geographic location. Not anymore. You seem well travelled, Baroness. Who are your friends? Which countries do they come from? Are they less than you? Do they deserve to be treated differently? I am sure these are not concerns for you, Baroness. I'm sure these are not questions you need to ask yourself. Do you belong? This is not something you think about. But for many of us, for most of us, these are questions we ask every day. And when you are holidaying in Nice or Spain or wherever it is you go, ask yourself about the people. Are they less than you? Do they deserve less because they were born in a different geographic location?

What do we live with? Our celebrities abuse children. Our leaders lie and cheat. Our heroes are people who steal other people's money in order to keep up their lavish lifestyles of excess. Who force people out of their homes, and then celebrate making money from it! Our country is a country of bigots and abusers. Violence and theft! A haven for the rich and a lottery for the poor. Is that the country you are trying to protect from us, Baroness? Is that the country you are trying to cling to? The freedom you are eager to protect?

The Baroness' tea is cold, still she holds it in her hand. She toys with the thin ridges of the cardboard under her thumb, aware of how her wedding ring feels against the paper, buckling under her touch.

Let me ask you this…

And the young woman sits back. Her arms fall to her sides, the thumb of her left hand against the metal of the chair. The right falling weightlessly, swaying slightly with the momentum.

Let me ask you this. You say that this is not your country. I suppose the argument would run that you did not have any choice in being born here.

Have you ever read Rousseau, Baroness?

An interjection. Unpleasant. The Baroness misses the bench where such an outburst would have led to severity.

Are you trying to opt out? Is that what you are trying to tell me, Ms. Guelmoussi?

And the sting is enough to silence her.

I have read my social contract, yes, if that's what you are asking.

Why do you deserve the state's protection? Indeed, if you are looking to step outside of it, if you are looking to break the social contact - as you alluded to there - then why seek it at all? Why... come back? You act against the interest of the state. Why should it protect you?

Because I have broken no laws!

Really?

Put me on trial. Put all of us on trial!

And the Baroness can't tell what angers her about this, what words give rise to her voice, but she can feel it in her, feel it in her hands, feel it in the words passing through her lips:

I suppose I'm trying to understand whether this intelligence is something of your own, your own thoughts and reasoning, or whether it is something that they teach you. Answers that they tell you to give. Reasons that they ask you to justify.

That's for you to decide.

Indeed.

You speak very well, Ms. Guelmoussi. Very controlled. Very passionate. You speak of the high-minded ideals of truth and justice but this week your group killed five Western hostages, the Baroness says. A British man, two Americans, a Dutchman and a Jordanian. That, however, is not the part that bothers me. That is not the part that, I believe, would bother you!

Your group executed five people while you were taking a flight out of Turkey. Two French aid workers were with them but when the French government paid up, they were released. Do you understand? These people? Your people? Who are trying to change the world? They did not bend their principles based on wisdom or conscience. Money! That was all they were looking for. Money, and we can all go free! You speak of justice and sacrifice, but this is a business to them, nothing more, nothing less. And as soon as they lose control of the oil fields and the French stop paying them, they will be gone as quickly as they came to be.

It is four am at the Hotel Intercontinental Kabul when the phone call comes in from the UK. Four-fifteen before they can raise the Judge.

A boy is dispatched from the front desk. The telephones in the rooms don't work, so there is a constant stream of young boys available at all hours, ready to ferry bottles and dispatches and clean towels up to the rooms of people for whom sleep is akin to battle.

He knocks without ceasing on the bedroom door, but the Judge doesn't wake. In her dreams she sees the boy in the street, watching their reversing car while his family tries to save themselves. Their worldly goods in the cart, circumnavigating the endless potholes. Lucas is there. He is telling her that the boy is on her docket. He doesn't have immigration papers. He doesn't have a court date. What is she to do…?

The bellboy, worried he might have the wrong room but certain he doesn't, goes back to the desk and tells a man who tells the woman on the phone that the Judge isn't answering. The woman is insistent however, so back the boy goes and this time the Judge answers the pounding on the other side of the door on the fourth attempt.

The Judge had drunk no more than four singles over the course of the evening, but neither had she slept more than a few hours over the past few days.

Sleep and ghosts go too well together.

The conversation in the bar took on many turns while she was there and still awake. Mariela had gone to bed soon after the introduction of the American in an abrupt way that told the Judge more than she wanted to know. Robert Darlington had however, to her surprise, stayed and the level of exchanges were raised thanks to his presence.

There were two types of journalist, the Judge decided. There were the junkies; hungry for the next rush, the next piece of news, the next big thing. They loved the world of corporate greed and warfare, and loved to hate it even more. The others were those embattled by the world, seeking salvation in one child saved, searching endlessly through war-zones for the redemption they so desperately needed.

The bar at the Hotel Intercontinental Kabul had a fine mixture of both, and the American salesman was the perfect catalyst to set them at each other's throats. There had been heated exchanges, and one of the Germans who had been propping up the bar attempted to show off his skills with Robert Darlington's football and got bared in the process.

Then the shelling intensified.

A lot of the reporters left then, including the anchor-man and his small and increasingly displeased producer. Robert Darlington grabbed a radio from behind the bar - where it was obviously always kept - and tuned in to a local station.

It surprised the Judge that the man spoke Persian so well, but no one else on that side of the bar seemed to think it strange, and they listened as he translated what he heard.

The shelling was outside the city.

Taliban forces had met with government forces.

People were fleeing.

Rabbani is too strong, offered one commentator, but the Judge noticed the passive incredulity in Robert Darlington's voice when he said that he shouldn't be too sure.

It's like Iran all over again, offered another. When did they say the UN plane was getting here, and the Judge noticed that the American didn't divulge the fact that he had a jet waiting at the airport.

The airport is to the north of the city, cited another. It'll be days before anything begins to happen.

They wouldn't dare touch the UN, said a third, but nobody believed that.

By the time one of the guests discretely nudged the Judge awake some hours later, Robert Darlington had gone. She made her excuses and headed upstairs to her room. It was one in the morning, and the Judge was unsteady on her feet. The shelling had stopped, or perhaps she had simply moved past the ability to hear it. She didn't undress, just simply flopped down on the bed without removing the cover and went to sleep, muscle memory kicking her shoes off one by one as she drifted from one dream state to another in quick succession.

The boy from the front desk is small and speaks no English, but miming he manages to communicate that there is a telephone call for the Judge in reception and she returns to the foot of her bed to collect her shoes before following him down.

Hotels are eerie affairs at four am. Even in a city where most lights have long since been extinguished, the lights within the hotel shine brightly but in patches, with one corridor as bright as the sun but the next shrouded in half-light and shadow.

The Judge follows the boy to the stairs, remembering halfway down that she forgot to collect her purse before leaving, grabbing only the room key, attached as it is to a large wooden stick-like object that has long since lost its significance and meaning.

At the desk the man hands her the telephone without a smile, and the Judge turns her back before speaking into the mouthpiece.

Hello?

Judge Armstrong? It's Kate Harring. From Lucas' office.

Lucas. Perhaps he'd had a change of heart and followed her out somehow? Perhaps a charter of some kind…

Yes, Kate. Hello.

I'm sorry to bother you at this time of night, but we were wondering if you'd heard from Lucas over the past few hours.

The Judge tells her that she hasn't. She has, after all, been on a plane for the best part of a day.

Only he didn't come into the office yesterday. Which we all understand, she adds. And we've tried to contact him at home, but there's no answer.

Have you tried his mobile, perhaps? It's an impotent question, but the Judge decides to forgive herself due to the hour.

We have – and there's patience in the young woman's voice now – but we're not getting any luck with that either. We knew you were flying… out and we were a little concerned, so we sent a runner round but I'm afraid there's no answer at your residence either.

Ms. Harring. My husband and I have just lost our son. Forgive me, but it does seem that a desire to be incommunicado can hardly been seen as a cause for alarm.

Well…

And there's lead in that silence. Heavy and portentous.

Well… He did leave the office in, understandably of course, but you know, quite a state. Ordinarily, of course… but with you out of the country…

Damn you, Lucas. Damn you for abandoning our son. Damn you for humiliating me with your secretary like this! Damn you all to hell, you selfish bastard!

The Judge's first call gets no answer. The home telephone rings out but no one picks up. The mobile is the same. The Judge then dials the housekeeper's number, but a quick check of the time confirms the lateness so she is not surprised when there is no response.

Goddamn you, Lucas. What in hell could make you disappear like this?

She phones the club. In thirty years of marriage the Judge has never called the club, and until now had no idea how much she prided herself on that fact.

Lucas is not there. They have not seen him in over a week. He has not signed in. Nor have any guests requested rooms for the night.

Damn it all to hell!

People are in your life for two reasons, the Judge has always believed. There are people who bring you joy. People you look up to or look after, but who you nevertheless simply enjoy the company of, and take pleasure in who they are. Then there are people you are tied to. People you can't untangle yourself from. Dead weights, pulling you down.

The Judge needs her mobile phone to find Bethany's number, so she returns to her room and scrolls through her list of contacts until she finds it just where she knew it would be, under; Wife, Richard.

She stares at the designation for some time, pushing a button to turn it back on every time the green light of the screen starts to dim. Finally, she selects it, and not knowing whether her battery will last she writes the number on a piece of paper, before trudging down the once-grand staircase again to place the call.

Rachel?

Not mother. Not Judge. Just Rachel.

Bethany. Hello. Were you asleep? I'm so sorry. I wonder if you could do me a favour…

She waits, the words hanging in the air, leaving them to sink in or for the phone to click off again, which, frankly, wouldn't be a surprise.

Rachel?

Yes. I'm terribly sorry to bother you but I'm afraid it couldn't wait. Did I wake you?

I thought you were in Afghanistan!

Yes, Bethany. I am. I... I'm calling from the hotel, you see.

She can hear Bethany thinking this through, grasping the concept; or is she being too unkind?

Are you with me, Bethany?

Is there a problem with Richard?

Apart from him being dead, you mean, the Judge thinks, but regrets it immediately. The woman has lost her husband, she tells herself. And her pay-check, another voice adds.

It's Lucas, I'm afraid. He's not picking up and we're a little worried that something might have happened.

The Judge pauses for a moment, gathering herself.

We're a little worried… Well, you can understand, I'm sure.

Silence.

Have you tried calling him?

The Judge breathes out.

Yes. I wonder if you wouldn't mind popping around to the house. Making sure everything is alright? I don't want to call the police if I can at all avoid it. Richard has a key. I believe you'll find it on the key rack. Leather fob with his initials.

More silence.

I don't want to have to call the police, you understand, if he's just taken a couple of sleeping tablets, but I'm afraid this really can't wait and…

She despises every moment of this though it's too late to stop now. But honesty, perhaps, at the end of it all, honesty is the only thing we're left with.

I'm afraid this just can't wait, and there really isn't anyone else I can ask!

It will be two and a half hours before the phone rings again.

In the interim the Judge steps out onto the front steps of the Hotel Intercontinental and looks out at the dying darkness of the capital below.

Private security guards man checkpoints leading up to the lobby and their lights are like landing strips for the city beyond, guiding it in to the microcosm of the world represented in the hotel. The denizens holed up in bombed out rooms, waiting for the next story to give them some worth. Waiting for death to give them something to do.

Well, she thinks. At least they'll know how to find us when they take the city, and she steps back inside to see if the kitchen has opened for coffee.

She watches the dawn from a room without windows, peering around a sorry pot plant to an open door and the kitchen beyond, using the faraway service entrance as a viewpoint out, waiting for Richard's wife to tell her that she, too, has become a widow and that Lucas simply decided to take one sleeping pill too many and she should look into matching plots.

But Lucas is not dead.

Bethany calls just before seven and tells her that he is fine, but that he doesn't want to come to the phone.

What do you mean? He doesn't want to come to the phone?

I think he's too upset. We all are.

Have you called a doctor?

But Bethany tells her that she is simply respecting his wishes. There's nothing to worry about. He's already messaged work to let them know he'll be taking a few days off until after the funeral.

The Judge blinks into the face of the concierge.

I don't understand.

He's just lost his son, Rachel!

Just like that. Like a slap in her face.

I see.

People deal with grief in different ways!

And all the Judge can think is how incredulous it all is. After all, he was fine enough to go to work…

Put my husband on the phone, please!

I really don't want to get in the middle of…

Put my husband on the phone, Bethany. Immediately. If you don't mind.

But Bethany doesn't put her husband on the phone. She puts the phone back in its cradle and the Judge can hear the click of it as she's cut off from three thousand miles away.

She stands there. Phone to her ear, listening to a dial tone as anger swells through every fibre of her being.

It is only later she realises that neither Bethany nor, by proxy, her husband have asked if she is bringing Richard home, and whether or not it will be in time for the funeral.

There was this boy…

The young woman is in full raconteur mode now, her hands bunched, her shoulders turned downwards, her eyes away, and the Baroness thinks about how long it's been since she's used English to express an opinion.

There was this boy, in the camps. When you first arrive there are a number of things that they teach you. A woman alone is a target. She is a temptation. Many of the men are young and inexperienced. So there is a boy. Harun. He was my… helper. My escort. When I went out he went with me to make sure I was protected.

He was my first real guide to the camps.

They gave him to me because he spoke French. I don't speak French but I guess they thought I did, because that's what the women told me. That he was given to me because he spoke French.

We would speak to each other, Harun and I, in Arabic. I was learning Arabic, you see. It's one of the first things they teach you in the camps. That you need to learn it. So, he would speak to me in French and I would speak to him in Arabic. Or words of it, at any rate.

These were the first days. You understand? Before I was married.

And… Harun, he was twelve. Thereabouts anyway. Just under, though I didn't know it at the time. He was Iraqi. Thick, thick hair brushing tiny shoulders. This transparent beard forming on his face. Just a few whiskers of it, but he was so proud. And he would stay with me, show me around the camps. Show me where things were. Talk to the men for me, though he rarely knew what I wanted until my Arabic got better.

I have no idea how he learnt French.

The Baroness is tired. She stretches her toes in her shoes and listens to them click under the table.

All of the women had them. The boys. They would live in one of the rooms, and we would live in the others. And we'd teach them. In return for their help, we would teach them things. They all had teachers for their studies. The Quran. Science. Things are not quite as Third World as you think they are.

The Baroness raises an eyebrow but it goes unnoticed, along with the rhythm of her toes.

We taught him cooking. I did. And he was good at it. Much better than me. He had the right sized fingers for it. You know? For the spices. A pinch. The right size fingers.

And he was with me. Right up to the wedding, he was with me. Then one day he was gone.

The Baroness leans forward and interjects. Sleep is creeping up on her.

Your friend? Ahmad?

But the young woman looks at her as though the name means nothing to her.

At the school?

She shakes her head. No, nothing like that, she says. One day he was just gone. He gets up in the morning and doesn't come back at night. There's a new boy. Younger. Eight or so. Frightened. Doesn't speak French.

But there was a lot to do. It was a busy time and I was still getting used to the place. I was still a stranger…

She leaves it there for a moment. Lost in her thoughts, and the Baroness leaves her there until she decides to return.

I saw him again, later.

When?

Six months, a little more. We were still in Iraq. And I saw him, on the edge of the camp. In a truck. He was… She pauses, unsure whether or not she should tell the Baroness. Unsure about how it will make her feel.

He had a gun. He was assembling it. He was just sitting on the back of a truck assembling a gun. Oil and cloth at his side.

And I called out to him. I was shocked, you see. Even then. I was new to the place. I was finding my feet. But I called out to him. Told him to get away from there, but he ignored me. So I called out in French instead.

Arrêtez-vous! Harun, arrêtez-vous! My French is terrible.

And he looks up, looks right past me, and looks down again, but I'm nearly on top of him now and I grab his arm. I want him to stop, you see? I want him to be safe. A child playing with guns.

And he twists out of my grip. I'm telling him my name and he twists out of my grip. And I forget. You see, he's twelve now. Actually twelve. A man. And he shouldn't be touching me. Shouldn't be talking to me.

You are the property of someone else.

But the admonition goes unnoticed and the young woman continues unabated.

What are you doing? I ask him. Playing with guns! You'll get hurt!

And he's angry with me, angry for touching him in such a manner, but I'm not listening. All I can see is this sweet boy who I taught to cook playing with a gun. Not the soldier that he now is.

And he tells me. He tells me, why shouldn't I fight? Why shouldn't I pick up a gun and fight when they are dropping bombs that kill us all? They do not discriminate against age. Why should we? If a child is old enough to drop a bomb on, then he is old enough to defend himself against it.

My brother, Baroness Armstrong. I love my brother. I love him as if he was my own child, but he should be fighting for his people, not stealing cars. He brings shame on us. He brings shame on me! When there are so many things in the world that need changing and all he can do is steal from people, then he deserves what he gets.

We have laws too, Baroness. I have sympathy, but we have laws, and God's are much harsher than yours!

The door buzzes open. St Thomas is standing there, all smiles and an apologetic demeanour.

Sorry to interrupt, Baroness, he says, but you have an important call.

He smiles at Zahra as if he has interrupted a polite conversation. As if he's breaking social protocol. As if he's her friend.

How are we getting along, he asks, smiling the smile that never breaks.

Mariela doesn't like sleeping alone. The bed, without breath to accompany it, has an emptiness that wakes her, so she lies there, deep within the pre-dawn light, a thin sheet pulled around her for comfort, a pillow, pounded into shape in the space where a lover would curl. Breathless.

She ignores the first rap on the door. It's gentle, hesitant, possibly one of the runners and there's nothing they can give when all she wants is out of this damn country.

Mariela has a place on base. A room, a shared kitchen, nicer than the bed she lies in now, but she can't face the hollowness of her surroundings there. The United Nations are just waiting for something to happen. At least at the Hotel Intercontinental Kabul the people are actively looking for events rather than passively waiting for them, so she stays here, amidst the life, the hopelessness, against orders and against protocol. A room in a hotel full of hungry people looking for new ways to avoid life

The second rap is more insistent. Louder, and clearly not one of the boys.

Yes?

And it's a woman's voice that answers, though it takes Mariela a moment to place it.

Mariela? Am I waking you? I'm so sorry.

She rises and pulls a gown around her before making her way to the door.

Mrs. Armstrong?

It is clear from her face that the Judge hasn't slept, but she still exudes the confidence of the British Establishment. Her clothes, though casual, are neatly arranged, and there is fortitude in her voice when she speaks.

I need to see the place my son was killed.

Just like that. Matter-of-fact. No prevarication.

Is that something you could do for me, the Judge asks. It's a lot, yes, of course, but I don't know anyone else and you have UN…

She leaves it hanging. Eyes red but firm. A mother asking a woman. A dignitary asking a secretary. The Establishment requiring a tool it fully believes is there for appropriation. A force of will.

Mariela sighs.

Downstairs, five minutes, she says before she closes the door. Front desk, she adds. Tell them we need a driver and a bodyguard and it can't be one of the boys.

There is smoke over the south of Kabul but it is from a single pillar, spilling out over the wind, and the morning is quiet.

It doesn't look like they're putting up much of a fight, Mariela says, her arm out of the window on the passenger side, staring out toward the mountains.

Doesn't look like much of one at all.

The site of the roadside bomb that killed the Judge's son is about half way between the airport and the United Nations compound. A nothing road pitted with houses and boarded up shops, washing lines strung out above, criss-crossing the road.

There are no signs, but even the Judge's shaky command of the local geography is enough to determine that left leads to the airport with right going back to the base just outside the city.

At Mariela's request the driver brings the car to a halt. His partner, a different man to the one who took them to the hotel the night before, rests his Russian-made-machine-gun out of the window, checking windows and angles.

On the far side of the crossroads a small divot is all that is now left to mark the spot where her son's car rode over a landmine, driving the wheel up through the floor of the car, killing him instantly and sending the car front-over-end, killing the driver and bodyguards far less painlessly.

Broken earth is the only marker. No flowers. No cordon. Not even blackened dirt marks the end of the man she gave birth to twenty-eight years before.

Were they going to the airport or away from it?

But Mariela doesn't know.

I don't see how it hadn't gone off before.

Mariela shrugs. The bodyguard in the front of the car moves his weapon, careful to assess something he sees further down the road.

It's a busy interchange, or at least it was before the city emptied, Mariela tells her. There are areas, markers. They put up flags. No flags mean they've checked and the area is clear. White and they're not completely sure. Red, and it's a minefield that they haven't been able to clear.

There are white flags all over the city, she adds. Whole areas of them. Trucks go through here, a lot of them. If I had to guess, she tells the Judge, I'd guess that they were trying to overtake one of them and the driver was forced to use that side of the road. I doubt they'd even see the flags.

The Judge doesn't hear them yelling as she moves. She hardly feels Mariela pulling at her trouser leg. And then she's out, standing in the morning sun, gulping in the dust air that her son inhaled moments before his death.

Or did he? Filtered and air-conditioned was more likely. Barely touching the soil that would end him.

Get her back in the car, now!

She can hear the bodyguard yelling at Mariela.

Get her in the fucking car!

The other one, the driver, pleading, softer, words she can't make out in a language the Judge doesn't understand.

Mrs. Armstrong?

Why isn't the bodyguard dressed in a UN uniform? The Judge hadn't paid attention to him since getting in the car but is sure he's missing the blue beret and insignia that mark him capable of travelling in a car with United Nations plates.

Mrs. Armstrong!

The Judge turns and sees Mariela standing on the other side of the car, one hand on the roof, the other on her head, pinning a scarf the wind has decided to play with.

You have to get back in the car!

They put toys on them, the Judge says. That's what I read. Before I came here. They put toys on the landmines, connected to the landmines. Candy. The Soviets. They put them there so that children pick them up and…

She lets it hang.

It's a questions of mathematics. At least that's what they tell me. An injured man takes people to look after him. A doctor, a nurse. People who could otherwise be fighting, so it's simply a question of maths. The more injured, the less people able to go out and fight. But a child? An injured child? That takes more. More than simply what is needed at the hospital. A family. It takes a family to look after an injured child. Both parents. Both…

But she doesn't know what she means by this. Richard wasn't a child. He was an adult. Following his father. Money and law. Not a fighter. Not a child.

The driver yells something and points back the way they came.

Standing in the middle of the road, the Judge turns and sees a rising dust ball heading towards them. She can hear the cries of Mariela, the bodyguard and the driver as they call out to her, but all she can do is stand there, watching as a parade of cars and trucks rocket toward her.

To her left, the bodyguard has positioned himself out of the car on the rooftop, his weapon trained on the approaching cavalcade, his eyes never leaving the sight. Next to him Mariela, still shouting, is pulling her credentials out of a bag while the driver guns the engine, unsure whether flight is even possible at this stage.

The Judge watches as Mariela waves her identification, proclaiming her to be someone who shouldn't be shot, one eye on the encroaching traffic, one eye on the Judge, still pleading with her to get out of the road.

Oh, Richard. What on earth were you doing getting mixed up in all this?!

The Judge steps to the side and within the protection of the car just in time to watch a metallic procession of Mercedes and trucks, armaments and men, flash past in a whir of black and grey. Dozens of forms of transportation carrying hundreds of men and munitions, green, white and black flags flapping in the dust on top of each and every one.

She stands there, her back to the car, watching them go by as they rocket north out of the crossroads, a barrel of dust and noise and heat, and then they're gone. A trailing breeze and settling earth the only indication that they had ever even been there in the first place.

Rabbani is leaving Kabul, says Mariela simply, watching the dust cloud dissipate.

We need to get back to the UN.

Ian St Thomas' hair has dried. His jacket has gone as well, no doubt airing on a radiator somewhere. His tie, however, is still present and accounted for, straightened, and he smooths it against his shirt as he talks to the Baroness, the line of his undershirt appearing and disappearing with every stroke of his hand.

They are standing in an office situated beyond the counter at the entrance. There is only one small window looking out into nothingness, but it is a welcome change from the stark interrogation room. The room is carpeted. Not well, but carpeted nonetheless. A cheap replica of a 19th century bureau sits at one end of the room, its plywood façade shimmering under the florescent lights, a tan faux-leather chair rolled behind it.

Ian St Thomas stands, inclined against the desk. The Baroness has declined a seat and leans instead against the browning wallpaper, a cup of cheap coffee in her hands to warm them.

There had been no phone call. They had been monitoring them, Ian St Thomas informed her, and thought it best if they took a break. Have a bit of a chat, as he likes to put it.

It's best you give them time to stew.

The Baroness informed him that she was pretty much through with the interview anyway, which seemed to displease the agent and he set about making her something to drink instead.

No, thank you. My driver?

On the phone, I would think, he says handing her a mug that reads 'World's Greatest Dad'.

We tried to call him but it's engaged. I'm sure he'll be back soon enough. Would you like to come through?

By the time they step into the office, Ian St Thomas is in full flow.

There are, he tells her, three types of people when it comes to questioning. Perhaps three types of people over all. The first are those who want to please. Most people fell into this category.

It has been instilled in them since school, Baroness. They crave the approval of authority figures. Give them a little praise and then make sure they understand you're not happy with them. Simply keep being disappointed until they give you all they have to give. People, Baroness, can withstand an awful amount of pain and suffering, but very little disapproval from someone they want to like.

The Baroness looks at him, wondering whether he thinks she is this type as well.

The second are people who need to rebel, to fight against something, yes? To rage against the machine as it were. These people don't want your approval. They want to think they've got the better of you, so they play it dumb and ask asinine questions. These are the easiest. Tell one of these people that you have never heard of anyone having grapefruit for breakfast and they will give you their complete dietary rundown just to prove you wrong.

The third kind, however, are game players, liars, or what Ian St Thomas informs the Baroness, we used to call good old fashioned sociopaths. They aren't interested in appeasing or brinkmanship. They want, quite simply, to extend the game for as long as possible.

The only thing they are interested in, Baroness, is the game, which makes them the hardest to read. They want to stay in it, you see. Never want it to end. They'll tell you anything as long as they have your undivided attention, and there's very little way to tell truth from lies.

And which one is she?

Ian St Thomas shifts a framed photo on the desk in order to make himself more comfortable.

Oh, number three, definitely. They all are, these types. You can never apply reason.

The photo on the desk is of a young girl, maybe eight or nine, playing in a garden, the warm summer sun glinting off her left eye, closing it slightly as she smiles into the camera.

Your daughter?

Ian St Thomas twists and looks at the image.

Good lord, no! Not my office. Anyway, he adds, turning the frame photo-down onto the table. Anyway, you are doing really well, Baroness Armstrong. It's always a good idea to give them plenty of breaks, make sure their next gambit is in place and ready, but we'd like you to keep at it, if that's alright. She likes you. The last twenty minutes have borne more fruit than the past few hours.

The Baroness looks at him over the rim of her mug. If this is not his office, then who invited him here?

I'm sorry, Mr. St Thomas, but you seem to have confused the matter. I am here in my capacity as a member of the House, as a senior subcommittee member, and as a favour to the Home Secretary, nothing more. My remit here is simply to advise the Home Secretary as to the viability of using Ms. Guelmoussi's circumstance as precedent. I'm sure you feel there is a lot to be gained from the woman, but that is not why I am here.

You like her, don't you, he says, brown eyes over an unmarked coffee cup.

My liking of the girl has nothing to do with it, Mr. St Thomas. The Home Secretary has a firm grasp of the affair, but I'm afraid Ms. Guelmoussi will not be able to help us in this regard.

And what regard is that, Baroness? But he is toying with her, and the Baroness knows it.

Now, I thank you for your help in the matter but I must return to London. The Home Secretary will be expecting my report.

Ian St Thomas nods, thinking, then twists once more and produces a manila folder from behind the upturned frame. He taps it gently against one hand, never opening it, talking while he does so.

That boy she was talking about. Ahmad? His full name is Ahmad Kastrati although he hasn't gone by that name in quite some time. He prefers the name Mohammed El Affie. She lied about him. A little bit. He is not who she says he is, or perhaps not who she thinks he is, it's always hard to tell. We held him once, in Somalia. Well, the Americans did at any rate. They thought him something of an asset. Thought they'd turned him. Low ranking intelligence gathering, that sort of thing. Passed them a few juicy bones. A few underlings that he wanted rid of. Perhaps even a few further up the ladder. We even traded them on some of his intelligence for a while, being the nature of our arrangement. Prime piece of real estate. Or at least they thought he was right up until the time he shot his handler in his head and set off a bomb under a high ranking official's car. This was eight years ago, or thereabouts. He was Albanian. Originally. Nothing to do with Syria. Though she was right about his family. We picked him up again in Kuwait. Setting up arms deals with, well, let's call them the less well-armed wing, shall we? He is, as of today, responsible for the bombing of three separate mosques, a marketplace and a school in Tikrit, not to mention the theft of a large number of armaments belonging to the Americans that they left lying around northern Iraq. Up until three hours ago, we thought he was in Egypt. In fact, the Americans were almost positive they had killed him in one of their little Xbox fantasies, though I doubt we were ever quite as convinced. Now it seems he is running a training camp somewhere in southern Kurdistan, looking after the little ones and singing Kumbaya. Though probably not the exact same words.

His thumb creases the edge of the folder.

Would you like to see photos of the school he blew up? They are quite graphic.

But the Baroness doesn't respond.

This is the first intel in a year. Very big for us. Very big for the Americans to be precise, which is therefore very big for the Home Secretary, if you catch my drift.

The Baroness is tired of being scolded. She sets her mug on the desk next to Ian St Thomas, silent in her condemnation. It's quite obvious they're not going to let her go, and without access to a phone…

She'd like you to call her, by the way. The Home Secretary.

The Baroness nods in acquiescence and tells him she'll need her phone.

Ian St Thomas reaches into his pocket and pulls out a thin slab.

Use mine.

I'd prefer my own.

I'm afraid that's not possible at the moment, he says, but the Baroness was expecting the retort and takes the cold chrome from his hand.

I'll take it outside, she says and turns to the door. I take it it's pre-dialled.

And she is at the door when he says.

The room isn't bugged, I promise.

The Baroness pauses, her hand on the door, and tells him that it's just as well the phone is then, before exiting.

The death of Dr. Najibullah marks the beginning of the end at the United Nations compound.

The streets have been lined for over an hour now with riotous crowds. Gunfire has been rampant, but there is an air of jubilation rather than anger to the mob, and they seem unopposed as they march through the streets, chanting and shooting in praise of their god.

Christ on a stick!

Robert Darlington watches through a window as the throng presses in. UN guards, stoically blue hatted and vigilant, have been told to keep their guns holstered unless fired upon. This is not their problem, according to Laurent Viviani, and the UN has no position on the internal political affairs of the nation.

Christ on a stick! The fucking army has gone over to other side.

The Judge remains silent behind him, buried in thought. Thinking about her court, the walls, the smell of leather, and the distance between the dock and the bench.

Ungrateful bastards. After all the money we threw at them as well. Where's the Frenchie, by the way, he adds, as if Laurent Viviani and the Judge are the oldest of friends.

On the phone. I believe he's finding out whether a withdrawal is warranted or not.

The American snorts.

Just like the UN to look for a decision days after one needed to be made.

I would have thought you'd have left, Mr. Darlington. Special flight and so on.

Robert Darlington holds her eye for a moment, and then shrugs it away.

We'd be on the tarmac by now if you'd stayed in the hotel.

The Judge thinks about this.

I'm not going anywhere without my son, Mr. Darlington. I should have thought you'd have gathered that much by now.

The American shrugs, considering.

After all the money we threw at these guys!

There is shouting coming from somewhere back in the compound. Then more. Then bullets. The pair flinch as the sound of gunfire rattles the doorframe.

There is shouting. Footsteps, growing louder and distinct.

They're storming the compound!

As one they move to the door only to see it burst open and a man, small and rat-like with a lanyard around his neck that confirms him as a local hire, enters the room.

He skids to a halt and closes the door, his breath coming in catches as he leans against it, listening.

Robert Darlington and the Judge watch him, comic in their inability to move.

He sees them, as if for the first time and turns his attention back to the door, still alert, still listening.

Outside there's more gunfire, further away than before, with shouting and the slamming of doors punctuating the sentencing blasts.

What…, begins the American, but the rat-like man extends a hand, pleading and commanding all at the same time.

Please, he whispers, tearing his eyes away from the door.

Please! They will kill me if they find me! Please!

And then he goes back to listening for his impending persecution.

Robert Darlington and the Judge look at each other, both stock-still below the neck, frozen in mid-movement since the arrival of their companion and the Judge is suddenly reminded of the story idea the journalist had shared with her the night before.

Robert Darlington breaks eye contact and whispers, asking the man at the door if the Taliban have taken the compound, but he waves his hand frantically once more. Eyes, pleading with them.

Please! Please! They will kill me if they find me with you!

His hand steadies to a pause and he fastens his ear to the door once more.

The Judge and the American exchange another look, but to them nothing has changed. Has the gunfire died down? Has it gotten further away? There is no way for them to tell.

Suddenly, their terrified companion pulls at the handle. He opens the door a fraction of an inch and peers out into the corridor.

Together the Judge and the American both take a step back. Beyond the door they can hear voices, footsteps running and the rattle of gunfire – when it does come – is loud enough to jerk them back another step further until they realise they are now standing with their backs to the window they were once looking out of, and as such visible to the crowd at the other end of the compound.

Thank you, their rat-like local hire says and slips out through the barely opened door, closing it behind him as he goes.

Screw this!

A full minute has passed since the local hire left the room and Robert Darlington has decided that is long enough for anyone to wait in safety.

The Judge watches as he crosses the room and looks out from behind the door, mirroring the body language of the man who sought sanctuary, before opening it an arms width and stepping out.

Left with no other choice, the Judge follows.

They find Laurent Viviani behind his desk in his office. Things have been smashed and the ceiling above now hangs, with broken pieces of cardboard lining sagging out, no doubt the result of warning fire.

He looks up as he sees the two enter but doesn't seem surprised or concerned. He simply sits there, taking them in as if they had arranged a meeting and he is now waiting for them to tell him the purpose of it.

What the hell is going on, the American asks.

They took Dr. Najibullah.

They overran your compound?

Laurent Viviani shuffles some papers on his desk and picks off a sizable piece of plasterboard from his telephone before dropping it into the bin.

It is not the place of the United Nations…

But neither the American nor the British have time to hear out the excuse.

Where did they take him?

Laurent Viviani looks at the Judge and thinks of his mother, though the woman before him is in actuality no older than his wife.

Najibullah. His brother. They just came in here and took them. Then they tied him to the back of a car and dragged him out onto the road.

The Judge looks at him, disgust in every pore of her being.

And you just let them?

But it is the American who breaks the mood by shifting into gear and looking around the room.

Right, he says. Time to get the fuck out of dodge! Coming, he adds, casting a look in the direction of the Judge.

She steps forward and places the full weight of her experience on the bench into a gaze that bores through Laurent Viviani and beyond.

Mr. Viviani, even you have to concede that there no longer is a government to whom you owe the fidelity of paperwork! Now, I am taking my son and I suggest you arrange for evacuation of all personnel to the airport, before they decide that killing an ex-president is lower on their agenda than they thought!

Laurent Viviani looks up at her and blinks. He is thinking about the gun that was just pointed at him. He is thinking about the ringing in his ears from the bullets that drilled into the roof over his head, and he is thinking of the eyes of the man under his protection as Najibullah was dragged past the room, his feet unmoving, his mouth already bloodied, pleading for his life.

And we're taking the body of the other British man as well, the Judge tells him as both she and Robert Darlington make their way towards the door.

He doesn't deserve to be buried here with you, she adds uncharitably, and leaves.

The outer office is military-grade clean. Three neat desks sit in contradiction to the counter, erecting a gauntlet that the Baroness has to walk through. There are three men there in all, Button Man prominent amongst them. Are the other two the same as before? The Baroness can't tell. That's the problem with military personnel, they almost always look alike. The thin one who brought them the tea is definitely not here, and his absence was conspicuous from outside the interrogation room when they left.

Six pairs of eyes watch the Baroness as she crosses the floor, the device cupped in one hand, the other in her trouser pocket. She has no idea why she holds it this way but the phone is about an inch from her body. As if contagious. As if someone was on the other end and the Baroness is worried about the unseemly pop and crackle of it rubbing against her thigh.

She moves wordlessly past the front desk and makes her way to the first of the double glass doors and then stops, waiting. Never intending to seek the Button Man's approval, she simply stands there while he rises from his desk and makes his way slowly across the office towards the door release while the night stares in at her. The lights of a plane drawing in to land scatter all around and are mirrored in triplicate across the window pane, bulletproof no doubt, glinting and dropping like snowflakes in tandem before they fall behind the hill about half way across the glass.

Beyond Button Man's footsteps the Baroness hears the door opening from the inner office and imagines Ian St Thomas standing there, nodding tacit consent, but she does not look. Button Man reaches his destination and fulfils his duty. The double doors slide apart, and the cold air of midnight braces the Baroness as she steps forward and waits once more while the doors close behind her, as if fearful of contamination from the outside world.

It is even colder outside. The rain has stopped but it hangs low, heavy, and the wind feels damp and turgid.

The car has gone and Jan along with it. There is a drier patch of road where they pulled up earlier so he clearly left recently, but the Baroness has no way of knowing how long ago that was.

The wind whips up and the Baroness pulls her suit jacket in tighter. She looks at the phone. A number she doesn't recognise with a prefix that doesn't exist looks back at her. A green square with a white bone inset tells her what to do. She presses it and lifts it to her ear, waiting for the dial tone.

Rachel. Thank you for calling.

The voice is rich, friendly, tired, but stripped of intention.

Helen.

No formalities, and the Baroness gets no further with her discourse.

We need you to do this for us.

The royal 'we' or are there more people in on the call?

We need you to do this for us. We need to know what she knows, I'm afraid. It's as simple as that.

There are flecks of rain in the air and the thin drone of an incoming airplane can briefly be mistaken for distant thunder.

I thought I was here on a fact finding mission.

There is breath on the other end of the line, though whether that is the Home Secretary sitting back or a third party the Baroness cannot distinguish.

You are. You are. Or, at least you were. I'm afraid matters have become… time sensitive.

El Affie.

El Affie…. El Affie might be the tip of the iceberg I'm afraid, Rachel. Just another in a long list. I know this isn't your bag. I know we're putting you in a difficult position but she's opened up to you, is opening up to you and that's what counts, I'm afraid. St Thomas tells me you're reticent?

But St Thomas hasn't had time to tell her anything between the office and the call and the Baroness tries to remember the phone on the desk. Looking for tell-tale signs of a hold light.

Yes, she says, letting the syllables linger. Who is he exactly?

St Thomas? Yes, he's a weasel, isn't he? I know. I'm afraid he's really good at his job. Is he treating you with the proper respect?

But the Baroness thinks to hell with respect, and takes a symbolic step out from underneath the portico into the newly picking rain.

No, I mean, who is he? Who are any of these people, Helen? No uniforms, no designations.

I see. Yes.

I'm on the House ethics committee, Helen, and you are placing me in a very precarious position. If you want my help…

I see. Yes.

There's a sound of fumbling and the Home Secretary asks the Baroness to hold for a moment, which gives her all the answers she will ever need.

She is not alone. This is not a friendship thing. This is not a Westminster thing. This is not about the law. This is about Britain.

The rain is coming down quickly now but the Baroness does not want to move back to the porch.

Rachel?

Yes, Home Secretary.

I'm sorry about that. Things are moving quite quickly, I'm afraid. I know I'm putting you in an awkward positon but, well, frankly… We need your help. We can hold her under the Anti-Terrorism Act for even knowing El Affie but I don't want to do that. Not just yet.

She pauses.

I think this is a young woman caught up beyond herself, Rachel. I want to believe that. I want to make the right case – the right public case – but like I say, things are moving quite quickly and we need answers. The men, I am told, are not in uniform because technically she's right; they are not on British soil.

Technically she's right.

The room is monitored in a number of ways.

There is the weight of silence.

Rachel? Use the child if you have to. I know it's shitty of me. I know it's a lousy thing to do with friendship, but if this is what we think it is then there's a lot we can do with it. Okay?

The Baroness sweeps her hair back with a disregarded hand and steps into the dry. A shiver runs down her spine and she almost drops the phone.

Yes, Home Secretary.

Rachel?

Yes.

Do you believe her? Believe in her? This girl?

A new plane is coming in to land. Lights taxi in the distance.

I don't think that's my job, is it? I don't think she's the right poster child, Home Secretary, no. I agree with you that legislation does need to be made, but I don't think this is the case to bring it. That's what I was coming out here to tell you.

Silence.

I see.

Home Secretary, I learned something, all those years on the bench. I learned something about me. About people. I think it might be of use to you.

Go on.

There is such a thing as objective proof, Home Secretary. No matter what I said in there, objective proof is a reasonable expectation but what I have learnt, from my years on the bench, is that we rarely, if ever, get to know it. At least not without hindsight.

I don't believe anyone. That's my rule. I don't believe in their motives, I don't trust their instincts. What people are looking for when they pass judgement is objective proof, and we rarely, if ever, get it.

But does she believe that? Does she think that way or is she simply passing on a message to this unseen third party?

I see. Well, Rachel. I just want you to know that I appreciate what you're doing for us. Keep me informed.

Of course, Home Secretary.

And she can feel the heat of the phone fade against her ear as the call is disconnected.

Behind her the doors, as if on command, swish open and warm air pools against her back.

The Baroness turns to see Ian St Thomas standing in the doorway, his jacket back on, his hair once more caught in the wind.

Everything alright, Baroness, he asks in an overly casual manner.

Yes. Thank you, she replies and, handing him the phone, squares him in the eyes before saying;

Why don't you take me to where you're holding the child.

Black body bags and blood-lined clouds, that's all the Judge can see from her seat on the plane.

They had thought about putting the bodies in the hold, but that seemed somehow disrespectful, so in the end they stretched them out on the floor of the aircraft in their plastic wraps and the pilot kept the air-conditioner as low as it could go.

The Judge watched the sun, setting over the clouds outside the window of the jet, and thought of the man she had met with the purposeful hands, translating a book about the British invasion of his country in a walled garden surrounded by foreigners.

It had taken nearly a day for the UN to be assured that they wouldn't be fired upon if they left the compound. It had taken most of the morning to be equally assured that they wouldn't be killed if they stayed, and both the Judge and Robert Darlington had advocated making a run for it during the confusion. But in the end cooler heads prevailed.

During that time news of the death of Najibullah had made it to international waters. A video had surfaced of bearded men in turbans beating him in the back of a car, before tieing a rope tied to the bumper and dragging him along the avenue.

His body hung from a lamppost on a street leading into the city alongside that of his brother's. They'd castrated him first.

In the end though, they'd left without incident. A UN plane was waiting at the airstrip to airlift a number of personnel out of the country but, almost without thought, the Judge had ordered the body of her son and the other British national onto the corporate jet instead.

If she had expected some form of protest from Robert Darlington, she didn't get it. Indeed, he barely spoke to her once they arrived at the airport. They simply arranged the bodies, closed the door on the heat and the dust and the death of it all, and took off.

Instead, the American sat at the front of the plane, in the same seat as the flight in, and spoke on the phone in hushed tones, no doubt debating whether or not to attempt a deal with people who only one day before he'd feared were going to shoot him.

The business world was such a strange place, thought the Judge, watching the last red tints fall away from the clouds, their hearts growing darker as they sped into night. One could forgive anything in the name of business. One could do a deal with anyone as long as it was within their own interests.

Were they considered people businesses would be deemed a danger, both to themselves and the world around them.

A young woman brought the Judge a drink, stepping professionally over the body bags on the floor while balancing a glass of whisky and an ice bucket on a flimsy wooden tray, and the Judge noticed for the first time since boarding that it wasn't the same woman who had served her on the way in.

The Judge asked her what had happened to the other woman, but the cabin-attendant simply didn't know.

Had the jet left Afghanistan and returned, she continued, but the woman could only shrug and ask if the Judge would like her to find out, which she didn't.

Excuse me, Judge.

Robert Darlington was standing behind the stewardess, an imposing looking cordless phone in his hand.

A call for you, he said, the phone outstretched.

Rachel?

And she wasn't aware of how good it was to hear his voice until she did so.

I'm fine, Lucas. Was that concern in his voice or was she projecting?

We've been watching the news.

We, the Judge thinks, but doesn't say. We?

It's all fine. And then, because there's nothing else to say, Richard is with me.

But is that static she hears or is it something deeper?

We've made arrangements for the airport.

The Judge looks down at the body of her son, lying on the floor of the corporate jet he probably flew in on - and no doubt expected to leave on as well - and wonders to herself if boat orchids might make an acceptable alternative to calla lilies.

You should tell them to go directly to Hastlemere, she tells her husband and there's a silence at this that she interprets correctly.

I'm not sure what time we are landing.

And there's that static again.

Yes, of course. Surrey. I'll make sure it's arranged.

The jet hits an air pocket and the bodies in front of her produce a thud as they rise and connect with the floor once more in a barely discernible movement.

And a car for me. Separate, if you would. To London. I'm not fit for the funeral like this.

Yes, of course.

I'm… And that really is static and the Judge has to ask her husband to repeat himself.

I'm sorry I wasn't able to come to the phone. When you called, he adds.

The Judge looks down at the body of her son and wonders if that is actually him, or whether the one further forward bears the last remains of the only offspring she'll ever have. It would have been the simplest thing to get them muddled, what with both bags being completely identical and all.

Rachel? Can you hear me?

Lucas.

The Judge swivels in her chair, looking out on the depth of night. A small light blinking at the end of the wing, and nothing but darkness from there.

I'm going to give you a name. Is that alright? Call Graig Russell at the MOD. It's on my rolodex. I'm going to need a contact number for a next of kin.

And somewhere to send the remains, she thinks, but doesn't say.

We all have to go home eventually.

Down the hall, past the interrogation room where they are holding

Zahra – no guard. Through an identical door - use your key card - is another corridor, another set of entrances. At the far end a different door – glass, metal mesh running through – is a room with garish colours on the inside. A stark contrast to the rest of the facility.

It's for the children.

Ian St Thomas swipes open the door and ushers the Baroness into a room replete with soft furnishings and colour-me-in dinosaur walls.

They have families in here from time to time and they need somewhere to keep the little ones, he tells her, but the Baroness has been in hundreds of rooms like this before. During her time on the bench the Baroness saw all kinds of misery in rooms like this. The sadness of people separated from loved ones and the lengths they will go to in order to secure a better future for their children.

A young female, no uniform, all black business trouser suit, cheaper than the Baroness', stands as they enter. The look on her face tells the Baroness all she needs to know about the woman, and they share a moment of solidarity over being entrusted with those things men believe only women can do because they would rather not do it themselves.

Sir.

This is Baroness Armstrong, he says, but there is no indication of a reciprocal introduction.

Yes, sir. Baroness.

And beyond the woman, the baby. A stray arm reaches out from under swaddling, cushioned on a makeshift cot of pillows and blankets.

Is this her?

He, Baroness. He's a he. Which, I suppose, given the religion is a bit of a plus, adds St Thomas.

He's just gone to sleep, sir, says the young woman with the inferred pleading of every parent everywhere.

The Baroness steps forward softly but Ian St Thomas stays where he is, disinclined to enter the child's personal space. She leans in, careful of noise, placing a light finger on a pendent her mother gave her to stop it swinging forward under her blouse, pinioning it just above the bridge of her bra.

Small, brown nostrils breathe from underneath a sheath of white.

Richard hadn't looked like this. Had been nowhere near as cute and round. Richard had been top-heavy and red and bloated. Angry at the world for having come to greet him. The baby's hands are clasped tight into little fists as if ready to fight the world, but his face is one of immense calm and beauty. A small freckle on his left cheek the only blemish on a perfectly round face. His already-thick, dark hair pushed long over his forehead in much the same way as Ian St Thomas wears his.

The Baroness straightens, releasing the protective finger on her breastbone.

How old is he?

And it's Ian St Thomas who answers;

Six months, give or take.

Does he have a name?

Solh, is what it says on the passport. With an H. No middle name.

The Baroness turns and looks at him, their voices still whispers.

He has a passport?

Of course. She applied for it in Turkey. At least, she added the name of the baby to hers. Perfectly legal under a certain age. Or so I believe. Not my field, obviously.

The Baroness looks at him and takes a step back. Her voice is going to take an edge and she has no interest in waking the child.

And how long does that take?

I'm sorry? Ian St Thomas looks at the other woman in the room as if the questions were some kind of code that only women could understand.

If she applied for a passport then we knew she was coming.

Ian St Thomas thinks about the rationale behind this.

No, we knew she had a child. Nothing more.

How long have we been tracking this girl?

Ian St Thomas looks at her, gauging. Assessing as he goes.

Baroness, he says and his tone is weighty, deeper than it has been before, boyhood charm devoured in exhaustion.

Baroness, perhaps I am not the one you should be asking these questions to.

She takes real tea back into the room. Hot Darjeeling, purloined from a drawer in the desk in the inner office, the only thing she can find. Two cups. Milk in one, packets of sugar pocketed in her palm. Pick one, she tells the young woman and Zahra decides on milk, which is what the Baroness had wanted for herself.

The boxes of food have been cleared from the room. An oily stain on the surface of the table and a slight odour the only remnants of an unwanted meal.

I'm sorry about the delay.

When can I go?

The Baroness ignores this.

I just checked in on Solh. It is Solh, isn't it? He's sleeping. Quite well.

And now it's Zahra's turn not to answer.

Why didn't you tell me about him?

The young woman sips her tea, eyeing the Baroness over the top of it and for a moment the Baroness thinks she is going to fling the hot liquid into her face, scalding her.

I thought you knew.

You mean you assumed?

You're the one holding us here, aren't you?

And yet you didn't ask about him.

She says it flatly. All accusation neutralised, and she can still see the hurt it causes and the struggle for the next sentence.

Is he alright?

The Baroness nods. He's sleeping. Or at least he was a minute ago. He's being well looked after. How old is he?

But the young woman is angry and not open to entertaining her captors.

The Baroness lays pen and paper on the desk. St Thomas had cautioned against this. A pen is a weapon, he told her, and not one that needs a lot of imagination to use.

You are monitoring, aren't you?

We are, yes. I don't mean that she'd… I think our carotid arteries are safe, don't you? But still… He pauses. Still inadvisable to take one into a room.

What would you suggest?

Oh, he says with a smile. We go Russian, when we have to.

Meaning?

We use crayons.

Which had been the final straw.

I'm not going back to kindergarten, Mr. St Thomas, so I'll just have to take the risk.

I want to establish a timeline, the Baroness tells the young woman.

A timeline?

Of events. Leading up to the birth. Leading up to your return.

Who is with him?

But the Baroness hasn't heard or doesn't want to answer.

I beg your pardon?

You said he was being well looked after?

Is that a concern? But it's the wrong thing to say and she adds to it before the woman can respond.

You are being held here. You understand that? While your status is reviewed and it can be corroborated that you have not taken part in any crimes, either here or overseas. Or, indeed, are planning to. Back home. You must understand that! You must have known what would happen, no?

The young woman looks defiant.

I asked about him.

I beg your pardon?

You said I didn't ask about him, but I did.

I see.

When they brought us here. All I did was ask about him. For hours! I pounded on that door!

Alright…

You know that!

And the Baroness asks her to calm down.

Don't tell me that I didn't ask after my child!

Calm down, please.

But her rage is up now and there's no option but to sit it out.

You drag me out of the line, rip… rip my baby, my baby from my arms, stick me in here and tell me that he will be taken…

Who told you? Who told you he would be taken…

My child!

Her hands are balled like her son's. The tea rattles on the table at her righteous fury and the Baroness half expects the door to buzz and Button Man or the thin guard to enter.

Solh. His name is Solh.

I know what his name is!

You are going to have to calm yourself, Zahra. You're going to have to calm yourself and… Otherwise they are going to come in. Do you understand? And then this conversation is over. Do you understand? For Solh's sake.

The young woman looks at her. Burning at the injustice.

I was wondering. Why Solh. With an H.

But the young woman isn't ready to answer, she stares at the wall, collecting herself, reigning in the emotions that are struggling to overtake her. She focusses on her hands, pressed flat on the table.

Finally, she turns, and it's a different woman who looks the Baroness in the eye and, with a different tone, asks her to repeat the question.

What did you ask me?

Solh. It just seems strange. It's German, isn't it? Unless you meant it to be without the H, and then it's Latin. Sun god. Which also seems strange given where he was born. I take it he was born in Iraq or Kurdistan or…?

The young woman looks at her.

He doesn't sleep without his bottle.

Well, I can promise you he was sleeping soundly a few minutes ago. He's being well looked after.

Pause.

It's his grandfather's name. Farsi. It means peace.

The Baroness nods. Which is strange, isn't it? Farsi? Not Arabic. It is not the usual language of Salafists.

Please. Do not try to understand our religion.

Isn't that the point?

You do not have to understand something in order to live under it. I do not understand British law and yet – she holds her arms out, encompassing – here I am!

I understand more than you think.

Do you?

I do, yes. I need to establish a timeline.

And she's thinking about Richard when she says it. About the man in the garden with the thick moustache and the desire to understand his history.

You left the United Kingdom two years ago.

Silence, and then a nod. Acquiescence. Expectation.

Yes.

September.

Yes.

You took a bus. A…

She checks her notes.

A Euroliner… to Paris.

Yes.

From Bristol.

Yes.

And the Baroness repeats the question.

Yes.

Why?

It was what they had.

Ticket-wise?

Yes.

I suppose what I'm asking, says the Baroness, is why you didn't simply take the bus from Newport. From where you were? We know there was one.

There were no seats.

It's the same bus.

The young woman shrugs. Slumps back in her seat. Sullen and silent. Daughter-like, though the Baroness has never had daughters. Never wanted them.

There's no record of you getting from Newport to Bristol.

A friend gave me a lift.

A friend?

I'm not going to give you her name.

Alright, let's leave that. You took a bus to Paris.

Overnight.

That's right. Then a plane to Turkey. Why?

Silence. The room is cold. A thin trickle of air has reached the back of the Baroness' neck and she can feel the tension there. Have they turned on an air-conditioner? Is this part of the manipulation?

The room is monitored in a number of ways.

The Baroness pulls her tea closer, confiding in it for warmth.

You didn't buy the ticket. I mean. It's all here. I'm just looking for some context, that's all. Some sense of… I suppose, help.

No.

You didn't buy the ticket?

The young woman shifts in her seat, seemingly coming to the end of an internal argument.

My husband bought it.

Your husband? Was he your husband at the time?

The young woman looks at her. An even gaze.

We were married in the camp.

And where were they?

Pause. Thought.

Northern Iraq.

The Baroness makes a note. Nothing new, just a figure she has invented from her time on the bench. A plus sign with a line through it, followed by three letters: E J T. Cryptic. Leading. Designed to confuse the subject looking at it. +E J T, E plus five, J plus ten; Multiples that the brain sees but the consciousness doesn't.

I see. And how did you get there.

Silence again. Those beautiful eyes. Intelligent. Searching.

A car.

A car?

Build a rhythm. Make them dance to it.

Yes. Whose car? Some friends. Of your husband? Yes. In Iraq? No. From Turkey?

But the young woman has had enough of this. She wants the story for herself.

I caught a flight to Batman. My husband sent me the ticket. It wasn't in his name.

Innocent as you like it.

What is your husband's name?

But the girl isn't to be distracted.

I noticed it on the receipt. For the ticket. It wasn't his name. I never met the man who bought me this ticket. I would like to. To thank him.

You flew to Batman?

It's a city in Turkey. East Turkey. There are many flights there.

But the Baroness knows where it is and waits for her to continue.

I didn't know anyone in Batman. I didn't know anyone in Turkey. I was met by this family. I had no idea who they were, but they knew me, from the moment I got off the plane. They were waiting for me. They just jumped up and down, waving! They had this little boy, Mensau, and he held my hand as we left the airport. Eight or nine. No more. Just took my hand.

I stayed with them. One night. It might have been two. I was very tired. And then I took a bus.

What kind of bus?

No different from the bus to Paris. A little newer, perhaps.

What was the name of the family? Mensau's?

She shrugs.

I'm not good with names.

The young woman watches as the Baroness scribbles something illegible and underlines something else. There is no understanding what she has written, though it appears to be some kind of shorthand. Only three letters stand out: E J T. She watches as the Baroness' pen – a Bic biro, black, see-through, cheap – underlines the three letters carefully before she continues.

They had been displaced. From Iraq. After the war. Many years before. Most people had returned but they'd stayed. I don't know what they did. Their house smelt of sandalwood.

I took the bus in the evening. It wasn't a very long ride, only four hours. I had never been in a foreign country, an Islamic country. This was… This was the greatest thing that had ever happened to me! To be there. Looking out of the windows. To see people like me. On the street. To hear the call to prayer and not think it was something to be afraid of.

The Baroness interrupts her with a question but she blows it off.

Does it matter? Turkish? Pakistani? Muslims. These were my people.

The bus only took four hours. But the countryside! I watched the sun setting over the hills and watched a glow encompass the land. The bus was full and there was lots of talking. People were louder. Livelier. But there was also a peace to it. A religious peace. I don't speak Turkish, but I know the name of God. I know the names of the Prophets, and they were alive on that bus!

I thought we were going directly to Mosul. That's what the family had told me. That my husband was in Mosul. In Iraq. The bus would take me there. Mensau's mother had told me this. And there were other people on the bus going there. I could tell from the way they were talking.

But you didn't?

The young woman leans back. Remembering the smell of the bus, the bump of the brakes.

I was nearly asleep. At the time. When we stopped. I was nearly asleep. And then we stopped. I remember… I could tell from the people around me that this wasn't a normal stop. That this wasn't part of the bus route.

Two men came onto the bus. Brothers. They had guns. They talked to the bus driver who waved them in. A few of the passengers were asking them questions but they didn't answer. They came up the aisle and looked right at me. Then they left.

I thought, I thought, maybe the bus would leave then, but a woman got on and came up to me. Zahra, she said. You are Zahra, are you not? And she had the kindest eyes. Perfect English. We are here to collect you.

Zahra sits back in her chair, the last of the tea warming her fingers, memory warming the rest.

What was her name?

Ishaf.

Ishaf told me that there were checks at the border, that perhaps they were waiting for me, but that they would take me to see my husband.

Your fiancé.

They told me he was in Turkey, or at least that they thought he was in Turkey. Mobile calls are dangerous, that's what they told me.

Who's they?

This is a family.

Ishaf's family?

There are many different kinds of family, Baroness. To be… British people do not have families in the same way we do. You have cousins you never speak to. You live nuclear. You live alone. Everyone stayed at our house when we were young. Everyone stayed at our house. All of them. Cousin, aunt, uncle… It's endless. Forever. Who's blood and who isn't is not the limit to our definition. Ishaf had brothers. Five that I knew of. I didn't think to question whether or not they were related by blood.

What were their names?

And the young woman looks at her levelly when she answers.

Mohammed.

Then continues.

So I waited there. This was south of Silopi, a small town called Aktepe. Another three days. He was coming, they told me. He was coming across the border for me. We would be married.

She knew him?

Ishaf? Yes. Since childhood. She told me stories of him as a boy. Showed me the river where he had taught her to fish. I began to get quite jealous. I began to feel he loved her. Or maybe that she loved him, I don't know. And I guess she must have sensed this. She would take my hand, look at my face with those beautiful brown eyes and tell me: he loves you more than life itself – he is coming for you!

But he didn't?

The young woman picks up her tea for the first time.

No. He never came.

The story is waning. The tea, gone. The back of the Baroness' neck has started to cramp from the cold and she rubs it fitfully to ease the discomfort.

The women slept in the house, but the men slept in tents in the garden. That's where Haras found me. I was hanging out washing. The winds are dry there, but the sun is too hot. You can only hang washing in the evening. Colours anyway, unless you want them to fade. I was there, and Haras just appeared out of nowhere and told me we were leaving.

I was excited. I thought maybe my husband had arrived, that he had come for me. Haras had me by the arm which… was unlike him. To touch a woman like that. He told me we needed to leave and we needed to leave now.

Ishaf was by the car, waiting. Another man, I didn't know him then, didn't recognise him, but he was standing by the driver's seat, urging us to hurry.

And it surprised me. Because the house was so full at the time. There were maybe fifteen, maybe sixteen people living there, but I could tell from the courtyard everyone had gone. We were the only ones left. I had been outside no longer than fifteen minutes and the house had emptied.

We got in the back. Ishaf and… I wanted to go get my things. My suitcase was in our room. Every morning, I repacked it; Ishaf had taught me that. Be ready to leave at a moment's notice because he will come for you. But still, here we were, leaving without it. And the washing on the line.

Ishaf and I got in the back seat. Haras and the other man got in the front. And I was begging, pleading with Ishaf. Let me go and get my things! And I was so used… She was the only one who could speak English. I was so used to people not understanding what we were saying to each other, it took me aback when the driver turned around and spoke in perfect English.

Little sister. We leave now or we die.

Just like that.

And I could see; through his beard, through his tan. This was a white man, an American, and it surprised me completely.

The Baroness tests the pen's resolve before asking his name and is surprised when she gets one.

Jon. Mohammed was his Muslim name, but he told me once, on the mountains, over the border. He told me he missed it.

His name?

People calling him by it. He said he was proud of his Muslim name but there were some sounds that were a comfort, you know? Like a TV in the background. A radio tuning. Things that reminded you of home. That sang to you. Your heart. That's what it was like, he said. Hearing his name spoken out loud: hearing his heart.

It never occurred to me there would be white men in the camps.

We were driving fast. Out of the town, but north, away from the border. I could tell from the hill lines. I asked them where we were going and they told me across the border, to Iraq, but that was behind us.

Ishaf just sat there, in the back seat, holding the armrest, looking out the window. Frightened.

I had never seen her like that.

It took us three days to cross into Iraq. Ishaf had my passport. And my prayer book. She had collected these things, these two things, from my room, along with the picture of my husband I kept inside it. She gave them to me the next morning, on the side of a hill. We had driven all night and were hungry, tired. I could see a town in the distance but I couldn't tell which side of the border we were on.

And whether because it's the cold or whether it's because she is tired of the romantic nature of the young woman's story, the Baroness decides she's had enough.

She stands, looks around her, micro-stretching her joints, one at a time, overcome with tiredness. Unsure of why she is still doing this.

How did you meet your husband, Zahra?

Zahra looks at the older woman in front of her. Her form contorted by age, the gold of her wedding band blackened by time.

Didn't you ever want to change the world?

There are two types of people. People who shape the world and people who are shaped by it.

Zahra thinks about this before responding.

Where I grew up, it's a pop song. Sally-meets-Barry-and-falls-in-love-and-out-of-hope kind of thing. There was this girl at my school…

133

Please, no more stories!

But Zahra is not deterred.

There was this girl in my class. I must have been what, fourteen? And she was twelve. Twelve! Two years younger than me. And… She was just so… incredibly pretty. Beautiful! You know, what girls like me dream of being. Blonde hair, blue eyes, tight ass.

The Baroness smiles. There is a click in her left knee and she shifts her weight onto the other foot to alleviate it.

We all dream of that, dear.

There she was, beautiful, perfect, this… flower and she was… a tissue. Passed from boy to boy. All the boys in my form had her. All the worthwhile ones anyway. Twelve. You can't think that's right. You can't think that's the way it should be! A child like that.

She was raped?

There are many kinds of sin.

The young woman matches the gaze of the Baroness evenly.

When my grandparents came here… When they came here they didn't engage. They didn't want to be part of the culture, but they didn't want to change it either. They thought of simple things. Food on the table. A house. The promise of a better life. My parents, they didn't see it like that. They wanted to be part of it. They wanted the pretty dresses and the nice cars. They wanted the life they saw on TV. The white life. The one the world was promising them. They didn't want to change anything, they simply wanted to belong, to be part of the promise their parents had bought them.

But… twelve! No crime. No condemnation. A perfect girl. A flower. Used as a tissue.

These boys were older?

Fifteen. Sixteen.

The Baroness sighs and reclaims her seat.

It's a difficult area.

It's really not.

There is silence in the room. The faint whisper of the air conditioner confirms the Baroness suspicions.

You have to look at the world around you. Don't you? You have to look at what we are, what we've become. This girl. She gives herself to these boys. She's twelve. What does she know about her choices? Where's her protection? Where are their judges?

The world needs changing, Baroness. It needs structure. My people. My family? We are not bound by countries, by borders – not any more. We are everywhere throughout the world. Every city. Every town. How can you say our way is not better?

The Baroness looks at the youth in front of her and sighs.

I think the naivety you ascribe to the girl is inherent in your argument as well.

Really?

You want others judged by the same truths as you judge yourself?

Is that so bad?

You want sin to be part of the law.

How it should be.

You want guidelines. Clear and stark. Crime and punishment.

We are a people without direction.

Are we, says the Baroness. Are we? What about the man who insists you should not exist? That you should be cattle? Slaughtered?

That is not part of our teaching.

Not yours, no. But others. Perhaps other religions. Other positions. What of them?

There are only three reasons to kill in Islam, Baroness. No others.

Murder?

Murder, unbelieving - breaking from the faith - and adultery.

Yes. But see, I don't agree with that. I don't think that breaking with religion, as you so put it, is a reason for anyone to be put to death. But let's take that as read, shall we?

What if they claim you cannot even exist? You want to take over the world and bring it under Sharia law for the betterment of the people.

A twelve year old girl!

But what if you are not strong enough? What if someone else beats you? What if it's the person who believes that you should not exist? What if he has all the power? What then?

Zahra leans forward, purposeful, only the smell of stale tea between them.

That is where I have lived my whole life!

A riposte. Nothing more. And the Baroness is tired of clever words.

We live in a world of wildly contrasting people and beliefs and ideals. We live in a country of them! One man's way of life is not another's. Neighbours cannot agree on the most simplistic of things. What you are talking about is totalitarianism, pure and simple. For the good of the people, perhaps, but totalitarianism nonetheless. The anarchist would argue the same. Abandon all laws! Allow society to grow naturally, without constraints. People will be forced to be better, be better to each other, if they do not have the constraints of the law holding them back.

But they forget the problem of the good king. And the problem of the good king is not that he will fail to stay good, but that he can't trust those who come after him to be good as well!

We need laws. Not absolute laws, which can be twisted by whoever is championing them, by whatever mouthpiece is being put forward in favour of them, God's or man's! We need legislation because legislation does not control the populace, it controls the people who control the legislation! A law, a good law, controls the government, not the people. It prevents the government from taking matters into its own hands. You can only go this far! You can only arrest a man for parking in the wrong place. You can only fine him. You can't chop of his hands. It stops the leaders of the country from, for example, banning your beliefs because they do not like what you are doing with the world!

The problem I find, as a Judge, both with the world you are proposing and the world of the anarchist, is that there is nothing to protect the ordinary people on the street from their leaders. They need protection from any power that deems them irrelevant. One leader has a different interpretation than another. Which is right, which is wrong, and, more importantly, when they are dead, when time has passed, when society has adapted and there are tools no one could ever have seen coming; how can they be sure that those coming after them are going to interpret their laws, their scriptures, in the way they meant them?

A country, a civilization, built on people – this can't work. It's simply not sustainable. People change, Zahra. You did. I have. Many times! People change and with them, their views.

We need laws, guidelines, or, as we call it, legislation, because… people die. Men. Women. We get old. People change and they are rarely who we wanted them to be in the first place! To give those people, any people, universal power…!

There are two phenomena; the most likely ways to change people. The first is money. Almost every single person who has won the lottery in the United Kingdom has changed who they vote for. If they were leftist at the start, they start swinging to the right once they see the tax man coming. The second – and she tells the young woman there's a name for this but it is lost to her at the moment – the second is that if you put a group of likeminded people in a room, any room, and they discuss the ideals they all believe true, whatever centrist viewpoint they hold dear, put them together in a room with people who think the same thing and they will all, without fail, move to the most radicalised position present at that time. Each one will leave the room more absolute in those views than when he or she went in.

We need dissenting voices. We need opposing beliefs and approaches. It is the only thing keeping us moving forward as a species! We had the immutable laws of God in the West for over a thousand years and look where it got us!

The law I came here to advise on… It would prevent you or your brethren, anyone committed to your cause, from re-entering the country. They would be stripped of their British passport, whether or not crimes have been committed. They would face deportation or prison, or simply be banned from coming home in the first place. Fight against the will of this country and you will no longer be a part of it! Which, prima facie, seems pretty fair, all told.

And what of our rights? As citizens?

It's not the first time this has happened, the Baroness tells her. It happened during the Spanish Civil war in the thirties. Germany and Italy were supporting Franco. Anyone with socialist, communist leanings wanted to fight against him, thousands of people were going over to Spain, fighting for a cause that, on the face of it, the British government didn't support. So the British government brought back a law from the century before. The Foreign Enlistment Act. Two years in prison. Two years for anyone who went over to Spain and fought against the very people that a few years later we would end up fighting anyway!

George Orwell, Ernest Hemingway; both could have been found guilty under it. Both of them went over and fought. Both held a gun, both killed people. Hemingway wasn't British, of course, but there were just as many who were.

Zahra has taken to playing with the emptiness of her paper cup. She pulls listlessly at the moulded overhang, peeling it back with her thumbnail.

If they were alive today, they would be in Guantanamo.

The Baroness smiles. Perhaps Orwell would have found it apt. But she is tired of the argument and snaps back quickly.

The people need laws, Zahra. Good laws. Not to protect them from each other but to protect them from overreaching powers, from future governments. You need strong, solid laws so that that boy in there – she extends her hands past them – your son! Is protected.

From a law designed to strip him from his nationality?

Zahra… If you don't mind me saying. There is a dichotomy. An… unfairness to the world you want to create, no matter how high-minded. You would strip that girl… The twelve year old you talked about? She'd be eighteen now. You'd strip her of her physical rights. Nothing to do with underage sex. But rather… love. Her right to marry. To wear what she pleases. You would do all that, yet you claim the right to citizenship is paramount. You say countries are an antiquated notion, and yet you rail against the government for thinking of stripping you of yours. Can you see the dichotomy?

We exist in a world of absolutely disparity. Disparity of beliefs, disparity of fortunes, and I would, if nothing else, like to afford you the same rights as everyone else. As a bottom line. The same rights, the same ideals. I have spent my life – I have spent my life, Zahra! – fighting to make sure that at the very least, no person, no government, can have any more control over you than they would over any other person under their control, as long as you live. As long as your baby lives! As long as we continue.

And yes. – The cup is destroyed now. A remnant of its former self in five strips, still on the table, still under the young woman's hands.

Yes. There are holes. Of course there are. There are protections we cannot give without taking freedoms away from others. Twelve-year-olds. And there are times when we have no choice but to remove those freedoms - like drug use or seat belts - from people because of the damage it does to those around them. But this balance… I would rather a thousand murderers go free than an innocent suffer, but I would also tolerate a million sufferings before allowing whomsoever comes next to use my laws to supersede the will of the minority!

She is feeling her age, the Baroness. It has not been so long since she stayed up all night arguing ethics but with that damn wind on the back of her neck…

That's what I do. That's what I have lived my life by. And that's what we are doing here today, she says. For the innocents. For tomorrow. For Solh.

And that is why you must tell me everything you know, Zahra, everything you did and everything you hope for! Unless you want to see your child end up without a mother!

The young woman looks inward and east, feelings flashing over her eyes.

He should be awake now. Don't you think?

The Baroness sighs. She cracks her knuckles, expecting a response, but doesn't get one.

How does he sleep?

The young woman shrugs. I never had a problem with him.

Were there a lot of babies in the camps?

You have to see it to understand it, she tells her. There are three camps. Always three. One for training and arms; a forward position. One for function; cooking, eating, the single men. And one for families.

How does it work?

The young woman leans forward and dips a lazy finger into the

Baroness' cup, then draws a triangle on the table.

They are always like this. The camps. Always in threes. Two clicks. That's the term they use. Clicks. American. Two clicks between the forward point, the training base. Then this, two clicks from that. Always qibla. Always towards Mecca. Then this, two clicks beyond. Four clicks off the first one. This is where the families are. Where life is. Houses, if they can be found. Tents, if not. The families are always closest to Mecca.

Do most of the men have families?

The younger woman nods. The leaders, she says. People in important positions. They are allowed. Their wives are the handmaidens to the entire camp. They provide the cooking, the cleaning, the… support.

Arms?

The younger woman looks at her, eyes flashing.

Many things.

Why did you leave your family?

My family is with him now.

Your husband or your child, the Baroness asks but she doesn't receive an answer.

There are many things you can stomach in life. Things you put up with. You can, for example, deal with being smuggled into a country in the boot of a car. You can survive being smuggled out again with your baby in your arms. But you cannot survive hypocrisy in your life.

Is that why you left the camps?

That's why I left my family! My parents! My family… They are not bad people. Smart people. Quiet people. Good, evil; you can't think of people in these terms. People aren't made like that. Evil is an erosion. Little by little, we accept what is around us, we accept what is happening. My family; they are not bad people. They believe. But their belief is… watered. Eroded. You say people should coexist but how can we do that? How is that possible?

What is the alternative?

There is no alternative. You cannot believe one thing and accept another! There was this boy, on my street. His name, his religion, was Christian. Who knows which once came first. Born, then born again. He was young and handsome, but he decided… I don't know when he decided… but he decided he was going to convert me. It became his mission. A new believer, you know? The fervour? And I suppose he saw me as something of a challenge because he kept posting me things. First online. Then… I didn't notice it at first. I was religious, he was religious, that's all I thought it was. He would leave little notes at the end of my drive. Just toss them there, but just when he knew I needed to leave for school so I'd see them. Notes with bible verses. He used to talk to me as well. When he'd see me on the street. Ask about the mosque. Ask about my faith. I was… thirteen? Fourteen. He was a year older.

It got scary. I mean, not scary-scary. I tried to explain this to my family. I tried to tell them that he wasn't a threat, not physically, but he was getting out of hand. Sometimes… Sometimes my father would find the notes. The little bible verses. He knew who was putting them there and it made him angry, you see, because he thought it was an attack on our faith. I told him it wasn't, told him it wasn't anything like that but he didn't believe me. My father thought it was anti-Islam, but it wasn't. He just wanted to save me.

Anyway, one day, my father came out and saw him, the boy, Christian, he saw him. Saw him wedging one of the bible verses between two loose bricks at the end of our driveway. And he chased him. Right down the street. Just chased him! Screaming after him to leave us alone.

He went to see his parents after that. Threatened to report him to the police and everything.

He was proselytising.

The young woman looks at her, quizzical.

What's that?

It's trying to convert someone to your own faith.

Yes. That's it. Exactly. Proselytising. I didn't know there was a word.

He came up to me, on the street later. I was with some friends. He told me that his parents had told him that he had to apologise, that he had to stop. But he couldn't and he wasn't sorry. He was trying to save my soul.

She pauses, remembering.

I called him a weirdo. Something like that. I told him he was a nutcase and he should leave me alone. And he said the truest thing. He said; if you believe in something… If you truly believe what you believe is

141

right and what you believe is that people who do not believe are in danger of going to hell, how can you live with yourself? How can you live with the knowledge that everyone around you is drowning when you have the keys to the lifeboat? No matter how hard they fight, no matter how hard they struggle. What kind of person would you be if you simply let them drown?

The Baroness thinks about this.

Is that what your family is doing? Letting them drown?

How can you live in a world that is imperfect and not try to change it? How can you live amongst people who say they believe one thing but then practice another? How can that be right? How can you accept that?

The air conditioner has stopped. The room is still icy but the Baroness feels herself relaxing somewhat. She has been crouched into her jacket and only notices it now that she starts to relax. A turtle coming out of her shell.

Maybe they noticed and turned it off.

The room is monitored in a number of ways.

I suppose, she says carefully. I suppose, a bit at a time. That's what I have always found. To change the world. Just that little bit at a time. Person by person.

My parents are good people, Zahra tells her. They are good people who are evil of the worst kind. There is a saying, in Islam. In our faith. When a man and a woman are alone together, the devil is the third person present. That's my parents.

The devil?

The ones who allow him to be present.

The Baroness reaches for her notes, thinking of something. Zahra remains silent as she flips through the pages. Looking for…

You have a younger brother, don't you, she says finally. Hadji. I take it you know about his situation?

But the young woman is refusing to be drawn.

You see, continues the Baroness. I've been listening to you for some time now, and I believe you. I do. I even understand it. But I'm not sure that's really the point, is it? I've never paid it much mind myself; religion. I think age does that. It makes one an atheist by default. The three stages of man; the young and the dying, they need to believe, but the rest of us, well, let's just say we're too busy living, shall we? But my parents believed, after a fashion. And I've seen men and women, those of conviction standing before me and... I believe you! You want to change the world. I've been trying to change it my whole life. We have a lot of similarities, you and I. The problem with atheism, or – the Baroness thinks this over – agnosticism, I suppose... I'm not really an atheist. The problem is there's very little to believe in. A better house. A better education for your children. More opportunities. Something decent at the Royal Opera House, you understand? These are small things to believe in. Petty, really. So I understand it. I believe you. Change the world. Change it! Make it a better place. But let's not pretend that's what you are doing, shall we? Let's not pretend that you, going where you went, doing what you did... Let's not pretend that any of that made the world a better place.

What happened to Hadji?

The Baroness leans back, loosening the jacket. Could they have turned the heater on now? Maybe it's a signal. She takes her own hand in an effort to test its warmth and is surprised by the paper-like quality of her skin.

How has she ever gotten this old?

Hadji was arrested. About the time Solh was born, I should think. Almost exactly.

Because of me?

I don't think that would have helped. But no. Not in the sense you mean it.

She looks at the papers.

Who was Kyle Sylvester?

But once again the young woman isn't responsive.

I want to know everything Zahra. Not these stories. Not the reasoning behind them. I want to know what happened to you. In the camps. I want to know why you decided that killing thousands of innocent people would help change the world and most of all – I want to know why you came back!

Kyle Sylvester was a friend of Hadji's. From our town. When they were kids.

A rap at the door and an unseen hand opens it. The women pause and the door closes behind the thin guard as he enters.

Baroness, he says in a voice that matches his child's eyes rather than his uniform and the women fall silent, unwilling to continue their conversation with a man in room, as though he were an interloper or a waiter. As if they believed no one had been listening all along.

He is close to the Baroness. Closer still as he leans over to deposit cups of steaming tea on the table. He has thin hips and a scent of cheap aftershave, though the Baroness cannot place it.

On his side lies the thick, plastic oblong of a firearm and the Baroness stares at the solid casing, fastened by a faux leather strap into an equally ill-moulded sheath.

The tea delivered, the thin guard straightens. He steps back and pulls a piece of paper out of his pocket.

Baroness, he says, handing it to her.

Taking it without acknowledgement she is quick to remind him that they should – under no circumstances – turn the air conditioner back on.

I am old. And unless you want the death of a former High Court Judge on your record, please see to it that the room is kept at an even heat, thank you very much.

The thin guard smiles and Baroness' her a third time before exiting.

He raps on the door and again it is opened, but the Baroness doesn't look to see who opens it and waits until it is closed again before unfolding the note.

Three lines. Simple handwriting.

You're doing splendidly, it commends her, and underneath, in an overly ornate scrawl, lies the signature. Ian St Thomas. Then, beneath that a third line. Back to legibility once more.

P.S. What is E J T. Question mark.

The room is monitored in a number of ways.

The Baroness refolds the piece of paper and places it in her jacket pocket before leaning forward to pick up a cup.

Zahra, who hasn't moved, does likewise.

He's dead.

The young woman sips, savouring the heat more than the sustenance.

Hadji?

The other boy. Sylvester. Hadji is in custody. Well, prison actually. There's a difference.

You think he killed him.

The Baroness immerses her face in the fragrance of the tea – what there is of it – and closes her eyes.

Every action has a reaction. Do you believe that?

She opens them again, and stares at the young woman between the billows.

Zahra? Do you believe that?

It's a law.

One of the immutable. Yes. Very good. A law, then. Every action has a reaction. And sometimes action is nothing more than a vacuum. The absence of something. In the place you once were. Moving objects simply because you are no longer there.

You and Hadji. You were close, no? Growing up? I have an older brother myself. Had. Passed on a few years ago now. But it's not quite the same, I'd imagine. Not the same as a younger one. Especially with that age gap. Three years. That must have made for quite a bond.

He must have worshipped you. Idolised you. Closest sister. Older friends. At that age. And then, twenty-one and you're gone. He's only eighteen. That's a very impressionable age. Eighteen.

Richard…

A very impressionable age. Still, it's amazing how a few years difference will change a person.

The young woman leans forward, a tired anger stings of stoicism behind her eyes.

You won't show me my son. You won't tell me about my brother. Is this how you write laws, Baroness?

Hadji was… Well, he was always in trouble. But you know that. You were there when he got in that fight at school. And when he got thrown out for fighting you were there then. Not Birmingham. Not London. You were still in Newport, weren't you? Still in Gwent, she says, savouring the syllables.

Zahra is silent. Her tea shakes slightly in her hand and the Baroness sits back, buttons pushed.

Hadji got into trouble after you left. I take it you knew he was using? Nothing too bad. Marijuana mainly, it seems. A little bit of ecstasy. Some dealing. Some not.

He started stealing cars. Not doing anything with them really. Just, what do they call it, joyriding? I suppose there'd be different term for it these days, but back on the bench that's what it was called. Joyriding. Not much joy for the people whose cars get stolen though, but there we are. And he had a record. And he was careless. And the police were looking for him. I would imagine we were watching him quite intently given your... travels, but car theft...

Anyway, it caught up with him. There was a chase. Not much of one. Nothing like in the movies. But a chase. In the lanes. Outside Newport. Gwent

And someone was coming the other way. A small lane. Two cars. You can guess the rest. Kyle Sylvester was with him. Died at the scene, I believe. Hadji had a broken leg but that was about it. A few bumps and scrapes. Nothing tragic. Outside of the accident, of course.

And then it got worse. Fighting, in prison. It happens. But he stabbed someone. Three months ago. In his cell. So that's two counts. And the car theft. And the drugs.

Every action has a reaction.

You're saying it's my fault.

I'm saying, says the Baroness, sipping quietly and looking at the younger woman over her glasses, that you're the cause. Equal and opposite. You abdicated responsibility. You left, he didn't. It's very simple.

You say you wanted to change the world, and I believe you. You say the world needs changing and I'm not in complete disagreement. But you wanted to change it for the better and you didn't, Zahra. You failed. In that regard you failed! You married. You had a baby. You spent two years playing revolutionary, and what did you achieve outside of a brother who lost his nearest sibling? The one he grew up with? The one who was supposed to take care of him? You wanted to change the world? I say you failed.

The anger is active now. The cup creased at the young woman's fingers as she clenches it tighter; the liquid obeying Archimedes.

There is a saying in our religion. A law, I suppose you would call it. You cannot save a soul that does not want to be saved. The world, for you, Baroness, is full of two types: people within the law and people outside it. Well, we have two types of people as well. Those who have chosen the righteous path and those who have not! The ones who have not can still be saved, they can still come to know the grace of God, but until they do they are ballast, pulling the ship down. A liability, drowning those who are following the path. And that must never be!

My brother loves zombies. Video games. Unthinking masses that can be killed with impunity. There is always a story. Some lone survivor with unlimited ammo while people who look like drunken cattle stumble towards you and try to to eat your brains. Try to turn you into them. It is the metaphor of our generation!

And I always used to say to him, what if there was a cure? What if there was? All these people you've killed, all these people you're slaughtering, what if there was a cure and you could save them instead of shooting?

And every time, you know what he'd tell me? Every time, while he was pressing buttons and blowing people up, he would tell me: they are the sacrifice so that I can live and I can find a cure and save everybody else. They are the martyrs, and I have to kill them so I can save the world!

The door unlocks again and the two women look up, the tea still largely untouched in their hands.

Ian St Thomas sticks his head around the door and waves a smile.

Hello again, he says to Zahra as if he has interrupted a social gathering.

Might I have a word, Baroness?

Ian St Thomas is ecstatic.

They stand in the office as before. The window is open, no doubt to allow for the trail of smoke that emanates from the desk, and a fine drizzle can be seen in the night-light outside.

The Baroness has to huddle into her suit jacket once more for warmth.

Seriously splendid. The Home Secretary is over the moon, as are we all.

The Baroness thinks of the tea, still on the table in the interrogation room.

She didn't give me anything on El Affie, I'm afraid.

But St Thomas is buoyant.

Oh, she gave us more than she thinks! A whole lot more.

I'm so glad you're pleased. But the irony is lost on him.

Indeed! Indeed! I have to say, I thought this was a fool's errand when they brought us in. A dot-the-i's and cross-the-t's sort of game, but it's played out better than we could ever have dreamed of! A feather in the caps of all of us, I would expect!

She still hasn't told me his name. Her husband.

St Thomas looks at her quizzically, then pulls a pack of cigarettes out from the pocket of his suit, taps one out, and lights it.

We knew that from the video. Months ago. Facial recognition software. One of the reasons they called me in on this. He's nothing major. We certainly never knew he was with El Affie. Well, I'm sure we suspected, somewhere. We usually do.

And the American? Jon? To my way of thinking that couldn't be his real name. Jihad Jon. It sounds a little…

But he cuts her off. Offers her the pack which the Baroness refuses, noting the immaculate nails on his hand as she does so. Why does everyone have such perfect nails!?

Oh, that. No, she's been giving you a bit of a run around, I'm afraid. But then we knew she would. No, Jon is Jon Stevenson. Not what he called himself of course, but that's what's on his passport. He was a Marine or some such. American, as she said. Arab descent. Lord knows why he ended up with a name like Jon Stevenson. I'm sure it's in the file. He's dead, I'm afraid. Little over a year ago. Drone strike.

The Baroness moves across the room and pulls the window shut, much to the surprise of St Thomas. Screw him, she thinks. If he's going to smoke, I'm going to be warm.

We don't know she knew that.

St Thomas looks at her, thinks, and stubs out the cigarette on the table, his exuberance gone.

No, she probably did, he says. The almost fresh carcass of the cigarette is swept into a corner behind the still upended photograph, the ash from his hands brushed onto the floor.

She's been obfuscating, I'm afraid. It's an old tactic. Giving information that is no longer of use. It makes it look like you're being helpful without actually helping. Same thing with the camps. The layouts and all that. Four miles, not two, and it's standard knowledge anyway. My nephew read it on Wikipedia I think, he adds, slicking his tie down once more now his hands are clean.

No, no. Quite unusable. That family, for example? The one in Turkey. The ones with the boy who held her hand? Quite touching. Arrested by the Turkish government last week.

And the Baroness can hear the sting in her voice as she asks about the boy.

Not my bag, I'm afraid. Not sure we'd even know.

No, he says. It's what she's not telling you that has us interested. For example: The story about the house? Well, we narrowed it down to a small number of strikes, given the intel they gave us. Given the time and the area we're pretty sure that was us, which means that, if we're right, if the reason they left the house was because we were about to drone it – or the Americans were at any rate – then that means there's a leak. We know what we can follow. So we'll have that soon enough. No doubt it'll turn out to be some contact in the ISI with links to MIT. Not the University, he adds quickly. Millî İstihbarat Teşkilâtı, the Turkish version of MI6, though why the Americans keep telling everyone what they are going to do is a mystery to me. Surely the whole point of drones in the first place is you don't have the accountability of a pilot! Anyway...

Then there's the woman. Ishaf. Which is what's got us really excited. Not her real name, of course, but you see, we think we know that one. We think we know what we're talking about here, which is part of the fun of it. Can't say too much, of course, but the Americans are very interested.

We think we're about four pieces away from collecting the whole set, if you follow my meaning. Which is just wonderful. Still, he adds, easing the cigarette packet back into his pocket, mum's the word, and all that.

The Baroness watches him. Thinking of anger and the power of it, but stays silent.

We'd like you to talk about drones when you go back in there, if you could. We need the whole story, you see? Just a few more pieces from her time in the camps, and we think talking about drones will help with that.

Do we, Mr. St Thomas. But if he notices the tone he's ignoring it.

Nudge her in the right direction sort of thing. Completely up to you.

I hadn't decided I was going back in, Mr. St Thomas.

But it's churlishness and she knows that he knows it. All those years on the bench. Too much control. Not enough practice at giving it up.

You're doing a wonderful job, Baroness, he says, and leaves it at that.

I'd like to speak to my driver, if you don't mind, Mr St Thomas.

Ah, he says, reaching behind him. Yes, I think the Home Secretary might like to talk to you first.

He holds the phone out to her. The same as before. Thin plastic slab. Pre-dialled. But even from here the Baroness can see a little light flashing in one corner indicating a call is still in progress, so she stays in the room this time. Stays where he can see her.

The room is monitored in a number of ways.

The Baroness looks at the screen and holds it up to her ear. No dialling.

Home Secretary.

There is silence for a long moment and the Baroness begins to think she has got it wrong. That the call hasn't been on the whole time. That, perhaps, the Home Secretary is on some hellish hold cycle waiting for the Baroness to summon her back.

She is all eyes on the thin man in the cheap tie and about to remove the phone from her ear in order to examine it when she hears a voice.

Rachel?

Home Secretary.

Rachel. God, he's a weasel, isn't he?

The Baroness looks again at St Thomas who smiles back.

Anyway, listen. You're doing a fantastic job. Truly. Can't thank you enough. I can't talk about it over an open line, even this one, but I really think we're saving lives here, Rachel. Real lives.

Friends have a way of disappointing you. We forget that friends are other people when they're not with you.

I'm not sure I'm comfortable with this, Home Secretary.

No one is, Rachel. No one is. But it is working and that's the test of it.

The law should not be used like this. Judges should not be made into agents of the prosecution.

Silence at this. Is she imagining it, or can she hear other voices off?

No one is, Baroness. No one is. If I could be there myself to do it, I would. But she's confided in you. Has shown that she's willing to. If we'd known this going in I wouldn't have asked you, but there it is.

She pauses, about to say something else, but thinks the better of it.

There it is.

I understand Home Secretary, she says, and is about to hand the phone back when she hears the voice again, and reluctantly moves it back to her ear.

She looks at the still smiling St Thomas but the tone has changed, the voice conspiratorial, so the Baroness turns away. Protective.

Rachel? Rachel?

Home Secretary.

Listen, while you're in there. Try to get back to asylum. And the Baroness has to ask her what she means.

We've got enough for our American friends, she tells her, or we soon will have, I suspect. Enough for his lot. But I want something for us as well. I want you to talk about asylum.

For her?

For the child.

Which hangs there. Over the phone.

The mother's nationality... but she is cut off, the tone losing its conspiratorial tone.

Well, yes, possibly!

No, Home Secretary. Not possibly. Actually! British law is very clear on this, I'm afraid. A citizen…

I'm talking of exploring it. That is what we do. Explore! The girl's grandmother was born in a different country, but the girl's mother is not a citizen of that country. She is British. The girl's son was not born…

Home Secretary. I understand what you are trying to do and I understand the thinking, but this is not the case and that is not the law!

Well, and there's a pause there. Hanging on the line.

Well. I'm not sure I agree with you on that, Baroness.

Has this girl broken laws? Yes, Home Secretary. Are any of them British? Probably not. Are any countries looking for extradition? No one even knows where she was! And the child? A maternity test, possibly. The state must be satisfied with the application, I understand that, but Home Secretary, I must warn you: The woman is incredibly sympathetic. She is extremely intelligent and more than capable of making an argument in her favour!

You mean she's the moderate face of extremist Islam?

I mean, Home Secretary, the Baroness continues, not enjoying the joke, that she'll interview well on Al Jazeera. The very last thing these people should have is a poster child of their own, I'm sure you'll agree.

Well, and that pause again. Thank you, Rachel. I thank you for your counsel, sound as it always is. But if you could, while you're in the room, broach the topic, we'd be obliged.

Naturally.

Thank you, Baroness Armstrong.

Of course, Home Secretary.

Put St Thomas back on, would you?

The Baroness holds the phone out towards St Thomas, who looks at it, an idiotic grin on his face, and points to himself in surprise, mouthing his incredulity. But the Baroness isn't playing. She simply puts the phone on the edge of the desk and walks to the window, staring out into the night sky, watching in reflection as St Thomas picks up the phone and speaks.

Home Secretary. Silence. Wind outside. No airplanes. Of course, Home Secretary. Of course.

There is a moment in the dark when night becomes morning, a

feeling of it in the air as chill as any two-AM excess. They are there now. The Baroness can feel it through the glass. She can sense it in the moment. Though dawn is still hours away, it is no longer last night.

St Thomas is looking at her through his reflection, phone to his ear. I'll ask her.

She looks at him in the window, unwilling to turn as he presses the phone against his chest in a faux gesture designed to convey confidentiality between the two of them.

Baroness?

But she knows he can see her watching him and waits for him to continue.

The Home Secretary is asking what E J T stands for?

Jan is waiting outside when the Baroness finds him. The air is crisp and saturated, the pavement full of errant puddles.

He clips his phone shut as the doors open and the Baroness walks out into the pre-light of morning, pulling her suit jacket around her in an innate fashion he has seen a thousand times since coming to work for her.

Would you like me to get your coat for you, Baroness, but she just shakes her head, eager for the air, gulping deep breathfuls of it into her lungs to ward off the tiredness.

I thought it better we talk out here.

Jan nods. It's one of the things he has come to enjoy about working for the Baroness. Her directness.

I was calling my wife, but the Baroness isn't listening.

I think perhaps you'd better tell me where you were this afternoon, Jan. When you were late at the club.

I told you, there were road works...

She waves him away. Yes, yes. But not for that amount of time. And I noticed we were low on gas while we were lost on our way here, which presumably is where you've just been. Unless there is something else you'd like to tell me.

He looks down, stubbing his toe into the tiny concrete ridges of the paving slab. He looks back at the car, as if expecting an answer from it, but the only sound comes from a bird, noisy in a distant tree, competing with the airplanes.

I think it's best you tell me, all told.

It's best I leave. I'm sorry, Baroness. You are a good employee, but…

He pauses, looking back at the car once more.

If this is about that ridiculous incident…

My wife doesn't like it here.

But now it's the Baroness' turn to look at the car, half expecting to see a woman, uncomfortable in the back seat.

She doesn't like it in England.

It's that little bit colder now, and the Baroness crosses her arms, ostensibly for warmth.

I'm not following.

That's where I was. Today. When you called. There were road works, I wasn't lying, but we are buying a house. I was at the estate agent. Or brokers, anyway. He's dealing with it for me. I'm sorry, I should have said.

You're buying a house?

In Trutnov.

The Baroness looks out at the darkness. The manmade hill is silhouetted by the lights of the airport beyond, casting an almost silvery glow. There is water in the air that she breathes in.

This is what I meant. When I said I should quit this afternoon.

I didn't even know you were married.

Last year.

And she's smiling when she says, no invite? And he smiles back at the thought of it, embarrassed.

So you're going back home.

Not home, no, he shrugs. I can find you another driver. There's no rush.

You're not from… Where was it?

Trutnov.

Trutnov?

No.

Then why go there?

The car yet again. A sideways glance, checking authority for the statement.

Life is less complicated. I don't know. Life here, Baroness… There is money, and that's a good thing. But my wife, she is pregnant…

You're pregnant!

I'm… We are. Yes. And life here is more difficult. More clumsy. I'm sure we can find you another driver.

She looks back at the building behind her with its double panelled entrance. Beyond that she can make out Button Man leaning on the counter, idle and bored.

And you're not part of anything to do with this?

But now it is Jan's turn to look perplexed.

Baroness?

You don't know anything about why they called us here?

He shrugs, sensing the meaning. The first I heard of this was when you called me.

Why didn't you tell me? About leaving.

He sighs. Baroness, you are… I have enjoyed working for you. I like driving you. It's interesting. I drove a rock star once. The most boring thing you can ever do. I drive you to parliament. I drive you to the courts. I drive you to the Palace!

He looks at her, thick eyes behind grey rimmed glasses.

How do you tell a woman like that you no longer want to live in her country?

The baby is anything but asleep, and jacket off, blouse clouded, the young woman looks anything but job satisfied as the pair of them bounce up and down. The woman toe to heel, the baby wrapped in her arms.

The Baroness can hear Solh's cries from the corridor as she approaches. She wonders if Zahra can hear them but doubts it, at least outside the way every mother continues to hear her baby cry long after they've stopped.

He won't sleep.

He's hungry.

But there is food there aplenty. Bottles of formula are stacked against Cow & Gate boxes of solids. A childless man's approach to buying baby food. Enough to last a month.

The woman is rattled, sleep deprived, daunted.

I asked them to ask her what he's on, but I know fuck all about babies, she says. Then, noting her tone, apologises.

Please, don't worry about it. I'm afraid it's something I should have thought about. While I was in there.

Yes, says the young woman. Me too.

The Baroness thinks about this.

They brought you in to speak to her?

It's protocol, Baroness. For these kinds of people, she adds, carefully avoiding the proper noun of it. There's a point when you want a man to go in there, rattle them, make them uncomfortable, but you can't establish trust that way.

The Baroness nods and imagines aloud that it must take quite a lot of training.

Three years.

This only takes nine months, the Baroness says with a smile.

Do you have children, Baroness?

But she doesn't want to think about it. Doesn't want to see Richard in these wails of exhaustion and despair.

I'm sorry, it's just…

The Baroness reaches out towards the child, and the young woman passes him over with a caffeine stutter that releases her hold on him before the Baroness has a comfortable grip.

Have you ever heard of the Stranger Situation, the Baroness asks the young woman.

No, Baroness.

It's a theory. A psychiatric experiment, I suppose you could call it. Back in my day, when we didn't mind scarring children for life.

She has the wail in her ear now, and the Baroness cannot tell if her levity has soothed the young woman or if she is even listening.

There are, she continues, according to these studies, though I have to say during my time on the bench I never put too much stock in them. There are, however, in the Stranger Situation, three types of children.

She is bouncing the child. Talking into his ear in measured tones. Pacifying him and, hopefully, the young woman as well.

There are, of course, names for these types, labels, but I've forgotten them. Anyway. The idea of the study is that you introduce a stranger into a room. While the mother is there with her child, you introduce a stranger and see how the baby reacts. Some go quiet. Some get louder. Some don't react at all. Completely understandable. Then, with the stranger still in the room, you remove the mother. She steps out, as it were, leaving the child alone with the man. It was almost always a man. No word of where she's going or how long she'll be. She just simply steps out. I've no idea how they found mothers willing to this, but it was the seventies and we were pretty open to the Philip Larkin form of parenting, as it were.

There are, it seems, three types of children at that point. It's funny how they're always in threes. There are those that engage directly with the stranger. Those that refuse to acknowledge him, and, of course, those who scream their bloody heads off.

Not exactly rocket science, one would say. Pretty much what anyone who has ever spent time with children might expect. But the interesting thing, or at least the interesting thing for me, is what happens when the mother comes back.

The first type of child runs straight to the mother. Maybe they've been talking to the stranger, maybe they haven't, but they run straight to the mother. Want to talk to her. Want to be held. Love and be loved. Nothing strange there.

The second type. They now actively blank the stranger. Doesn't matter whether they were playing with him a minute ago. They completely ignore him, worried that the mother might not approve. They are looking for positive reinforcement. They don't want her to know that they've betrayed that love, that they might even be capable of enjoyment with somebody else, so they ignore the stranger, going so far as to be hostile if he tries to re-instigate contact.

The last type though. This is the type that interests me. The other two you can expect. Confidence is about the only mark of it. Put a stranger

157

in the room, and if the baby's confident of his place in the world and his mother's love, then no problem. If he's not… Well.

The last type, however. When the mother comes back into the room, the baby quite simply ignores her. Won't talk to her. Won't acknowledge her. Shuts her out completely.

The baby has quietened. She can feel his breath on her shoulder. His chest against her breastbone. His weight in her arms. So brown. So beautiful. The warmth of his head a thing to undo.

They, she continues, are the interesting ones. They have, whether they've shown it or not, been hurt, however slightly. They have been betrayed and now they are lashing out. They have no interest in being brought back in to the fold, so to speak. No interest in forgiveness. They have been hurt. And so they refuse any futher attention. As punishment.

She speaks softly into the shell on the side of his head, wondering which type he is.

The Baroness turns to the young woman and sees she has lost her attention. She is sitting on one of the soft stools that are dotted around the room, staring out into space, eyes heavy and clouded.

She looks up at the silence that fills the room when the Baroness stops speaking and the Baroness looks down at her, offering the child back.

They do the same thing. Radicals. Three types. Always three.

The Baroness smiles.

Keep talking to him. Low voice. Lots of diaphragm. He'll eat when he's ready. Though you're better off with the bottle than that stuff. Rice, if you can get some. Plain with apple. He should be used to that. Sultanas.

Were you there when they picked them up, the Baroness adds as an afterthought and the woman answers in the affirmative.

What happened to her head covering? A chador? Niqab? Anything?

She wasn't wearing one, ma'am.

On the flight?

Not according to the flight attendant, no. I think she thought it would get her through security.

The woman still hasn't risen, and the Baroness has to unpin and proffer the child before she does.

I take it you don't have children… She leaves the sentence hanging, looking for a name that doesn't come.

No, Baroness.

The child is back in the arms of the agent and both women can tell from his breathing that he is unhappy about it.

Well. Shouldn't be much longer. The Baroness is curt, straightening, muscle memory running a hand over her shoulder for spit stains in a move that she hasn't performed for nearly forty years.

One day, she says, and she is not sure whether it is meant as comfort or admonition. One day you will have to do this all over again.

And then she leaves.

The Baroness is met in the hallway by Ian St Thomas, though whether he's been hanging about waiting for her or was on his way to get her is unclear.

He smiles his smile and asks her if she is ready.

Do you have the papers I asked you for, Mr. St Thomas?

He smiles again, looking at her through crinkled brown eyes.

Is that wise, Baroness? You have after all been gaining her trust, as it were. Such a shame to undo all of your hard work.

But the Baroness holds out her hand and he reluctantly parts with the papers in his own.

There is a child in there, Mr. St Thomas. A baby who needs its mother not an agent trained in interrogation. If such a thing is going to happen, the less time this charade goes on the better.

The younger man nods, thinking, then smiles his smile.

Well, you know best, Baroness. He says it with a twinkle. You know best.

He leads her silently back along the barren halls. How many parents have been deprived of their children here? How many families split apart by boundaries that belong to her grandfather's way of thinking? The government, thinks the Baroness, is not of a rule for all. We are an empire that chooses who to rule and when to rule them, one at a time.

She knows the name of each and every case in front of her that ended in this way. Can recall every angry face of parents who were refused asylum, every child whose parents could not join them and every one of them knew corridors like this, in one way or another.

They take the final turn. The thin guard is standing at his post outside the unmarked room, and straightens noticeably at their appearance.

Sir, he says clearly as they approach, moving to allow for a key card to be applied, or perhaps to apply it himself, but the Baroness stops, St Thomas almost running into her from behind.

The Baroness asks the thin guard if his charge has asked for anything, and he looks at St Thomas over her shoulder for permission before he answers her.

No, madam.

Baroness.

Yes. Sorry. No, Baroness.

St Thomas, believing they are finished, reaches forward with his access card but the Baroness is not done and he has to arrest himself once more.

What's your name? Come now. You surely know that? I am a member of the House of Lords, after all. You don't need permission from a man in a suit to tell me your name, do you?

No, Baroness, he says carefully. And then, when the unseen permission comes, Bartholomew, Baroness.

Bartholomew?!

Yes, Baroness.

That is quite a name. Not one you usually hear this side of the ocean!

My parents are big Bible people, Baroness.

But that came without permission and a look from St Thomas tells him as much.

St Thomas leans forward, breath in the older woman's ear.

Baroness?

An apostle of Christ's, Bartholomew. Not a famous one. A follower. Is that what you are, child? A follower.

But this is more for St Thomas than the confused young soldier and she turns to him when she says;

Well? Someone open the door, for crying out loud! We'll be here all night, otherwise.

Ian St Thomas looks at her, the smile for the first time completely faded from his lips. Then he steps around the Baroness and plants his card on the reader without looking at either the of them in any way, shape or form.

Zahra is asleep.

For a moment the Baroness wonders where the observation room is. But then, she supposes, they are probably watching them on their phones, or on a laptop, or, more probably, in another building altogether along with big screen close-ups and barometric readings. Somewhere comfortable with a decent table for the Home Secretary to drum her fingers in expectation.

The Baroness hasn't expected the young woman to be asleep. She pushes the door shut gently and takes in the slight figure at the table. She has used her hair – thick, matted – to block out the light and so she slumps, head forward, arms folded into pillows, her head turned to the left and her hair in her eyes. The grey cold of the metal reflects badly off what little is viewable of her face, giving her an age that the Baroness had never seen before.

With quiet ease, the Baroness pulls back the plastic chair and sits, arranging the papers on the table in front of her, but the young woman still does not move.

The Baroness envies this. She has never been able to sleep anywhere other than her own bed. Not the car. Not her office. She remembers this, putting her head down on the desk, closing her eyes, blotting out the world, but never sleeping. She has never been able to do this.

Richard could. Lucas can. She remembers him telling her about it.

It's one of the gifts of travel. One of the perks. Travel long enough and you learn to accept sleep where you can get it. It's also a young man's game, he'd added. As you get older sleep becomes more and more important to you. Which is strange. Being young, you'd think it was the other way round. Staving off the ending, not wasting time. Nevertheless, he told her, you're twenty and a traveller and you can put your head down just about anywhere.

The older woman looks at the sleeping form in front of her and considers letting her rest. Then she leans over and pats her arm.

Zahra shifts in her sleep, her mind protesting the invasion. The Baroness pats once more. Firmer, feeling the cheapness of the sweater under her fingers. Not cotton.

Zahra moves and then, accepting her surroundings, pulls herself upright. She rubs her eyes, looking at the Baroness. She doesn't seem perturbed, doesn't seem shaken. This is what she expected. Even in her dreams.

The Baroness watches her as she comes to consciousness.

How long was I out? A mumble, and the Baroness has to ask her to repeat herself.

I'm not sure. Minutes, possibly. Not long, I would think.

Is he okay?

He? Solh. Though what okay means the Baroness has no answer to.

He's hungry. When did he last eat?

The young woman puts her palm to an eye, pressure and yielding.

Airport. Moscow, she says.

Is he on solids?

Zahra nods.

I thought he might still be on formula. Given his size.

The younger woman looks at her before asking when she can see him, which seems to trigger something in the Baroness.

So, she says, spreading her hands out across the papers in front of her, decades of judicial practice embedded in her movements, missing only a wig.

So, Zahra. Where did we leave it?

But the Baroness knows full well where they left it, and catches her gaze over the rim of her glasses before continuing.

I like you. You are a sharp and intelligent young woman. You want to change the world. Which is not the worst sentiment I have ever heard. But you are not helping yourself, and by dint of that, you are not helping me either.

I want to show you a few things.

The Baroness has had no time to order the mass in front of her and while she is saying this, she shuffles through the papers. Finding where she had decided to begin, she holds it out for Zahra.

I can't read Arabic.

The Baroness looks at her. Isn't that what they teach you? In the camps? I thought that was the first step of it, becoming a Salafist? Learning Arabic?

But the young woman remains stoic in her appraisal, refusing to be drawn, and the Baroness continues.

This is only a few days old. It would have come about after you left the camps, but this is by your group. And, I need you to trust me on this, Zahra. If I tell you what this is about, I need you to promise to believe me.

Why?

I am not interested in a discussion on theology. I am not interested in changing your mind. You are an intelligent woman, and I have no intention of trying to hold up the flaws in any piece of religious text. They all have things we would rather were not in them, and I think a discussion on literary criticism is best left for other minds, don't you agree?

The woman is careful. Groggy. Untrusting.

Okay.

Okay. Good. So I am not about to attack your faith. I have no interest in it, the old agnostic that I am, and I want you to remember that. I want you to bear that in mind. Alright?

What does it say?

This is a… The Baroness pauses, unsure of how to continue and tells her so.

It is a handbook. Of sorts. By your group. The group you were with in Iraq. With El-Affie. With your husband.

She lets it sit there, the name and the lack of one, but there is no reaction from the young woman.

I don't know who it was written by, but it's a handbook. On how to rape women.

Again, and again nothing.

It seems that there have been some… difficulties, within your group, on how best to rape the women they capture. A problem for us all, no doubt… But the Baroness can hear St Thomas in the quip and regrets it instantly, dropping her voice as she continues.

Over three thousand women have been captured by your group during the last two years. Perhaps you haven't seen them. Perhaps you know nothing about this. Perhaps…

Silence.

And there is a… debate. On how to proceed with the raping. When it is right to, when it is not. Who you can rape, who you cannot. This, of course, is not new. Some countries have this. Some… Not your group, I know, but still… Some countries, when a virgin needs to be executed, they rape her first because virgins have an exalted place in the next world.

This…

The Baroness' fingers are wide across the writing, strident and holding. The young woman in front of her passive but listening.

This tells the men in your group who to rape. When it is allowed. The women they capture, they are slaves, not wives and there are several passages in here about duty. About the duty of raping someone. The obligation.

I brought this to you, Zahra. I brought this to you because you were so concerned about that twelve-year-old. Worried. And I wanted you to see this, to hear about it, because this is not the world you were telling me about. This is not what you said you wanted to change it to.

There is a passage. In here. There is a passage that says that young girls can be raped. Before they reach puberty. They can be raped. It says that they are slaves. It says that this is not being unfaithful to a man's wife, to his family. It says that this is a duty! In here. Do you believe me?

Zahra looks at the older woman in front of her and thinks about her mother. She remembers her mother's smell. Her voice in the kitchen. Her hands on her in the morning, straightening her dress. Wiping her mouth.

I read a lot of philosophy when I was young. I know you know this because you had a file on me. Philosophy. Before I dropped out. In Birmingham. Back home. So I know how the world works, Baroness. Marx predicted that it would take one hundred years of socialism before communism could truly take form.

But the Baroness isn't listening, she pulls out photographs from the middle of the pile and places them one by one on the table as she has seen a thousand barristers do before her.

Men. Twenties to forties. Different sizes. Same look. Five in all.

These are the people I was telling you about. Journalists… She pauses at one photo, her finger tap-tapping against his brow like the hand of God reaching down and marking Cain.

This one. This one was an aid worker. He helped people, Zahra. He helped the women and children who that document says you can rape. For your pleasure. And again, all of this is after you would have left. The last few days. I am not saying that these people's blood is on your hands. I am not saying you are part of any crime, except in the larger sense…

But Zahra has pulled at one of the photos. Not the aid worker. Another man. Thinner. Whiter. A hint of a smile somewhere on his face. Perhaps the eyes. Perhaps the laugh lines.

The Baroness asks if she knows him but Zahra isn't ready to answer yet. So she tells her that the man's name is Remon Duboir. Dutch-French. Or at least, he was. He is dead now, she tells her. Beheaded. His family couldn't get the government to fund his release along with the other French prisoners because he was Dutch and the Dutch government has very strict rules about this sort of thing that the French weren't willing to break. So he was beheaded. At a camp. Perhaps your camp. The camp you were at. They aren't sure when but they think five days ago. Maybe ten.

You know this man, don't you?

Zahra nods.

You've seen him before.

In Syria.

The Baroness looks at her, then takes the photo from her hand.

Why don't we start at the beginning?

Zahra can remember first seeing the camps. She can remember standing on the mountains with Ishaf. Her niqab billowing in the wind looking down at the small cluster of houses and tents that made up the northernmost camp.

She can remember the dryness. The heat of the sun and the bite of the air. She can remember how broken the ground was beneath her feet, crumbling at each footfall.

She can remember Jon telling them about himself. About how lucky they were. People from another world, witnessing the birth of this one.

We are here at the start, he said. The world is changing. There will be no trace of us in the years to come. No record of the world we came from. People do not want iPhones. They do not want anarchy. They want God. His justice. His peace.

She wasn't listening. She was thinking of the hills above her hometown. She was thinking of playing there as a girl, the rebel even then, swings over streams and swords out of sticks. She was thinking about how different the hills looked here. How less green, less fertile, yet richer.

Jon had told her then about his wife was also in the camp. He told her that he had promised to return to her and how he had promised he would bring his friend a beloved of his own.

Ishaf was quiet.

How did you cross the border, the Baroness asks, but Zahra doesn't know. I was in the boot of a car, she tells her. There was a crossing of some kind. I could hear voices, but nothing more.

Instead she tells the Baroness about life in the camp. About how, when she got there, before the wedding party, there was tension. Things had not gone well and there seemed to be a lot of waiting. And then when she saw Ahmad… She had almost wanted to leave. Almost wanted to…

When she met her beloved he was everything he promised to be. He was tall and slim and warm and firm. He had trouble growing a full beard and it leant him an air of uncertainty, of vulnerability. She liked that. He told her that it was because of age and that he would be able to grow a full one soon. She liked that as well.

Ishaf was the sister of Vadi. Zahra never found out if the two were related or not, but they were sisters, inseparable. Vadi was married to Jon. American-Mohammed as the men liked to call him, but he didn't like that. Together the sisters were her guides, teaching her the ways of the camp, the duties.

They taught her about the morning prayers the women often held together, though many chose to do so alone. They taught her about the kitchens where they would cook together behind curtains, standing behind the shroud until the food was ready and then departing, the silence telling the men it was safe to come into the kitchen and gather for themselves. They taught her about the scriptures and how they had been corrupted by the weak and the West. They taught her about the Sunnah, the way of life prescribed by the prophet. They taught her Al-wala' w-al-bara and all that was right.

They taught her about the satellites. About the hours they could and could not go wandering around the camp. They taught her about the garden and about caring for the animals. They taught her to watch out for the goats and their bad tempered bites.

And then there was the wedding. The one the Baroness had seen. The video. She told her about the lead up to the day. About how excited the women were. She told the Baroness that she had been nervous, yes, but ready. Ready to move on. To become one. To serve both her husband and God.

She left out the wedding night. The Baroness was old and Zahra doubted she would appreciate it.

She does tell her about the weeks after though. She tells the Baroness about the camp without the men. The men who had left to carry out holy orders. And she tells her that, at first, it was like a window had opened for the women. All alone. Vadi is teaching her Arabic to add to her Farsi. Some women stop wearing the full niqab, it is just them after all, but Zahra prefers it.

The men are gone, but they will be back again soon.

Then a day passes, and another, and through the window seep in doubts. Will they be back? Will they be victorious? They listen to the radio in snatches and discuss possibilities. But they do not trust the radio, and some of the older women eschew it completely.

Tensions rise.

And then reports from the training camp. The men have returned! News filtering in. Arrivals at the dining hall. The men still have work to do, so they are not allowed to return to their wives yet. Their wives not allowed to spend time at the training camp.

War takes time.

Zahra tells the older woman about the snatched minutes behind the dining tent in the valley, under the shadow of an outcrop. Holding hands. His arm is hurt. He fell badly, he says. It is nothing, he tells her. But he cannot raise his arm above his head.

And then the men trickle back to camp. The Imam's first. The older men. Leaders. Planners. The younger men still have work to do.

And this is how it goes. Some men never return. Not each time, but some men never do. Their wives are lauded, and then escorted back to their home towns. This, this is the saddest thing. Not the men who don't come back. This, after all, is war. But the women who have no place. They take their children and go. Gather them in their arms or watch from the back of a truck as it pulls out.

This is the hardest thing.

Vadi is pregnant. She tells Zahra. Ishaf first, of course, but then her. She likes Vadi more than she likes Ishaf. They get on better. They all have husbands but Vadi has Mohammed, and that gives them a connection.

This is her first baby.

Then one day, Mohammed does not come back.

This is how it goes, she tells the Baroness. The men go, some don't come back, but this was not during a battle. This was a supply run and they were hit out of nowhere. American-Mohammed is not coming back.

Ishaf is broken. Vadi will need to leave the camp. There will be a funeral – even without bodies there are always funerals – and she will have to go. She is heavily pregnant, but she will have to go.

The men are worried about the camp. Unsettled. They have decided to move across the border. Syria. The war is taking on different fronts. The funeral will have to be quick. There is a sense that this is because he was once American but no one dares say it.

Ishaf talks to the older women. She pleads for her sister. Let her have the baby in the camp, she begs them. Let her come with us. Ishaf's husband has promised to marry her.

They tell her this is not needed. She will be taken care of. Her husband is a martyr. She will want for nothing.

But Ishaf will not be shaken.

When the trucks pull out, Vadi is with them. She travels with her hand tight to her belly. The women leaning against her to ease the rock of the road.

Ishaf never lets go. For the entire trip, for all the days on the road, she holds tightly onto her sister, while she in turn cradles her unborn child with both hands.

Bartholomew has brought tea yet again. Sandwiches that smell of chicken in bright wrappers with neon text proclaiming them pulled from an airport staff lunch room.

This time he is accompanied by Button Man. This is the first time the Baroness has seen Button Man and Zahra in the same room and the discomfort is palpable. Button Man averts his eyes, failing to look even once at the small dark figure on the other side of the desk. And Zahra, for her part, stares fixedly at his head, willing him to see her, her anger a thing of heat.

Was it this man, not St Thomas, who questioned her before? Perhaps Button Man, not the slick-tied Cambridge graduate, was the one who threatened to take Solh away.

It's protocol, Baroness. For these kinds of people. There's a point where you want a man to go in there. To rattle them. Make them uncomfortable, but you can't establish trust that way.

Fitting punishment then. To be relegated to being the man with a finger on the button that does nothing more than open a door.

The thin guard smiles at the Baroness.

Thank you, Bartholomew, she says, though she knows this is breaking protocol. Can see it in the tension it adds to the room. But the Baroness is too old for such silliness. Too old a goat to be played like a fool. If someone wants to track down a soldier named Bartholomew working out of a Heathrow bunker, well, good luck to them. She doubts they'll have much joy.

Baroness… Button Man's voice is deep and hateful.

Baroness, we were asked to remind you.

He doesn't say what and doesn't need to.

But the Baroness just smiles at Zahra, and thanks Bartholomew by name once more before they leave.

What will happen, Zahra asks her when they are alone. What will happen if they enact the law you are proposing? If it passes parliament.

For you?

For everyone.

Well, I'm not proposing anything, for a start. I'm advising. On these sorts of thing, it's quite different. Though I would imagine I'll be on the committee.

She thinks about this.

For a start, they are already arresting anyone they know to be fighting with the militants. Anyone they know or suspect of committing a crime, per se. But they need to go bigger than that.

Why?

Well, you said it yourself really. We are in a global community. You sat in your house and dreamed of changing the world, of fighting for what you call 'your people', but how many of your people dream about coming here instead?

Britain has over a million visitors to our shores every year from Islamic countries alone. Hundreds of thousands of students. The nature of the problem is that these fighters, these people who executed these men, who wrote this handbook, they are mostly not people like your husband. Not people displaced. The frontline is formed, at least in part, by holiday warriors. Students taking the summer to go and wage holy war against the very countries they then come back and resume their studies in.

And what should we do? How can we contain this? How can we stop another King's Cross? Another Paris? Milan? You tell me - how do we stop every country turning into Jerusalem?

Leave our people alone.

Yes. The Baroness sits back. I wish it were that simple.

Isn't it?

A smile. I know you know this because you are not a stupid person, but governments do not control the world. They run it, give or take, but that is not exactly the same thing.

And this is what we're talking about, when it comes down to it. Do we limit ordinary people's freedom? Do we limit the banks on their ability to invest offshore, or a petroleum company that owns interests in the Middle East to stop selling here? Would that appease you? Would that stop people coming over here and killing innocent people on the street? I think not.

The Baroness brushes back a strand of hair from her eyes.

So we have a choice, she says. We can limit the freedoms of the companies and bankers who are operating inside of the law. We can spy on each and every person in the country, monitor their communications, share the results with whatever government is interested in them, and imprison people for even thinking about committing a crime… and then keep them there. After all, It's not like once you lock someone up they're going to be on your side, take up lawn bowling and move to Gloucestershire. We can do this. We can do this to everyone. We can do it to one minority. A minority who, no matter how well-intentioned and well-behaved it is, is affiliated with people like you.

She pauses for effect. Allowing the sentence to sink in. Watching it in the young woman's eyes.

Or we can simply ban you from being here. You, or whoever we believe might hurts us. However slight the provocation. However well-hidden the intentions. Simply exile you all and let you deal with it somewhere else.

That's what will happen. If this law passes. Not immediately, mind you. These things always go in steps. But the British, the British like you, who join groups overseas, who join groups affiliated with attacks on our soil, who join groups which won't denounce these attacks? Well, they may be imprisoned. Go through the court system; which I would prefer. They may be refused re-entry unless they take some sort of special course. But one day, and this is where it is going, Zahra. One day, they simply won't be allowed to board a plane coming back here. Their passports will be revoked. Globalization will be at an end, and only the very few will be allowed to travel. Others will stay in the country they are born in. Though, obviously, that country might not want them there either.

This is for you to decide?

The Baroness unwraps a sandwich. American. What she's reliably told is a 'wrap'. But she's hungry, so she pulls it apart and start to make herself a salad out of the miserable pieces.

That, it seems, is the problem. The problem is that most of these things… Well, there're too many of them. Too many people to keep track of. So, initially, it will be through algorithms. It almost always is these days. Metadata. Likelihood. No doubt the people who do these sorts of things will have a star rating sooner or later. Like hotels. America already does, do you know that? When you apply for a visa. Security risk ratings! One star if you are of a certain decent. Two stars if your family had connections. Three stars and they revoke your visa. It's right there on the paper they put in your passport!

And that's what we'll all have, eventually. And then that, in turn, will be passed on to the analysts. A group of tired men and women in a back room somewhere who have looked at too many of these things, and they will examine the data and make an assessment. Then, perhaps, it'll be a judge, or a panel of judges, who will say, yes, you are still British, or no, you are not.

But the thing is, Zahra. Imagine how quickly this will need to happen! Imagine the turnaround! For someone like you. For someone flying in from Turkey via Moscow. Even if that person is using their real passport? The whole identification and assessment process will have to happen in, what, six, perhaps twelve hours? At the most. From suspicion to exemption! An immigration case in front of me will often last no less than three months, and here we are talking as little as three hours!

There will be mistakes. There will be families separated. There will be innocent people stranded in countries they do not wish to be in because their government has disowned them, labelling them terrorists!

But, and this is the thing, Zahra. Something like this will have to happen. Eventually. We cannot be a country composed of calculated killers. A country whose people murder and rape in other countries and then travel back here to resume their normal lives in the streets and the shops, in the mosques and the community. We cannot be a nation of people who travel overseas in order to harm others simply to try to make a political point! We will not become that. I won't allow us to become that!

And mark my words on this. At the moment this is just one sided. Muslims answering Jihad. Like you. Now, how long before white boys from Shoreditch are fighting against you in Turkey because they have decided to form a holy war of their own? How long before people pick up a gun and start protecting their own in much the same way you are now?

She watches as the young woman digests this, her own sandwich untouched before her.

Though I suppose you could say that is already happening with the drones, adds the Baroness, feeling a smile from St Thomas on the back of her neck.

The young woman looks at her across the table and picks up the sandwich.

Why do you think they are white, she says, unwrapping it and pulling it apart all at the same time.

Syria, Zahra tells the Baroness, is not like Iraq. In Iraq, she tell her, there are roads but they are blown and broken. Half end in desert, half in catastrophe. In Syria the roads are like American movies. Two, three lane highways. Stretching on.

The benefits of a dictator, she muses.

My husband told me that the men stay off the roads. They are not interested in getting blown up by drones or anti-aircraft guns.

But by the time we come along in our trucks the roads were safe enough.

Vadi is driving. She wants to remain useful. Ishaf and Zahra sit next to her.

We were in charge of a goods truck. Food. Munitions. That sort of thing. Vadi is pregnant, morning sickness – so she needed to drive. The moment we cross the border she starts to throw up and we have to stop. The only way she copes is driving. She is still sick but she simply keeps the window rolled down and her foot on the accelerator. When she needs to lean out, Ishaf steers.

The Baroness asks her if it is unusual for the women to drive and is told that everyone has their role. Everyone has a place in the cause.

Zahra first starts looking after the prisoners in Deir al-Zor. They take over an old hospital there. It is obvious that there had been some battle in the building. There are beds and mattresses which is a welcome relief, but there are also bullet holes and bloodstains in places even hospitals shouldn't have bloodstains.

Zahra tells the Baroness that she found the prisoners while she was looking for a toilet on the first day. They had just moved in and the men were unloading. They were setting up beds for the women on the top floor, but the bathroom there had been damaged and the plumbing wasn't working, so she ventured down a floor and followed the signs.

There are no men there. No guards. She just opens a door and finds a man, sitting in the corner. He isn't wearing handcuffs. Isn't restrained in any way.

He is dressed in a simple grey tunic, Rachel. He was malnourished and his beard unkempt but he seemed fine apart from that.

The door is unlocked.

She is wearing her niqab, so he doesn't look surprised. He has turned his face to the wall, obviously hearing her approach, his hands on each side are pressed against the tiles, but he is watching her out of the corner of his eye.

It is not immediately clear that he is white.

The young woman tells the Baroness that she froze. Stood there. Unsure what to do.

He releases his hands slowly and allows himself to ease to the floor, his eyes firmly away from her.

It is only when he whispers the perfunctory Arabic greeting that she can tell he is European.

She goes out and closes the door.

Her husband is angry. Why has she gone in there? What has she told the prisoner!?

The men look at her differently, suspicion clear in their eyes, and she is glad her face is shrouded.

Even her husband becomes a figure of distrust.

She must set this right, she tells her husband. She must prove her loyalty. She talks to Ishaf and together they agree that as well as their duties in the kitchen, they will cook for the prisoners. For the guards and for the prisoners. This will prove her loyalty. This will show her atonement.

Every morning, after the men have been fed, Zahra returns to the kitchen to make special food for the prisoners. Before this they simply got rice. Now, they get figs, rice, beans, the same as the men.

Some of the guards speak to her husband. This is a blessing, they tell him. This is good in the eyes of God. A prisoner must be treated properly. Perhaps the women can help further? One of the prisoners has problems with his teeth, he howls at night, disturbing the guards. They have beaten him but still he howls.

There are pain killers in the camp. Basic ones, Vicodin. She gets them from Vadi who works with such things. They grind them up and put them with food specially prepared for the man. The guards are unsure about this. They are not sure that this isn't aiding the enemy, but they are tired of the cries so they allow it and the man's cries decrease. When the imam's find out they are not so pleased. The man, they claim, is suffering from spiritual pain. He is a member of another faction. The faction that held the hospital before them. His pain is with God and he must suffer it. No, says Vadi, his pain is with his tooth.

No one tells her not to, so Zahra continues the medication. The hospital quietens once more.

At night they can hear the prayers of the prisoners. Plaintive and impassioned they reach up in Arabic throughout the building and bring peace on the families that live there.

Zahra asks her husband about this. Are they all Muslim? Her husband tells her that most already were. He tells her that they are from warring factions. People who fought against them.

She asks him about the westerners. Have they all have converted to Islam? Yes, he tells her, but they have done so to prevent mistreatment and aren't to be trusted.

Now they know, he says. Now they know that nothing can save them!

Several months later Zahra is laying out food on the table for her husband and his friends. A man sits with them but alone and she thinks that perhaps he is a new recruit, lost in the conversation of men who have been together too long.

She serves him tea and figs. He thanks her in thick Arabic and it is only then that she hears the lilt of French in his voice and recognises the man as the prisoner she met in the toilet those many moons before.

Her husband shrugs when she asks him. Has he converted to Islam? Her husband says he has but that is not why he is free to wander. He is a reporter, he says. Harmless. And besides, he has nowhere to go.

This is when she is happiest, Zahra tells the Baroness. When she talks about happiness, she talks about Syria. Solh is conceived in there. Solh is given to her in Deir al-Zor. This is where she goes in her mind. While they are holding her here. If they send her to prison.

The desert is where she goes in her heart. But the derelict hospital is where she goes in her mind.

The Baroness has another piece of paper for her. She lays it out on the table, a spreadsheet of figures and numbers. Columns stretching down the page and onto the back.

Zahra pulls it towards her, her eyes running over the telephone-like numbers that make up the columns. The Baroness has circled one of the figures, though the young woman has to count the numbers before she can come to an approximation.

What's this?

This is revenue. As best we can tell. Of your group. This year. I'm pretty sure they won't be paying tax on it either.

She taps another number with her finger.

This is for oil. Several of the prisoners you captured, several of them were part of this. When you took the oil fields, this is the profit.

Zahra asks her why they shouldn't make profit. After all, it is on their land.

I think the Syrians might disagree.

And who created that distinction? You, Baroness? Your grandparents? Someone who knew nothing about the people living there stuck a finger in the sand and called it Syria.

Actually, I think you'll find it was the French.

If you had seen it, Baroness. If you had seen Deir al-Zor. The people there. A city, broken by airstrikes, ravaged by war. Being healed again, being brought back to life once more. These men and women. Holy warriors! They weren't people interested in material gain.

You say that, answers the Baroness, you say that, but couldn't it equally be the other way around? The Taliban, in Afghanistan, they were created out of the greed of the Mujahedeen. People who had fought for years in squalor against the oppression of the Soviet's suddenly had all the money and land they could ever wish for and they lived like kings, ignoring the everyday man on the street who had suffered along with them. Is it any wonder the young clerics rose up and killed them? Human nature is stronger the divine.

Isn't that the same argument here? The West is rich. Their puppets in government are rich. Let's rise up against them and sell the oil for ourselves!

The older woman turns the page. Another number is circled in red. Smaller, readable, but impressive nevertheless.

This is how much your group has made from kidnappings, the Baroness tells her. If they won't pay, or won't pay enough, their heads are chopped off and the videos put online to make sure the next one gets the right price. And they get paid, the soldiers, they get money every month to send home. Just like anyone else. Just as if they were working in a factory. As if this were an army and this was just another way of waging war!

Tell me something, Zahra, the Baroness asks her. Tell me. You say we have taken your countries, slaughtered your people, and stolen your gold. That you are the blessed, you are the chosen, and we are the cursed.

Tell me. Why then are you acting in exactly the same way? If this is about God and freedom and saving the people from themselves, then what is the purpose of profits and wages?

Ishaf is not speaking to Vadi.

Zahra has no idea why. Neither sister will tell her. They are each fine with her, laughing and chatting as usual, but neither one will talk to the other, and will certainly not talk about what's happened.

Zahra talks to her husband and asks him if he can find something out from Ishaf and Vadi's husband but he tells her that their husband, Manteghi, is neither a talking man nor prone to spending time with his wives as he should.

There are things that men do not talk about, he tells her.

Vadi is busy with her baby. They have named him Nahin. He is a big boy, thick black hair from the moment he is born in their hospital, but his skin is pale beneath it and he has the brown of his father's eyes rather than his mother's.

Zahra does not like looking after Nahin. She is frightened she will break him, frightened she will lose the love of his mother if he cries, the love of his aunt if he falls. But the boy is taken with her and the sisters have elected Zahra his nurse. She is the only one who can feed him the fig and rice puree they make for him.

By this time Zahra is heavily pregnant herself. She does not like looking after the infant, but it is good practice and she reasons it will help her prepare for motherhood.

Ishaf and Vadi are not speaking, however, and both Zahra and Nahin are caught in the middle.

Every morning, before cooking for the men and the prisoners, Ishaf will boil the rice and figs for the baby. She will blend bread and milk with it until it becomes a sweet paste, and then leave it with Zahra before moving on to her duties.

Vadi will bring Nahin, but she will not stay with them. She gives him to Zahra and makes excuses before returning to her rooms, away from them both. Ishaf is pleasant but will not take care of Nahin, and so it is up to Zahra, with the baby propped in her arms and his legs resting on the unborn in her stomach, to feed him and quiet his screams when he has had enough.

Once Ishaf has gone about her day, Vadi will return and gather the child from Zahra, retreating again to her rooms, before repeating the routine all over again before dinner.

Still, this is a happy time. Their unborn baby is healthy and Zahra's husband dotes on her. But she is more worried now when the men go out. When he is not at the hospital she is fearful he will not return.

She tells herself stories, tells Solh, asleep in her belly, stories that she remembers from TV. She cannot remember all the good ones that were on children's television when she was young, but she can remember the shows she loved as a teenager. She tells Solh stories from popular soap operas, from American sitcoms. Dressing characters up as animals she tells him about the bear and the fox who were on a break at the time. She tells him about the eagle and the rat who run a pub in the East End.

When her husband comes home he tells her belly stories about the Prophet.

They have to move from Deir al-Zor. Pro-government troops are closing in. Empowered by the Israelis, they have refurbished and are in striking distance of the city. They hear mortars late at night, and the men meet pockets of resistance while traversing the city.

They lie as they always lie. Her husband's hand on her belly, on Solh's head, a Quran in his other hand, and together they listen to the sounds of barrage from far away.

They are raping the women, her husband tells her. They are letting non-Muslims rape them, so that they will forever be unclean.

He tells her this with his hand on their baby, the Quran firm in his palm, and the sound of bombs far away in the dead of the night.

They do not leave Deir al-Zor by road this time. They take the mountains. Three convoys, no lights. Stopping and starting. Starting and stopping.

The transportation is better, however. Her husband gives Zahra the keys of a Japanese SUV, and she rides with Ishaf, medicine and food in the back.

Vadi will not ride with them, instead lodging herself alone in the back of one of the trucks, Nahin loud in her arms.

The night is dark, the sound of gunfire sporadic. The only lights they can see once they leave the city are the bright flashes of bombardment and the fires that trail behind them. They are returning to Iraq, but they are told it will take several days.

They are in the second convoy. A first went to set up camp a day ahead of them and Zahra wonders about the prisoners. She has not seen the European in several days but Vadi tells her that they have sold him to another group.

What other group?

Anti-government.

Zahra is confused and tells her so. The man with the toothache was anti-government as well, but Vadi just shrugs and tells her to ask her husband.

It is the morning of the second day when they reach Iraq. Zahra is cramped and in torment. A lot of their journey has been under the blanket of radio silence, but Zahra needs to stop and Ishaf is worried for her. Thin spots of blood stain Zahra's fingers when she puts them between her legs.

They call on a phone and tell the convoy they are stopping, then disconnect the phone once more. Zahra is scared. She is scared for her husband who has stayed to be with the last men out. She is scared that there is something wrong with the baby, and she is scared because she cannot tell what has happened between the two sisters that has caused them to be this way.

They stop the SUV on the side of a hill. The morning is cold but the sun is hot, and they look for shade before pulling in.

Zahra's knees hurt and her stomach is cramping, but she does not think she will be sick. She walks away a little from the car while Ishaf digs through the backseat to find more water.

By the time she joins her Zahra is crying. She is walking stiffly but the cramping is better. Still, tears flow down her cheeks and she cannot seem to stop them.

Why, she asks the other woman. Why aren't you talking to your sister!

Ishaf looks at her and laughs. Why am I not talking to my sister, she asks. That is what's troubling you?

There are cars in the distance. Their own perhaps, but the two women stop talking and watch as the dust cloud moves towards them.

The phone is in the car and Ishaf heads back to get it.

Zahra squats on the ground and places a hand between her legs once more. The cars are still some way off. Stragglers from the convoy, no doubt.

She removes her fingers from between her legs and studies them as she watches Ishaf lean over the passenger seat, reaching for the phone. Wet, but no blood.

Then the car explodes.

Rocked back off her haunches by the blast, Zahra's body finds the ground, her legs splayed in front of her.

The car is a cup of fire and metal. The roof gone. The chassis buckled.

The cars from the horizon approach her and men from their group jump out.

They wave guns in every direction and ask her what happened, but Zahra just sits there, watching the body of the woman she has been with for the last year burn brightly in the hollowed out car. A leg, trailing from the car, the part recognizable in the glow.

They scream at her in Arabic and tell her she must leave, but they are afraid of touching her, and she has to stand on her own.

The men take her with them. The rest of the convoy is untouched. Later, in the new camp, the men ask her husband to ask her why her car had been a target but she cannot answer. She does not know.

This, she tells the Baroness. This is what life is like under the drones.

You live every day with the promise of death. Never knowing where it will come from. Knowing there is little you can do to stop it. Being outside becomes a fear. Being inside, well, you know you are just as unsafe but at least you can pretend.

You begin to dream of them in your sleep.

She is thinking about cigarettes, the Baroness, and nearly misses the denouement of the story. It catches up to her and she swivels her head, almost expecting St Thomas to be standing behind her, but the grey room is silent.

The Baroness hasn't thought about cigarettes in a long time. Cigarettes mean sleeplessness, and sleeplessness is usually combined with Richard or Lucas, so cigarettes are an annual indulgence. Christmas perhaps, or birthdays.

The young woman in front of her is spent. Long hours of transit. Long hours of questioning. The dregs of a soul, dressed up in jeans and a man's pullover.

Where is your headscarf, the Baroness asks once more, but the young woman is still lost in reverie and doesn't answer.

Instead the Baroness leans forward and pulls at the sheaths of paper in front of her.

Your mother wrote to everyone, it seems. She wrote to the local clerics, very impassioned. She wrote to the Prime Minister, though it didn't get there. They were worried about you. When you disappeared. When you wrote to them from Turkey... Well, I suppose that's when they really got worried, isn't it?

Our Jihadi daughter.

The Baroness sits back, thinking.

You are not wrong about changing the world. Your world anyway. I don't know about the bigger one.

You speak of your parents as second generation. Pacifying themselves to find a place in our society. Westernising. Your father has been to mosque every morning since your disappearance. He has attended every prayer meeting, talked to every cleric. Sent letters to... is the term, Mufti? These are not my areas of expertise.

I don't know if they are more right-wing or leftist than they were when you started but they are certainly more devout. - your brother is a different story, of course, she adds hurriedly.

All our photos of your mother have her wearing a niqab, though her social media profile, before you left...

She lets the thought hang in the air, and when she continues it is with a careful air that the young woman attributes to an honesty of thought.

Most terrorism, the older woman begins. Most terrorism... and I'm not implying that you are...

She continues, flailing at the language in a way she is uncomfortable with.

The point of most terrorism is to radicalise your base. You push the powers-that-be, and they respond punitively in order to protect the populace. Your base is… ostracised. Marginalised. And soon they start to agree with your point of view. They too, they realise, are oppressed. And if not before, then they certainly are now!

Stronger. Her words ring more confidently now.

But that doesn't take into account how marginalised it makes the families feel. The damage it does to them.

Your parents know nothing about Solh. Nothing about your time in Syria or Iraq. They know, of course, about the marriage. They've seen the video. But that's it. Months. Silence.

Two months ago your mother flew to Switzerland. I would imagine we were taking a long hard look at her then, but she went anyway. Your mother has become very active since your brother's arrest. I think before that she saw all this as an embarrassment, nothing more. Perhaps a challenge to her belief systems but not much more than that, I should think.

Since then, however, she's been very active. One could say radicalised. Not in service of your cause, you understand. But in service of the families, of the parents whose children have deserted them and taken up arms in the Middle East.

So, she flew to Switzerland. One hundred women. Mothers. All of them with children who have taken it upon themselves to try to save the world. And, she pauses, it's not about you. It's not about getting you back or doing anything like that. It's a support group. It's about helping families come to terms with the damage that has been done to them. To their lives. By their children.

A smile.

She was one of the key speakers

'They fuck you up, your Mum and Dad...'

But the Baroness ignores her.

The group was started by this… woman. This mother. An amazing woman really. Her daughter, just like you, ran off to fight. Just like you she was married, and just like you she crossed into Syria.

Well, this mother – she was Dutch I believe – decided to do something about it, so she flew to Turkey, crossed into Syria, found her daughter, and dragged her home.

Zahra nods.

I know this, she tells the Baroness. I know. And I know she was arrested, the girl, upon arrival at the airport. I know all this. I have always known this. We all do.

Well, says the Baroness. That's who asked your mother to speak.

Yes, says the younger woman, being a mother changes everything.

Solh is born in a village in Iraq, a few miles into the mountains close to Snuny.

A doctor has been brought in. He seems nervous, under pressure, unsure of himself. Vadi is berating him, telling him this and that, and he tries to swat her away like a fly.

Vadi has been inconsolable since the loss of Ishaf. For a time, the raising of Nahin was left solely to Zahra, but the elders soon talked to her husband and suddenly the child who she once hated looking after is gone, given back to his mother. Zahra is bereft, a baby taken from her arms while she waits to receive another from inside herself.

It is only in the final weeks leading up to the birth that Vadi returns to see Zahra. Nahin is almost walking now. He struggles forward like a marionette with his mother holding onto his hands, controlling the strings.

Vadi begs her forgiveness. She begs her forgiveness for abandoning her which, she says, Ishaf would have hated her for. She begs her forgiveness for abandoning her child. Zahra wants to ask why the two sisters had become estranged, but doesn't. She simply holds the other woman in her arms, her belly and Nahin snug between them, and forgives her.

Vadi tells Zahra about another pregnancy she dealt with. It was before Zahra arrived in the camp, but she knows the child, a sullen young girl with a silent stare belonging to one of the elders. Vadi tells her that the birth had been difficult, the baby's head squashed by the walls of the vagina.

I used a vacuum cleaner. Sucked it onto the head and pulled, the woman tells her with a smile that does nothing to alleviate her young friend's anxiety as she pictures the dormant stance of the four-year-old who has never spoken.

Vadi pats her stomach and tells her that everything she needs is right here.

The birth comes a week early. Zahra wakes Vadi in the middle of the night, who in turn walks with her and helps her practice her breathing.

Word is sent to Zahra's husband but there is no expectation of his return.

The birth takes almost a day. Solh is waiting to see the sun, Vadi jokes, and then the moon, and then she is silent. She frets and brings towels and water, and Zahra is careful to check that there is no vacuum cleaner inside the house.

When Solh comes he is silent. It is she who wails. Then she is silent, and it is his turn. He is dark, with more hair than even Nahin, but lacks his light eyes.

Have you seen him, she asks the Baroness months later, having forgotten what she has already been told. He's so beautiful, she says, lost in her mind's eye.

It is two days before her husband returns, and she can see from his face that it has been a hard trek. Still, he is full of joy to see her.

He carries the baby out amongst the men, and Vadi helps Zahra dress and follow after him.

There are sounds of gunfire and shouting. Praises of God and his mercy. Prayers, but no singing.

Zahra emerges to a wall of faces. The elders have gathered, and each kiss a blessing upon the baby's head and pretend he is not screaming protests in return.

You have a great weapon, they tell her. One day, may God be willing, he will be a great martyr to our cause. He will take the struggle to the very doors of our enemies! But she neglects to tell the Baroness this.

Zahra does not enjoy her time in Snuny. It is not as dry as Deir al-

Zor but all the same Solh develops eczema within weeks of being born and scratches furiously, meaning she has to constantly keep his arms pinned to his body in a swaddling cloth.

Her husband is not home enough. They are too far from the fight and he is away for weeks at a time. He kisses her on the cheek, and then the baby's head, and is gone, leaving her alone with their precious charge.

Then her husband returns. He has been injured. They tell Zahra that a driver braked too hard, was going too fast, and he was thrown from the truck again.

The same doctor that came for Solh's birth is summoned, and he tells her that the head-wound is superficial but that his leg is badly broken and will take several months to heal.

She sits with him but Solh is intemperate and she is worried about impacting the head-wound, so Zahra removes herself and the baby to another part of the building.

She is woken in the early hours by her husband. He has tried to rise and instead aggravated his leg. Nevertheless, he seems bright and engaging though naturally frustrated, and Zahra begins to think there might be benefits to him staying home.

Zahra does not see much of Vadi these days. Her friend is rarely amongst the others, and stays hidden in her room during visits.

Nahin she sees often.

He is a curious one-year-old now. Fascinated with Solh, he reaches out to grab the baby whenever he can. Solh, passive as he will ever be, doesn't complain, though Nahin's fingers are sharp, his grip uncertain, and he often leaves marks on the newborn.

Zahra has taken to looking after the boy in the afternoons and, between the two babies and her bedbound husband, it takes all of her energy and willpower just to make it through the day.

This, she thinks, coaxing Nahin's grip off a wailing Solh, is why pregnancy lasts nine months.

One morning, several days later, her husband enters her room and gives her a gift. This is the first time he has shifted out of his bed, and she sees he has fashioned a crutch out of a broom she thought was in the kitchen.

Here, he says and gives it to her. For a moment she is excited. Her husband rarely plays with the baby. Even when she leaves Solh on her husband's bed with hopes of the pair bonding, she always finds him unattended and her husband disinterested upon her return.

The gift is simply one of the baby's clothes, a one-piece hand-me-down from the other children in the town. She thanks him and he sees from the look on her face that she is disappointed, so he takes it back and shows her. See, he says. I have sown the arms to the body so he cannot move them. Now he can no longer scratch his face.

Measles accompanies new faces.

Men move in and out of the town all the time, but now a number of families have taken up semi-permanent residence and schools run daily.

They are far from the front and they will not be moved again until spring. Unlike the early days, command structure remains largely the same, and with it the wives and children become familiar faces that Zahra sees every day. She knows everyone by name, as do they all, and as such the new arrivals are treated with caution and suspicion.

They are introduced as Sayed Mudallah and his family. Sayed's wife is called Khadijah. Zahra doesn't know if the woman's husband is aware that she has measles, being unsure of their relationship, but she does recognise the disease.

She asks her own husband if he has ever contracted the disease but he does not know what it is. She asks him if there is immunisation. He shrugs his shoulders and continues to flex and stretch his leg. He wants to get better, stronger. He needs to leave. Home is no place for a man.

Zahra goes to see Vadi. She won't leave until the woman speaks to her. When she sees her she is shocked by the transformation. Ishaf was always the prettier of the two, but Vadi had a full, round face and sharp eyes. Now she is sunken, her cheekbones visible, her hair thinning and grey.

We need medicine, she tells her, for measles, and she tells her of Mudallah and his wife Khadijah.

Vadi sits there, Nahin next to her, untouched on the sofa. Paracetamol and time will take care of the symptoms, Vadi tells her. Khadijah should drink lots of water and stay away from others until she is feeling better.

What about the other children, Zahra asks, but Vadi tells her it will be alright.

Within a couple of weeks a number of the men have contracted the disease. Within a few more, most of the school children have fallen ill.

Families that once met daily or weekly are now alienated, and her husband tells her that the men have moved up to the mountains to pray until it has run its course, though Zahra sees his frustration at being left behind, due to his leg.

The doctor is called once more but there is little he can do. The children need immunisation, not treatment. Vadi asks him if he can get his hands on any serum. He thinks he can, but will have to travel south for any chance of it. He says this in a tone that tells them all he thinks it would be too late, but they ask him to go anyway.

The doctor is given one of the SUVs and he leaves, honking the horn and waving from the window as if he is an old friend departing after a gossip-filled visit, rather than a doctor on his way across the country with little more than a letter and a map of the roads to protect him.

Zahra never sees him again.

The first death comes the week after. A slight girl, no more than three, passes away overnight. She had been sick for no more than a day.

The little girl who Vadi delivered with a vacuum cleaner is next.

It only takes three more days before Nahin's first symptoms creep over him.

Vadi and Zahra sit with the child, praying and comforting as best they can. Listening to his wails subside into breathing, his wakefulness into disconnected sleep.

Zahra's husband drives into the mountains to tell Manteghi, Vadi's husband, about Nahin and get counsel. His leg is still splinted, so he uses the broom to pop the clutch and changes gears with the other hand. He is gone two nights, and when he returns Nahin is dead.

We should move, Zahra tells her husband. Go into the mountains until the disease has run its course. The pair of them and Solh, but her husband tries to soothe her with inshallah, inshallah.

Still she insists. Zahra is familiar with measles. Hadji had it when he was eight. Her family was on holiday in Bournemouth and had to return early. Zahra went down with it a week later. She still remembers the painful sweats. The fever dreams. With their son in her arms she begs him to let them move up to the mountains.

They go together up to the council. Zahra drives and the baby sits in her husband's arms. It is a difficult journey, taken at night, but it is the longest her husband has held their son and there is a warmth to it. She watches them. Eyes on their snoring child, balanced on her husband's chest.

At the camp in the mountains Zahra makes her case. From behind a hastily erected sheet she talks to the elders, explaining the dangers of leaving children in the grip of an epidemic.

This is our future, she tells them. Our heritage. What we are fighting for.

They tell her that it is in the hands of God.

She tells them she believes she is pleading for the survival of her son.

They tell her that all men have an appointed time to die. If God wills it, then the baby will live. If God wills it otherwise, then the baby will not.

Her husband makes one more plea while Zahra waits by the car. Alone and without a sheet she believes he will have more chance. More chance of changing the minds of men who cannot let a woman guide their judgement.

The baby is awake now. Hungry. She feeds him rice and figs that she keeps in her pockets and bounces him, soothing him with prayers.

Her husband returns. The elders will not be persuaded. God will take care of them. They drive back in silence.

It is two days before her husband comes to her again.

She finds him sitting on her bed, holding the baby in his lap. This is eight days after the death of Nahin, two days since their return to the town. Zahra has been taking care of Vadi, alarmed by the appetite for life she has rediscovered now that her child has passed.

He tells Zahra they have to take a trip. He tells her that the elders have changed their minds and they are leaving until it is safe for the baby. He tells her to pack enough things for a few weeks, but that she must travel light.

The brown suitcase with wheels she naively brought from home but baulked at disposing of, lies open on the bed.

They leave that night, the stars still in the sky. Zahra wants to tell Vadi she is leaving but her husband is insistent. We leave now, he says. We leave and we tell no one. This is what has been decided.

They drive that day and the next, north into the mountains. And for a while Zahra thinks they are going to join the men, but she has learnt a lot in the eighteen months she has been here and even without the stars she can tell where they are headed.

It is only once they have crossed the border into Turkey that she demands answers from her husband, and he tells her what she knows.

There is a world, he tells her, where we will be together, as a family. God has decreed this to be a world worth fighting for. Their child is innocent, he tells her, and God loves innocents. In her country they will protect him from disease. Soon it will be like that for all children, everywhere. This is what they are fighting for. This is what they are dying for. He believes this. It will happen. It is the will of Allah.

She is crying, tempting him, begging for him to stay with her, to go with her, or at the very least to stay in Turkey with her, but she knows he won't.

They drive for two days more. Neither speak Turkish. Her husband doesn't have a passport or papers, so they stay on back roads and away from prying eyes, sleeping in the car and drinking water from a bottle. Solh loves the car. He loves the motion, and stares out of the window at the passing trucks and forgotten countryside, content.

They are heading to Batman, to the family Zahra stayed with when she first arrived, but when they get to the house it is empty, boarded up and unlived in. They drive by twice without stopping and continue on. He has the address of another family who will help them, he tells her and Zahra is pleased to see that Mensau is with them when they arrive. He is shockingly older, thick hair, same smile. He holds Solh while they talk to the family. His parents have been arrested the family tell them. Weapons charge, but they are safe here.

Her husband plays football with Mensau in the garden. His leg is healing but he is still shaky so he plays three legged while the boy plays two. Everyday, out on the street. Uphill, downhill, score one and change while Solh watches on from the shade of a bassinette.

These are golden days. To fit in she sheds the niqab and reverts to the simple chador favoured by the family. She feels the sun on her face and dreams of a day when they will build a home of their own with a garden full of fig trees.

At night, they lie in each other's arms, Solh asleep beside them or chirping in a way that promises the oncoming of speech.

She doesn't want him to leave.

He tells her he can't stay.

She tells him she can leave the baby with the family and return with him, but they both know she is lying and he holds her that little bit tighter in the darkness.

You must return to your home, he tells her again. Our son is the future and he must be protected at all costs. She must be strong, no matter what happens to her, regardless of what they put her through. She must make peace with her family, help them like a good daughter, and raise Solh until they can be together once more.

There is no point fighting for a future, he tells her, if the future is killed by the lack of a vaccine.

She tells him that they can get it here, that they can go to a doctor and…

He stops her.

You are going home, he tells her. Our son will not die like his father.

He stays with her for five days.

By the last day she is angry with him. They stand in the garden, the soccer ball under his bad foot rocking back and forth, his eyes on the ground. He stands there while she tells him that he is destroying her faith.

How can I call myself Muslim? How can I abandon the fight and live within the Ummah? I have sacrificed everything, she tells him. You are asking me to sacrifice more. You are asking me to give up my faith for the sake of our child! You are asking me to sin.

And he tells her that this is God's will.

It is not, she rails at him. This is not God's will! If this was God's will then they would be together. If this was God's will then they would have no need for a vaccine in the first place!

And he tells her that that is God's will as well.

I am a sinner, she tells him. You are forcing me to sin. If I return to my country, for this, then I am forsaking my husband, I am forsaking God.

She pulls off her scarf and holds it out to him, the wind free and open in her hair.

If I am forsaking God then I am not worthy of protection from other men!

But he does not respond.

He says goodbye to her on the doorstep while Mensau holds Solh a modest pace or two behind.

They will be together, he promises. They will be a family once more. If God wills it, they will have many more children. But now they must fight a different fight. They must do what they have always done and protect the innocent.

Their child must grow.

Their child must be safe.

She tells him she will not observe her faith until his return.

He does not look back.

Measles.

So it would seem, yes.

They are in the inner office. Ian St Thomas seated behind the desk, Button Man leaning against the wall by the small window and the Baroness with her back to the door, keeping both men in view.

A laptop is open on the desk and St Thomas closes the screen.

Abrahamic, don't you think? Saving the child, and all that.

Do you have children, Mr. St Thomas?

Button Man is angry, his arms folded. Whatever they had been debating before the Baroness entered had not gone his way.

St Thomas smiles his smile.

Six months, I believe, he says, intertwining his fingers in front of him on the desk. Six months is when they vaccinate, which, all things being equal, puts it at about the right time.

He opens his palms to the world.

But I'm no expert!

So simple, in the long run of it. And St Thomas just smiles even further.

It usually is, when it all comes down to it. People and children.

We're letting her go, he adds, drawing a puzzled look from the Baroness and a re-affirming of the crossed arms from Button Man.

She's committed no crime. Not a real one anyway, and we've learnt all we can learn from her right now. We'll keep her under tabs, of course. No passport. We don't want to stand in the way of true love, but still… No, there's no real crime in setting out to change the world.

Aiding and abetting a Terrorist? Harbouring terrorists?

St Thomas shrugs.

Not in our country. Anyway, we'd have to lock up half of Ireland and the Catholic church if we were to go that route. A child playing crusades? There's no damage that she can do outside these four walls. Not right now, at least.

And, he adds, before the Baroness can interrupt. I don't think she'll be a good candidate for your lot either. A radical who gave up radicalism because she wanted to get her child vaccinated from measles? Not exactly the demon in a hijab you were looking for, I'd expect.

That's up to the Home Secretary.

St Thomas gestures towards the laptop and nods.

Well, I gave her my opinion, though I think we are of one mind. We told her about the baby, the Home Secretary, after you were called in, but still with enough time for you to be contacted.

He lets that sit before continuing, and then stands up and comes around the desk towards her.

You were very passionate in there, Baroness. I can see why they hold you in such high regard. Still. What you're proposing? What the Home Secretary has got you looking into? It's ghettoising. Pure and simple.

He stands up and comes around the table and leans against it, habitual.

Button Man looks down at his feet in an attempt to hide his anger.

And here's me thinking that's what I was here to prevent.

St Thomas slicks his hair with one hand and his tie with the other, weighing up her words.

Is it, Baroness Armstrong? One rule for one and one rule for another?

The Baroness looks at him, anger defeating tiredness.

And what is your job, Mr. St Thomas? Because it seems to me that this whole exercise has been a bit of a sham from start to finish! I don't believe that this young woman just happened to get off a plane. You've known she was coming for weeks! You knew she had applied to add her child onto her passport. You even knew who the father was! You knew that she was with people like the American, and I don't believe you're only now finding out about El Affie, either! Yet you pull me into your little games! You pull me in and use the law – use the House – as if it was just another puppet on your strings and… I tell you, Mr. St Thomas. I still don't know what we've achieved here.

St Thomas nods, smiling, agreeing carefully with every barb.

To his left the Button Man has perked up.

I agree with you wholeheartedly, Baroness. I can see how it must be… frustrating, as it were, to be on the other side of the coin.

No. You weren't used. At least, not in that sense. She liked you. Related to you. And that's all it was, Baroness. You see. You work in laws, Baroness. I work in people.

Your desire, and if I may say so, it's a noble one… But your desire is to, how did you say it? Draw four lines around reality and contain it?

The fact of the matter is; people are always going to try to kill us. We're always going to kill them.

He indicates towards Button Man who finds himself the unexpected centre of attention.

Brown here was telling me, before you came in, about his father. Killed in the troubles. So, if not them then somebody else. This is the nature of things. A bloody mess is man, and he will spill or be spilled from it! At least, that's what my Classics professor used to tell me.

So we balance, Baroness. We prune. That's all we can do. They bite here… A finger in the air, he indicates surgical precision. We slice off there. They lop off an arm, we cauterise the wound! Increments. That's about the size and shape of it, I'm afraid. It's all just gardening.

People are going to kill us. We are going to kill people. Our job, yours and mine, is simply to make sure it doesn't get out of hand.

You've been very helpful tonight, Baroness. Very helpful. Naturally, he adds quickly, I can't go into the details of it but you've been fantastic. Truly fantastic for us, I shouldn't think, and I'm sure the Home Secretary will want to add her praise as well.

But the Baroness is beyond anger now. She stares at his cheap suit and cheap tie. His slicked hair and pat smile, and there isn't a person in the world, alive or dead, that she hates more at this very moment.

You may keep your garden, Mr. St Thomas. You may keep your gardening. Just tell me one thing. Was he working for us?

Was who working for us?

St Thomas' smile crooks and his eyes narrow at her understanding.

The husband, you mean? Was he working for us?

And then it's back. Full and bright. Beaming in her cleverness.

Not for us. No. Nothing like that, Baroness. You've got a little bit caught up in it all. We are not the all-seeing, all-powerful Oz you paint us out to be, I'm afraid. His grandfather did, I'm told, but that's not exactly out of the ordinary, given the time. He was killed by the Taliban, the grandfather, so we've had eyes on him in one way or another, but working for us? Her husband? No. This is not a game of Rudyard Kiplings, I'm afraid.

The other side as it were, they need a great Satan and we might as well be it. They need a reason why their lives are not the way they want, and quite often we are the cause, if not the effect. So imbuing us with superpowers, Baroness? I understand it coming from them. But I have to say, it's a strange thing to have someone from the establishment thinking that about us as well.

In the corner Button Man coughs into his hand in amusement, and St Thomas casts him a hard glance.

Forgive me, Baroness. The hour. Shall I let you behind the curtain? Shall I tell you why tonight has been such a success?

The Baroness doesn't move, doesn't speak, but St Thomas continues anyway.

Social media, Baroness. Six degrees of separation. The information, or more importantly, the lack of information. That is what we were looking for here tonight. That is what we happened upon, so to speak. The sisters? Well, he says, checking himself, not sisters, but we thought we knew who they were. Thought we could figure out that much. Turkey. Syria. Kurdistan. And then one blinks off the grid. American target, so we were pretty sure we knew who that was and, more importantly, why the Americans would target her.

And now we know. And they know we know. And they know they got the wrong woman, which is what makes it so valuable, if you catch my drift.

There are, so it seems, some young men in New York who will be picked up tonight. Some young men with some very not-on views who will be disappearing in the afterglow of all this, and that's because of you, Baroness. All because of who she was friends with.

But the Baroness has already turned to go. Already marked the floor with her heels as she straightens, ignoring the Button Man in her momentum towards the door.

Baroness?

St Thomas calls out and she pauses, her hand on the door.

It's people, he tells her. Mothers and children. We all want to make the world a better place. We all want to leave it a better place for our children. But the lesson we take from Abraham's example is that when it comes to our little ones, God doesn't want us to sacrifice anything at all.

The Baroness stands there, eyes unflinchingly forward.

You can't believe anything she's told you, he adds. About herself. Maybe they let her go, maybe they're planning to strap semtex to the baby carriage. I doubt we'll ever really understand what went on in those camps. For a woman like her.

Mulling this, she flails at the thoughts in her head, but with nothing to say she simply turns the handle and doesn't look back.

At the inner entrance she pauses, her back to the office, half expecting a plaintiff cry from St Thomas telling her that she is no longer allowed access, but the only echoes in the room are footsteps as Button Man emerges and fulfils his function one last time.

Zahra is awake when the Baroness enters.

She can sense him before she can hear him, but she hears him outside the door nonetheless, a chirrup that shouldn't escape the corridor but resonates into the room a fraction before the click of the lock and the electronic beep that signifies a visitor.

Solh.

His brown face is buried deep within the white of the older woman's blouse and he is wrapped in a blue scarf, but a clenched fist and lined bare feet is all she needs to see.

She rises, but the Baroness is not alone. The young man who brings the tea is with her, the one the Baroness called Bartholomew, and Zahra pauses, the chair tilted against her leg.

I thought you should see him, the Baroness tells her.

Are you leaving, she asks the older woman but it sounds curious, even to her.

The Baroness pauses and then, holding the child close to her chest, reaches out and proffers the blue scarf.

You are going to need this. When they let you go.

But the baby is still pressed close to her so Zahra doesn't move.

The young soldier behind the Baroness is watching and Zahra's eyes dart back and forth from one to the other, fixing on Solh and then the soldier, the Baroness peripheral to her judgement.

The Baroness, seeing this, steps forward and drops the scarf onto the table before lowering herself into the opposite chair, the baby still held tight.

The young man is alert, watching, so Zahra sits slowly, controlling herself from reaching out and snatching the child away from the old woman's embrace.

Satisfied, the soldier steps back into the corridor and closes the door behind him, his eyes the last to leave.

Zahra watches the brown bundle in the older woman's arms and remembers the weight of him, his breath against her. The child twitches, adjusting his still-too-heavy head as it slams into the breastbone of the Baroness with a resonance she can hear from here.

Before we let you go, the Baroness says, I thought you could tell me about his father?

Zahra's husband was born in Paris twenty-three years ago. His family returned to Afghanistan when he was eight, high on zeal and renewed hope for their country.

Zahra does not know a lot about his childhood but she knows he still has family there, still has people, though he doesn't send letters anymore. She asked him about this once, and he said he was born in an American prison. As simple as that. She doesn't even know the name he was born with, but life is never simple, and there are a number of things she learnt during her time with him.

Zahra learnt that he had gotten into trouble early. He had been arrested at the age of fifteen for trying to buy a handgun. He had an older brother, now dead, and they wanted to buy it together. They had brought pepper spray so that they could shield it from dogs at the checkpoints and were going to spray the gun with that and sell it in the city, or perhaps use it on rats, but the men they were buying it from had been under surveillance and they were arrested the moment they drove into the parking lot.

When he was released, he went to Pakistan. He was there for a few months, but caught a boat and ended up in Basrah. He joined the Jihad but was captured by the Americans once more. Here, he tells her, he was born.

In prison were many elders from the group they are now part of. The American prisons were harsh but better than captivity back home. The men had access to the Quran and there were a number of great teachers amongst them who taught them the word. They were allowed to pray together, talk together. They wrote each other's contact details onto the elastic of their boxer shorts and promised to keep in touch after they were released.

The men in that prison had two things in common. First of all, they were young. To be thirty was to be considered an elder, a wise man, one of learning. And secondly, they saw the corruption in the world around them and hated it. Each of them had seen what started as a desire to change the world shaped by greed into tribal warfare. They knew where their weaknesses were. They knew where they were vulnerable. They knew as men grow older they dream of living. As men know comfort they seek to hold on to it.

It is a powerful thing to feel comfort and give it up again.

It was in that prison her husband was told the story of the people who had killed his grandfather. The Taliban he had come to hate. How they were clerics who had witnessed the atrocities of the warlords in the years after the withdrawal of the Soviets from Afghanistan. He heard how they rose up to free local girls who had been taken as sex slaves by a former Mujahed. They started with a town, kept marching, and pretty soon they had a country. Countries were respected, they told him. Countries were what the West looked towards, but countries were also what divided them. They were not Iraqis. They were not Syrians. They were not Arabs, not Persians, not Afghans, not Turks. They were Muslims, and what they needed was to take back the world for the glory of God. Only a world under Islam had any chance of creating lasting peace.

Here her husband changed his name. He cast off his family and accepted that he would never return home. He had no home and if he wanted one, he would have to build it with his own two hands.

When Zahra's husband was released he tried to make contact with the men he had met in prison, but sweat had clouded the numbers written onto the elastic and the only one he could make out was disconnected.

Instead he crossed the border into Syria and joined the fight there. He was a good warrior, strong and smart, and though no one knew his background he rose steadily, taking command of his own troops.

Then he started to hear about the others, news about the men he had served time with in prison. About how they had taken up the cause, but he had no way to get in touch. Then he heard that they had declared war against the very group he was involved with and he was afraid, not for his life, which he had already sacrificed to the will of Allah, but that he had somehow – even while fighting against people who wished to destroy

Sunnah – lost his way.

Rumours started to circulate. Soldiers went missing in the middle of the night. Some whispered that they had been killed, but others were certain they had defected gone over to the group that began those days in the prisons of Iraq.

Some said they paid more.

A friend of Zahra's husband gave him a number. He said he could call this and, if he said the right words, he would be allowed to defect. His friend offered to tell him the right words, but Zahra's husband said that he already knew them.

He called that night. The man on the other end of the line asked him what he believed, and Zahra's husband repeated the words he'd learnt in prison. The words he had spoken before he changed his name.

He knew better than to say who he was on the phone.

The man on the other end of the line gave him the name of a café in town and told him to be there in the morning.

He was.

They had captured the town several weeks before and life was beginning to return to normal, so Zahra's husband sat outside the café and watched the market sellers as they struggled under the sun. A man sat down next to him and asked him his name.

I am your commander, he told Ishaf. You will do what I say, when I say it and tomorrow you will be in Iraq.

Zahra's husband told her that he had been allowed to take a wife after he showed his leadership in taking an American built prison not far from the camp where they had met. The prison was well fortified but they took it anyway, freeing many prominent leaders of the movement.

One of the top teachers took him to his home, washed his feet, and told him it was God's will that he should take a Muhaajirah as a wife. You speak Arabic, Pashto, Farsi, English, and French, he told him. You have saved many lives and the men respect you.

This was the life of a freedom fighter. This was the life of those answering Jihad. Twenty years old and he had served two terms in prison, fought a war in three countries, and helped overrun an American penitentiary.

Who wouldn't want to live like this? They were rock stars in a culture that forbade music. They were movie stars in a culture that forsook idolatry. Who wouldn't want peace at this cost?

God has seen fit to give you a wife as a reward, the teacher told him. Your children shall reach to all the corners of the globe and bring peace upon the earth for generations.

Zahra tells the Baroness that when she read his letters she wept. They talked. They shared. They saw the world around them and wanted to make it a better place. They saw injustice, not just against their people, but against all people everywhere and wanted it to stop.

He was a Sunni fighting for his people and she was a Muhaajirah, an immigrant, unable to sit on the side-lines and watch her people die.

A world, they agreed, that was not shaped on spiritual values was no world at all. God had willed it this way and who were they to stand in defiance of God?

When they met she knew who he was and believed in him. When they met he knew what she was and accepted her.

They fell in love.

BOOK THREE
ZAHRA

I am a stranger in my own world.

I keep thinking this. I keep looking for Muslims. I keep looking for covered heads, as if that will remind me of the world I came from and then, when I see them, I realise I've forgotten the crazy amount of money that goes with that propriety on the streets of London.

Paddington has changed. The last time I was here I was four years old, and now I can't find the directions to the tube station. I am a stone in the tide as people push past, left, right, Solh heavy on my hip with a protective arm around him.

A man in a rush – grey suit, morning traffic – catches me with his bag and turns to apologise, looking longer into the Hijab I have fashioned out of the blue scarf than I am comfortable with. And then he is lost to the crowd, caught in the ebb and flow of morning workers going to jobs they don't realise have been created simply to keep them occupied. Simply to keep them from questioning their place.

My suitcase tips. I feel the edge of it going over and catch it with my free hand.

Where am I going?

In the end I follow the throng. I need to get to Victoria but I dread the time it will take to get there.

Instead, I go to an ATM and enter my pin, resting Solh on the metal ledge of the machine as I do so. There is grit in my purse that smells of other places and I have to guard against following those thoughts back there.

No one, in the history of withdrawing money, has been more certain that their card has been cancelled, and the what-then questions begin. Call my mother? Beg on the streets?

But the green lights tell me that there is eight hundred and seventy pounds in the account. A ransom, far more than I thought I had, but it will only let me withdraw three hundred at a time so I wait, prayers soothing Solh while the money is dispensed. It doesn't fit into my small purse so I tuck it into the folds of Solh's trousers instead.

Let them take him. Let all my worldly goods be with him when he goes.

Solh has never seen the likes of London. There was a TV in the house in Snuny and he would fixate on the broken reception and squalled colours on the screen for hours.

He's like that now. Enraptured. Mouth gaping. People hurry around us and there is a queue for the cash machine so I move away, Solh only half in my grip. But he is happy, staring out in wonder at the people who move around him like summertime mosquitoes. Like the bluebottles in Deir al-Zor. He watches as women in trouser suits push past old people with suitcases.

Back in Deir al-Zor there was a man, a brother, maybe forty. Kind. Thin beard. But Solh would freeze open-mouthed whenever he saw him. There never seemed to be a particular reason but as soon as Khalilizad entered a room, Solh would become transfixed, never taking his eyes off the man.

And here he is, twisting in the sling and looking out at London, enamoured. A stranger in his own land.

I didn't expect to have so much money. My goal was to get to Victoria and take a bus back to Newport, far cheaper that way, but now that I have enough I might as well go home by train.

The next train to Newport doesn't leave for an hour. There are earlier trains via other routes but they are more expensive, so we wait. I squat on the side of the concourse, my back cool against the wall and sit Solh on my lap looking out at the world around him. A few feet down four plastic chairs stand empty, but I have had enough of plastic chairs and prefer the cold comfort of the marble floor beneath me.

He doesn't seem sleepy. He doesn't seem upset. He should be hungry but I have no idea what they've fed him during the night, so he sits there, looking out at the world, the sound of his mother's prayers always in his ear.

I wait, breathing into his hair with one arm wrapped around him for protection and together we watch the world around us. I listen with him to the sounds of the station, the mix and colour that it brings, the people who pass through it.

So many brothers without proper beards! So many sisters without their hair covered. So many people lacking respect for themselves and their God.

An old white man has claimed a position on one of the fixed plastic chairs. He leans forward and watches Solh with a smile.

How old is he?

I catch him with the corner of my eye.

He's loving his day out, anyway.

I think about this for a minute and then turn to the man. Older. Resting for tiredness. His grey hair cut short and fading from his scalp.

Six months, I tell him and he smiles.

They grow so quick!

I nod. The man seems to be having pain in his knee, and rubs it fitfully, like my grandfather used to do. Like my husband did before I left him.

You have children, I ask and he tells me that he does. Grown now, of course. Grandchildren as well, but he says he's always believed that this was the best age.

When they speak, that's when they start to lose it, he tells me. The cuteness.

He has an umbrella and a small black briefcase, but his clothes are casual. Even from here I can smell the fresh-soap-and talcum powder of aged skin.

Once they speak they start to demand things. That's when they lose it. Right now everything is new, everything is special. They look out at the world and it's one huge series of fireworks. Then they get used to it a little bit, and then suddenly they're talking. It's like they've got no use for language until things become regular. They don't speak until they get bored of it all. Then it's one demand after another.

His accent is London. South, if I had to guess, though I'm not good with accents. It has that foreignness of age, as if coming from a different time. As if it's been put on to mock.

That's true of all of us, don't you think? First we wonder at things, and then we demand them?

And I smile and tell him that there is some truth in that.

We sit for a while, he rubbing his knee, and me whispering prayers in Solh's ear, all three of us watching the world move by outside of ourselves. Then he offers his goodbyes and leaves, bending to pat my son's head as he goes, his blue eyes catching mine while Solh gazes up at him in wonder.

And then he's gone, favouring his right leg as he makes his way to the train he's been waiting for, the umbrella a slight crutch every second step.

I wait until Solh is asleep. The smell of feet near me is nauseating. Sand cleans feet. Mountains clean feet, but I had no idea until I left how badly the feet of city people smell, trapped as they are inside rubber moulds. I wait until Solh is asleep and then slowly move to make a phone call.

I rest him against my chest and feed coins into the slot. Most pay phones now are card based, and calling cards are bought with bank cards, and bank cards are assigned to a person and are to be avoided at all costs, so it takes me a while to find one that accepts coins and I stand there, in the middle of the concourse, watching the tail end of the morning rush disappear past me into the rainy morning while I insert my sixty pence.

The number is unrecognised.

I try again, focusing on the keypad this time in case I made a mistake, but there is no such number. I try it a third time and hang up.

From the shop I buy a tub of baby food, cooling bits of cooked fish in a plastic container, a carton of milk, a cheese sandwich and a bottle of water too. I am not hungry but it's a long way to Newport and I have no idea what's at the other end anymore, so I buy for the day. I wish there were figs and fruit. But the apples are all green and the figs expensive, so I make do and then, at the checkout, I add a banana as well. For me as well as for him.

And then I wait for the train.

For a moment I am reminded of the car ride out of Turkey, eighteen months ago. The boot of a car. The shock of the sunlight. I wonder why I am thinking of it, and then I see the light at the end of the track running into the station and understand.

I follow the voice announcing the track my train will depart from, wet from Solh's sleeping drool as it soaks through both sling and sweater, dragging my suitcase behind me.

The train is not ready. It has pulled in but the doors are locked and so I stand with a few bemused passengers, waiting for them to open.

From where I am I can see inside the train. It is full of women, cleaning the carriage, each one of them a sister. They bend and straighten, arrange seats and headrests covers to protect the fabric from browning with hair colour. They vacuum the floor.

Is this what I am going to have to do? Will I have to get a job cleaning trains to make sure Solh is fed? Just one more job created for no good reason other than to keep people small, to keep people from being proud of their lives?

I step forward as they exit, eager for the comfort of a padded seat. Solh is heavy on my hip but I look into the faces of each of the women as they exit, eyes down, chattering in a language that I don't understand. Demure in their mix-coloured company-supplied, cleaning frocks, proclaiming their worth only with their uniform black head coverings.

What does it matter if the headrests are straight?

Can't people put their own rubbish into a bin?

Where is the dignity in a life like this? And why are we working if there are no real jobs to do? A woman's place is in her home, helping her husband, and raising her children in the ways of God. The support system for a country. The bedrock on which family is built. This is made to demean us! This is made to make us suffer!

The train is empty so I take a booth, a table and four chairs. I lay Solh gently on the padded seat and wrap him, then push my small suitcase under the seat in front of me, the better not to be disturbed.

The women have missed a serviette. It sits on the floor, folded in half, glaring white against the anti-wear carpet of the carriage.

Solh is still asleep so I pick it up and produce the Baroness' pen that she had left on the table from my pocket. The plastic is clumsy under my fingers and the ink soaks too quickly into the serviette, slowing my hand.

I am going to change the world. I am going to unite my people. I am going to bring peace to warring nations. I am going to help the people rise up and overthrow those who oppress them. I am going to be a force for change. I am going to change the world.

There is a coffee stain on the table. Engrained, it stands in stark contrast to my words. Next to me Solh stirs. He's going to be hungry in a few minutes and I have little that he'll want from me.

I am going home and I hate it.

I've been to London a few times though it's still unfamiliar to me. I am, like most people from this island, familiar with the landmarks, the circles and circus', the dark river and austere buildings. The door outside Number 10, though we never really see it in person. These are the things we all carry within us, embedded.

And this.

The trains that rattle out of the city past peoples' back gardens, sooted and fenced with hundreds of passing trains and a million more flimsy planks of wood. People barrelled into their homes along an artery of industriousness.

The window shakes as another train comes the other way and we start to speed up.

I cannot understand suburbia. It is a form of defeat that I just can't get my head around. Live in the city. Be part of the city! That I can understand. Live in the country, stay away from the world, that I can understand as well. But this life, this desire for domesticated gardens with walls, houses without industry – it's simply another form of dying, isn't it? Another form of acceptance? Leave me alone, it screams. Give me just enough space to hear myself breathe and I will leave you alone as well, and wouldn't that be better for all of us?

How is that any different from what I'm doing now?

The train is busier than I thought it would be, but no one will sit next to me. A few people stare, I had somehow forgotten that in my time abroad. They glance and release. Taking in the head covering. Waiting until the third or fourth look before letting themselves linger. Men. Women. It doesn't make a difference.

I wonder what they would think of me if they knew where I had just been?

I wonder what they would think if they knew that one of those terrible people, one of those fearful people who were willing to stand up and fight for her beliefs and her people, was sitting right here on their very own train?

Fornicators. Paedophiles. Masochists. Bigots. Racists. The cruel, the mean, the unenlightened. They would all be terrified by this woman with a child who cared more for her people than she did for her own life!

And the thought nearly kills me.

I am going home.

I look at the gardens again. The billboards, the streets, the passing traffic en route to nowhere.

I am no better than they are.

Solh is awake, crying in his quiet way. I lift and rock him. I don't want to get the food out yet. I want to slip into slumber.

I touch the edge of my scarf and think about the woman who gave it to me. What life must have been like for her. How closeted her views are. All those years of looking at life in that single narrow way. How could she ever have imagined that she could understand us?

I am glad of it, however. The scarf. It was wrong of me. It was pride that made me judge my own worthiness. Only God can tell who is worthy and who is not. The rest of us must simply keep up the attempt.

We are pulling into a station. An army of people waiting on the platform glide past, vacant-eyed and staring ahead of them as they wait for the train to stop. I watch as a brother slips by, his beard thick, his eyes careful. A woman is watching him. She stands with her hands on a pram, eyes boring into him, though I suppose it could be just lust.

Solh has never been on a train before. He squeals gleefully at the passing people. I am worried about the drying effect of the heater on his skin, sensitive as it's always been, so I pull the collar up on his little shirt and sniff at his nappy, but it will have to hold. I only have one change and I doubt the other passengers would take kindly to a dirty nappy exposed to the over-zealous climate control of the train.

A woman motions to the seat in front of me and sits before I can answer.

She is younger than the Baroness, but without the benefit of money to compensate for it there is an age about her that speaks of bad diet and poverty.

She is white. Green eyed with laughter lines. Her dress would have been something to behold twenty years ago, but not now.

Are you coming from London, she asks me, and her accent is Bristol by the sounds of it. A familiar lilt.

I nod and she asks how old he is.

One. But that's been my answer for quite a long time.

I was visiting my daughter. She's a bit older than this one, though.

She has a smile and good teeth, but the breath she pushes out reeks of fried food and false mint.

I am going home.

And where do you come from?

It's always the hardest question to answer. Harder than anything about faith or morality or understanding. Where do you come from? It's a question that's been with me since I could talk.

When I was a child, I never understood the question. Where do you come from, they'd ask and I'd think, the same place as you. But then you get a little older and you understand a little more. No white person is asking where you come from in terms of a street and a number. They're asking what you are doing here. They are asking why your family brought you to their land.

I tell her Newport and Solh bangs on the table, so we talk about that for a while.

The question has changed since I was young. Where-do-you-come-from has changed to what's your heritage. I remember a teacher telling me that it was only because people were curious and that they were interested and wanted to understand me. And I remember telling her that no one would ask her whether she was Roman or Celt. But she had no answer for that.

Is his father Welsh?

The question comes suddenly and she can see it on my face.

Not that it's any of my business.

Afghanistan, I tell her and she nods, as if she understands everything.

My Sheila's oldest was over there. Couple of years ago. Horrible what they've done to the place.

For a moment I think she means the Americans, until I realise she is talking about the people who live there.

The children look so lovely.

Solh is hungry and I twist the top off the food jar and let him get at it with his fingers to keep him occupied until he starts to create, and then I switch to using the plastic spoon I picked up at the coffee shop counter in Paddington for exactly this occasion.

Must be better for you. Having him here and everything. For the baby.

I nod, not understanding.

We've got this couple on our street, and they're the most lovely people. Middle Eastern. Very warm. They're always bringing us things. For the neighbours. And I think… It must have been terrible for them. Growing up in such terror. Never knowing what's going to happen one day to the next. It's always terrible like that, isn't it? When bad things happen to nice people? It's always a shame.

And he works. All hours. Engineer of some sort I think, or so Danny tells me. Danny's my husband. He gets on well with them. Always polite.

They've got this service. You must know it. Just happened. One of their holy days. Around Easter. I've forgotten what they call it. At least, I'd be embarrassed trying to pronounce it. And, anyway, they bring round this gift. Rice. And my youngest? Her daughter was staying with us at the time. Jenna. Very sweet girl. They're a little worried about her weight but I tell her mother that kids grow into it, though they won't have it. Anyway, she was with us at the time, and they brought her this goldfish. In a bag. They told her that it was part of the celebration, which is nice and all, and that if we were okay with it, we could have it, but… It was nice of them, but she was only with us for the week and, well, we thought it wouldn't last, didn't we? The goldfish. Well, they don't last, do they? We used to get them at the fair, when we were young, though I don't suppose you can do that nowadays. Animal cruelty and all that. But they gave us this goldfish and Jenna named it and everything, and three months later we had to get a bigger bowl! It just kept on living and I couldn't stand to see the little thing cooped up like that, so I got it a bigger bowl. So it could swim around a little. Stretch its legs, so to speak. And we kept it clean and everything, and I thought okay, so it's going to survive 'til she comes back in the summer. It's going to be here the next time there's a holiday. And then, couple of days before she was due back, our Jenna, it died. Just stopped swimming. Dead. I thought they were supposed to float to the top but we had to fish it out. Drop it down the toilet. Of course, we had to get another one. Before Jenna noticed. But it was a nice gift all the same.

Solh has fallen asleep on my chest, his head tucked into my arm. I can feel the warmth of him against me and my eyes begin to droop. The woman is talking but I only see the hills of our homeland and smell Karmal's scent in Sohl's hair.

When I wake the woman has gone. We are in a tunnel, and for a moment I think I am back in the boot of the car, crossing out of Turkey, but I am only under the Severn and Solh is in my arms.

I was born on the 28C bus route between Newport and Bettws. That's the best way I can explain it. Born on the 28C bus route.

My mother explained their choice to me once. She said that they had felt, after youth with my grandparents, the need to spread their wings but it seems that their wings only reached half-way up the hillside.

I grew up on one of those sloped streets that both exhilarate and frustrate. Great for riding bikes down, hell for carrying bags up.

How can anyone who has seen the mountains of the Halgurd live like this? How can I be crawling up them, Solh heavy on my hip, fear and humiliation dragging my every step? Still, fear and humiliation are the two main lessons I learnt living here under siege. Under perpetual difference and passive hatred.

It's barely two pm, but my brain is still hardwired for the afternoon bells declaring an end to the school day, attentive to the onslaught of mean boys and white girls that flood noisily up the hills, promising barbs that I should be well past by now.

The things we do for our children.

I think of his brown hands on me as I call my parents from the train station. I think of his abraised fingers running across my face and down my spine as I wait for an answer that doesn't come.

I have no mobile and I don't know the mobile numbers of my parents. I only have the number of my childhood. The number of late nights out. The number of pickups and pleadings, curriculum vitaes and next-of-kins.

Am I looking to be picked up?

I don't think so. I want this punishment. I want to force myself to take the humiliation of the bus with its rattle and the driver's eyes in the rear-view mirror and the comments from the young men, returning from signing on. I want to see the world as unchanged. I want to remind myself that this is why I left in the first place. I want to never allow myself back into that cocoon again.

I also don't want to surprise them with a child in my arms.

But the phone rings without response, and I remember what the Baroness told me about my mother, how she had taken to helping families of people like me. Those who didn't want the world to change. Those who were too scared to look out of their windows.

I remember that my brother is in prison.

I feed Solh on the bus. Milk tipped into a half-empty jar of baby food and shake, then help him pour it into his mouth. It's messy, but is the best I can do. A mother watches me with disdain from the priority seats, her own child crying noisily from the comfort of a three-wheeler rocked back and forth. I must seem completely third-world to her with her pushchair and bags of disposable nappies and formula and wet-wipes loaded up in case of emergency. She looks coddled to me. Cattle and calf.

The miles around the home of our youth. Is there any road harder for us to travel?

I get off the bus at the bottom of the hill. One of the wheels of my suitcase has locked and drags on the pavement, trying to turn a perpetual left.

I have no keys to my family home. I jettisoned them when I left, along with all forms of identification other than my passport and bank card. You have to burn bridges. Even if you need to rebuild them later, you have to burn them to prevent yourself from walking backwards.

Down the road is a car, a neighbour inside it, watching so hard she barely makes the turn before speeding by. I keep my eyes fixed ahead of me, looking for something I don't realise until I see it.

It's bin day. Wheelie bins are lined along the street haphazardly. All empty. They stand like the poplars of Syria, lining the way forward, and it takes me a moment to see past them to the house I grew up in.

It's a good house. Placed nicely enough. Set back from the road by a well-positioned garden. I was reminded of it in Snuny when we lived there, though at the time it was one of the reasons I didn't feel I belonged.

This, if I had to choose a place, was where I was happiest as a child. This is where I remember wanting to fit in.

The house is ringed by a small wall, no more than three feet high and guarded by my mother's rosebushes on one side and the public verge on the other.

This is where we would play. My sisters. My brother. My parents. Me. This is where I learnt badminton and taught it to Hadji. This is where we would play volleyball and my father would outreach us, laughing as we jumped to armpit height. This is where I watched as my eldest sister wept, getting into the car of a man I have seen neither before nor since, outside of photos on social media where he smiles in a way I doubt he does off-camera.

At least that's my memory of it.

A central path runs to the door. A good door. Solid. Blue, though I always think of it as white and larger than it is. I can feel the weight of it on my hands. I know the stiffness of that final jerk before it opens. I know the lock intimately from a thousand unsuccessful attempts to pick it with a hairpin in the early hours of countless teenage mornings, hoping not to wake my parents, failing every time.

The garden and the door are as close as I can get to heaven this side of the Severn.

Solh is silent. His eyes nuzzle against me as I open the gate, a familiar sound that usually draws a twitch to a curtain in the left-hand window of the house, but this time it's still as I reach the door, and like the child I never wanted to be again, I knock.

No answer.

I wait. Looking out at the street. Wondering how many of their windows have noticed me already.

I knock again. No bell. And still no answer.

Solh is heavy on my hip. I raise him and he snorts angrily, defiantly moving towards sleep.

Surely they wouldn't have let me go if they had picked up my family as well? But would they have let me know if they'd moved?

The suitcase is awkward against my arm and I twist it, putting it down face up in front of the door, then remove Solh from my body and lower him onto it. As an afterthought I wrap the sling around him for warmth. He grumbles at first, devoid of the body heat, but then senses the lack of movement that accompanies it and closes his eyes once more.

I look at him there, on the soft lid of the case, his brown face crinkled in thoughtful determination to sleep, and then step back.

I look at the windows above the door. My room. My brother's.

Would I open a door if I knocked on it? Would I hide and hope I go away after my child put me through eighteen months of questions and accusations and a son whose life went off the rails without direction because his sister chose to squander hers?

Would I stand behind the window and look down on my third daughter, waiting for her to leave me alone?

I walk back onto the road in search of a car I know isn't there.

A white panel van is rumbling up the street and I can hear the noise of children, still a good street away yet, squawking at the end of their school day.

It's starting to rain.

I turn back, with no option but to stand the humiliation of waiting on the doorstep of a family I have rejected, hoping that there might be some room at the inn.

The things we do for our children!

I don't see them when they take me. I don't see the van or the driver, or the hand that clamps down firmly over my mouth. I don't see the man who twists my arm painfully behind me. I don't see the body that lifts me off my feet.

I see Solh lying on my parents' doorstep, wrapped in a sling and his father's sweater, silent, as his mother is pulled backwards into the van and the door slides closed in front of me. I see my parent's door, the door my life came out of, blue against the background of school children's voices in the distance. I see the garden I played in a million times, that I loved and hated in equal measure.

I see the wheelie bins left out for the dustmen to take.

I see the street I grew up on.

I don't see the men who rip me from it. I don't see where they're taking me or their faces or what they have planned for me once we get there.

I only see the world that I was trying to change.

THOMAS

Japan, 1945 – A Family At War

When a wandering priest escaping a troubled past is taken in by a prominent family, a quiet city in northern Japan is forced to confront the dark shadows of war seeping into their lives in ways they could never have anticipated.

THOMAS ALEXANDER

A Scattering
of Orphans

With its townsmen scattered throughout the farthest ends of a desperate empire in a final defence against the encroaching West, the idyllic northern city of Morioka, far removed from the harsh realities of the front, is largely left to itself.

But when a prominent doctor is conscripted and sent to Manila, his sister is left as head of the household and must deal with a young priest living at the bottom of their garden with a large collection of maps and strange knowledge of English.

As the cold hand of war approaches, each person must choose their own destiny and place in the new world.

THE OTHER SIDE

ALEXANDER

Commemorating the 70th Anniversary of the end of WW2! A trilogy spanning the length of the war from the viewpoint of an ordinary Japanese family.

Thomas Alexander

The Disingenuous Martyr

Thomas Alexander

Beyond The Noonday Sun

Offering a unique perspective through the eyes of a rural Japanese family into the impact of history's bloodiest war to date, *A Scattering of Orphans* is one families attempt to make sense of a changing world amidst the desolation of war both home and abroad.

OF THE SUN

www.ingramcontent.com/pod-product-compliance
Lightning Source LLC
Chambersburg PA
CBHW070815120626
46556CB00002B/512